MIDNIGHT SHADOWS

FEATURING AUTHORS

TOR ANDERS-ULVEN ~ ASHLEY BURNS ~ ELIZABETH DAVIS
BRANDON EBINGER ~ DAVID GREEN ~ S.O. GREEN
JOHNNY HEMPSEED ~ CHRIS HEWITT ~ JOEL R. HUNT
BLAISE LANGLOIS ~ CHRIS LILIENTHAL ~ TIM MENDEES
MICHAEL D. NADEAU ~ ELIZABETH NETTLETON ~ KIMBERLY REI
MCKENZIE RICHARDSON ~ AUSTIN SHIREY ~ K.T. TATE
V. A. VAZQUEZ ~ WILLIAM WELLMAN

AN EERIE RIVER PUBLISHING ANTHOLOGY

MIDNIGHT SHADOWS

Paperback ISBN: 978-1-7772750-9-9
Hardcover ISBN: 978-1-990245-00-8
Digital ISBN: 978-1-7772750-8-2
Edited by Alanna Robertson-Webb
Cover design by Michelle River
Book Formatting by Michelle River

ALSO AVAILABLE FROM EERIE RIVER PUBLISHING

NOVELS

STORMING AREA 51

SHORT STORY ANTHOLOGIES

Don't Look: 12 Stories of Bite Sized Horror
It Calls From The Forest: Volume I
It Calls From The Forest: Volume II
It Calls From The Sky
Darkness Reclaimed

DRABBLE COLLECTIONS

Forgotten Ones: Drabbles of Myth and Legend

COMING IN 2021

It Calls From The Sea
It Calls From the Veil
With Blood and Ash
With Bone and Iron
Dark Magic: Drabbles of Fantasy and Horror
The Sentinel
In Solitude's Shadow
The Void
A Sword Named Sorrow

Stories

Dedication and acknowledgments

This anthology was created over the last year, so it is only fit that we dedicate this collection to everyone that lived through 2020 - the year of uncertainty, panic, loss and revolution.

We want to thank those that stayed home to keep us safe, those that worked the front lines tirelessly so we could survive and the medical staff who saved countless lives.

There were those who barely hung on while the darkness consumed us, but hung on you did, and we are happy you are here. This is for you, for being with us and to thank you for everything you do.

We also want to acknowledge the ones lost during 2020, and we send our condolences to all of the families who have faced that trial. You have our support, and wishes for a happier 2021.

Thank you for reading,
Eerie River Publishing

Tasty Treats
Tim Mendees

"A clown can get away with murder."
— *John Wayne Gacey*

On a cold, wet day in November, the circus came to Betyls Cove. It sprung up overnight in a muddy field behind Chycoose Manor. The large yellow and red striped tent was visible from the road and was spotted by dozens of pairs of excited eyes on the school bus from the village of High Bend. The news spread through the school like a particularly virulent pox and by the end of the first lesson, teachers were sick of hearing about it. By lunchtime, they were contemplating burning the tent down.

Nothing exciting ever came to Betyls Cove, no fun-fairs or live bands. It was a small fishing town that even the locals struggled to find on the map. All it had was a small, run-down pleasure beach and a dilapidated pier. It wasn't the most stimulating of places to grow up, so the news of the circus quickly whipped the town's youngsters into a frenzy.

In fact, the only student in the school to greet the news with sullen indifference was fifteen-year-old Simon Fletcher. He had only recently moved to Betyls Cove from the nearby city of Truro, and hadn't been in town long enough for the ennui to have set in properly. When his friend John Angove told him about the circus, all he got from Simon was a shrug of the shoulders and a dismissive "So?"

"Come on, Si." John pleaded. "It'll be fun."

Simon snorted derisively. "They don't even have animals. It's one of those stupid *human* circuses. Just a bunch of creepy clowns throwing juggling balls at the audience."

"I hear they get members of the audience up and throw knives at them." John grinned.

Simon snorted again. "Yeah, blunt ones. You don't think they would be in any danger, do you? It's all tricks and sleight of hand. None of it's real."

John thought for a second. He needed to tempt his friend somehow. John desperately wanted to go but he didn't want to go alone. Not that he would ever admit it to Simon, but John hated clowns. "They have candyfloss and toffee apples."

Simon shot him a dirty look. "I'm diabetic... Remember?"

"Oops...Yeah." John shook his head at his own stupidity. "Sorry, dude."

Simon shrugged. He never had much of a sweet tooth in any case, and it was type-two diabetes. He didn't have to inject insulin or anything like that so it could have been a lot worse. He picked up his rucksack and turned to leave the classroom.

The final bell had rung, and John needed to think fast. "Um...Sally Green is going..."

Bingo!

Simon stopped mid-stride and looked over his shoulder at his friend. This put a whole new complexion on things. "Alright, Angove, you're on. I'll meet you by the church at six. We can get the bus from there."

John grinned like a manic Cheshire cat. "Yes! Thanks, Si!"

Simon didn't understand his friend's eagerness one iota, but the thought of Sally Green made him feel all fuzzy in his special places. "Just don't embarrass me by volunteering to be sawn in half or some shit...Okay?"

"Deal..." John carried on grinning as he threw on his coat and skulked out of the classroom after his lanky friend.

The two boys went their separate ways at the school gate, John to the Dockside Estate and Simon to a large barn conversion out in the sticks. Simon's thoughts were consumed with what he was going to wear. He couldn't mess up this golden opportunity to impress Sally Green. John, on the other hand, couldn't stop thinking about candyfloss. One of the banners on the roadside claimed that this particular circus troupe offered the best candyfloss in Europe... John was fixing to put that audacious claim to the test...

⊹⊱─◦─⊰⊹

"Roll up, roll up, to Mordiggian's circus!"

Simon winced as the irritating clown on the unicycle barked in his ear through a megaphone. Simon hated clowns as much as John, but not because of fear; Simon just found them incredibly annoying. That goofy, fake laugh that a lot of them put on just made him want to slap the stupid grin off their faces.

"Step inside to witness death-defying displays that will thrill, chill, and excite you!"

Nothing was thrilling or exciting about standing in a long queue in the pouring rain, especially while your best boots sank into the mud. Simon cursed himself for agreeing to attend the circus. Sarah Green was miles ahead of them so they wouldn't be sitting even remotely close to each other, and knowing his luck he would end up with a stinker of a cold.

Though, right now, a blocked nose would have been a small mercy. The air was thick with the cloying smell of sickly-sweet candyfloss and congealed, toffee popcorn. John's hand was coated in the sticky popcorn gloop, and Simon winced with revulsion as his friend began licking it off his stubby fingers.

"Get your free 'Tasty Treat' before you enter, and experience the best candyfloss in all of Europe!"

This latest announcement elicited a mighty cheer from the snaking line of fidgeting children and bored parents. Simon rolled his eyes. Further down the line the crowd passed through an old, rusty turnstile adjacent to the ticket booth. On the other side was another clown, this one was handing out small cardboard cups with a swirl of bright pink floss inside.

"You can have mine," Simon said sullenly.

"You can have a little taste, can't you?" John asked.

"You've got to try a little. It's the best candyfloss in Europe...See," He pointed at a huge, garishly-coloured board emblazoned with the bold claim. "It says so, right there!"

Simon's left palm met his forehead in a blatant display of despair. John really was a gullible prat at times. "That's just a marketing ploy, you muppet!"

"How do you know?" John shot back with a petulant smirk. "Don't knock something until you've tried it, my Granny always said."

Simon huffed. "Fine, just a little taste. Then I can tell trading standards about this bunch of frauds!"

John bristled at this statement; Simon's constant running down of things he enjoyed was starting to grate on his nerves. "You can be such a miserable wanker at times..."

Before their bickering could escalate to the calling of names, punching of arms and mocking of mothers, the line started to move. John fished the ten-pound note his mother had given him out of his overly-tight jeans, handing it to the clown in the ticket booth. "Two, please." He said politely. The clown took his money, gave him change and stamped his hand with a sinister-looking clown in smudged black ink... It definitely looked more Pogo than Coco.

Simon flinched when her hand touched his to give him a stamp. Something about her cold, clammy fingers made his flesh crawl. He managed a forced smile as he moved along, though the clown had spotted his discomfort and seemed to delight in it. Her yellow eyes, contact lenses of some kind, flashed with almost sadistic glee.

It was only now that he looked at the clowns properly that he noticed just how sinister they were. He had never found clowns the least bit frightening, but there was something feral about this troupe. All of them had an almost canine aspect to their faces. Their grease-paint was elaborate, and looked as though it had been designed to distract from their features rather than enhance them.

"Tasty Treat?"

Simon nearly jumped out of his skin as another clown stuck a pot of floss under his nose. "Eh?" He stammered in reply.

The clown's mouth hung slack, displaying a row of gnarled, yellow fangs. "You want a Tasty Treat?" He barked. His voice was rasping and harsh, like it had been chewing sandpaper. "Take. It's free!" This sounded more like a demand than an offer.

Simon gingerly took the cup and attempted a weak smile. "Ugh...Thanks?" He looked around. Everyone was tucking into the free floss and wore ecstatic grins.

"You try!" The clown insisted.

Simon smiled again and lifted the cup to his mouth. *What the Hell?* He decided. *Just a little won't hurt.* Flicking the tip of his tongue out like a snake tasting the air, Simon brought the floss to his mouth and licked the tip.

"Holy shit!" Flavour exploded on his tongue. It was unlike anything he had ever tasted. He had always imagined candyfloss to be sickly, overpowering, but this stuff had the perfect flavour balance. The corners of his jaw started to tingle as he began to salivate.

"Is best candyfloss in Europe, yes?" The clown's eyes danced with delight as Simon nodded emphatically. "You go in, now. Show about to begin!" The clown took a sweeping bow and gestured to the flap in the tent.

Simon hummed and sucked the flavour off his lips. In front of him the tent flaps opened, and he was swallowed by the warmth and smells of the circus. Brightly coloured lights dazzled and disorientated him as he stepped over the threshold. The joyful music rose and swelled between his ears. His whole body tingled as though he had just inhaled paint fumes. The candyfloss was indeed a revelation.

"What do you think of the candyfloss?" John's nasal voice broke the spell in an instant.

"Um...What?" Simon shook his head from side to side. "Yeah...Not bad."

John reached over and took the cup from his friend. "Gimmie that! We don't want you going into a coma do we?"

Simon looked at his friend. For a fraction of a second he could have broken John's nose for taking away his Tasty Treat. He took a deep breath and thought rationally. "Yeah...Go for it." John didn't respond to his comment and simply commenced shovelling the pink floss down his gullet.

The interior of the tent was just as brightly coloured as the exterior. Panels of red and yellow canvas alternated down an entranceway, which seemed to pitch at a slightly skewed angle. Though the tent had been erected on a perfectly level field the floor seemed to dip and lurch, as though the circus was burrowing into the ground. The closer they got to the arena the more outrageous the angles of the tent became. On more than one occasion Simon had been forced to grab hold of a tent-pole to steady himself. Nobody else seemed to have any difficulty navigating the labyrinthine passage, however.

"Check out these portraits…" Simon nudged John and pointed with revulsion. The corridor was lined with grotesque portraits of oddly misshapen clowns. Some of them were so twisted that they walked almost on all fours. "Talk about a freak show." Simon shuddered.

John's eyes twinkled. "I think they're beautiful."

Simon looked in utter bewilderment at his friend. John wore a euphoric smile that seemed to be firmly welded on to his freckled features. Looking around, Simon noticed that everyone in the procession towards the arena wore the exact same expression. He felt like he was standing amongst a production line of particularly creepy mannequins.

Something was wrong here…Very wrong. A feeling of deep unease started to gnaw away at Simon's lower intestine like a hungry rodent. Everyone was acting like they had been drugged, and even Simon felt docile and light-headed. He'd always thought that religion was supposed to be the opiate of the masses…Not candyfloss!

As they moved steadily onwards Simon was suddenly hit with an urge to flee, to just get the Hell out of there. He couldn't quite put his finger on why but he was slowly overwhelmed by a feeling of impending doom. He tried to turn and walk out, but the tightly-packed column of grinning humanity prevented any deviation from the forward surge.

Simon tapped frantically on his friend's shoulder. "John?" He hissed. "Something fucking weird is going on here."

John continued to grin. "Isn't it magical? Look at those beautiful clowns." He pointed to the widening aperture that led to the arena. The entrance was flanked by two hulking clowns that looked more dog than man. They seemed to be checking everyone as they entered the arena...But for what?

Simon watched in horror as they methodically *sniffed* everyone as they passed. Then it struck him; they were checking that everyone had consumed the floss. Thinking fast, Simon snatched the almost empty container back from John, dipped his forefinger in it and wiped the sticky substance around his lips while taking the utmost care not to ingest it. Next he mimicked the crowd's glassy-eyed vacancy and manic grins, praying that his deception would work.

The larger of the two clowns leaned forward and stuck its twitching snout in Simon's face. It took every fibre of his being to stop himself lashing out as the clown sniffed his breath. Its yellow eyes glared into his as it scrutinized his reactions. Simon kept staring at the back of John's head. He didn't know what would happen if he flinched... Nothing good, he imagined.

A glob of sticky drool dripped from the corner of the clown's twisted grin. It hung there for a few agonizing seconds before dropping with a disgusting *splat* onto the toe-cap of one of Simon's boots. The stench of the clown's breath was making his eyes water. Simon was seconds away from breaking when he was finally shoved forwards and allowed to enter the big top.

Simon took a deep breath, then quickly wished he hadn't. The air was heavy with simulated smoke that tasted like soap. It was so thick that it completely obscured the floor, and judging from the metallic clatter they were walking on metal grates of some kind.

Green and red lights flashed in the smoke, making navigation tricky. Simon reached out and held a metal guide-rail that led up into the stalls. John and the others didn't seem at all phased by the ambience of the tent. They just filed down the aisles and took their seats like well-behaved cattle.

When the line stopped Simon took the seat behind him, noting that they were three rows back and off to the left side. With wide, bewildered eyes, he gazed around at the bizarre interior of the tent. It was much smaller than he had expected, and there could only have been fifty or sixty people in attendance. The floor sloped down in a funnel shape and terminated in a circular performance area.

Below them was a circular board, complete with rusty manacles and suspicious-looking, brown stains. Dry ice had settled in the arena, and other strange objects lurked in shadow. Before his eyes could adjust to the lights the tent was suddenly plunged into darkness. The piped-in music rose to a deafening level as a drum-roll built to a crescendo. The crowd gasped in perfect unison as a cymbal crashed, and a dazzling spotlight beamed down and illuminated the clown on the unicycle with the megaphone.

"Welcome, ladies and gentlemen, to Mordiggian's *human* circus!" The clown howled.

The audience roared in appreciation as Simon looked around for the nearest exit.

"We hope you enjoyed our Tasty Treats. They were made by the great ghoul, Mordiggian, himself!"

The crowd stood and delivered a rapturous round of applause.

"And the best thing about them…? There's more!"

As the crowd whooped and cheered a small platoon of clowns, with trays strapped to their bodies, moved roughly amongst the audience and jammed a large tub of the floss into everyone's hand. Simon took his without comment and joined in the mindless show of delight that raged around him.

As everyone returned to their seats and started to eat the addictive floss, Simon pretended to join in. The clowns were carefully watching for anyone who wasn't completely under the spell of the insidious sweet.

"Without further ado...Can we have some volunteers?"

Everyone in the tent shot their arms in the air and began to chant, "Pick me...Pick Me...Pick me..." Simon joined in, desperately praying that they didn't pick him.

The spot-light circled around the room, and Simon's heart pounded as the clowns started herding people into the ring. There were ten people in total, and each was led to a different device. One man was loaded into a cannon, while one strapped to a bed of nails. Others were driven up ladders and pushed out onto tightropes. Simon let out a yelp of alarm when he noticed who was being strapped to the ominous disc...It was Sarah Green.

The unicycle clown pedalled over to the disc and produced a large axe from behind it. The crowd went "Ooooh!" as he pedalled back to his starting point. "Can we have a drum-roll please?" The clown grinned menacingly.

Another clown grabbed the handle on the side of the disc and gave it a good yank. The crowd went "Ahhhh!" as the disc started to spin. Round and round it went. The clown gave the axe a playful swing, then hoisted it behind his head...Ready to throw.

Simon started to panic and fidget in his seat. All over the arena the restrained members of the audience were joined by weapon-wielding clowns. The drums started to pound faster and faster, louder and louder. The lights flashed and danced. The smoke and dry ice swirled.

'Splat!'

The crowd roared with appreciation as all ten volunteers were dispatched in perfect unison. One man was impaled on a bed of nails by a hulking brute with a sledgehammer. Another was fired from a cannon into a pile of bricks and broken glass. People were tossed from the tightrope, while others were skewered with knives, swords and even a javelin. Poor Sarah Green was neatly decapitated by an expertly thrown axe...Simon screamed.

Everyone in the audience fell instantly silent and glared in Simon's direction. The clown on the unicycle pointed at him with a gnarled finger. "Someone hasn't been taking their medicine...Grab him!"

As John and several other members of the audience reached out to grab him Simon dropped to his knees then slid under his seat. There was a short drop to the ground below. He landed awkwardly and twisted his ankle.

"Treat clowns!" The ringmaster boomed over the raucous music at the clowns with the snack trays. "Find our unwilling participant!" Footsteps started to pound on the wood and metal bleachers as the clowns started to come for him. "Now!" The clown had regained his jovial tone. "Can we have some more volunteers?"

"Pick me! Pick me! Pick me!" The chants were deafening.

Simon limped towards the rear of the tent and scrambled behind one of the bass bins as the first of the clowns appeared under the seating. It had discarded its tray and the top half of its costume, revealing a hunched, scabrous body with tufts of wiry hair. It sniffed the air in an attempt to locate Simon.

Luckily the air reeked of freshly spilt blood and candyfloss, masking Simon's fear. It skulked off in the opposite direction, and Simon was finally able to take a breath. He had no idea how long he had been holding it. His mind was in turmoil. How could this be happening?

He found himself gazing in confusion at the floor. It looked as though the circus had burrowed itself into the earth. It sloped downwards towards a vast pit under the arena. There was a walkway that corkscrewed around it and went down, presumably to the bottom. The floor of the arena was entirely constructed of metal grates. Blood dripped down from the punctured and broken cadavers like a foul rain.

Disgruntled barking from the opposite side of the seating area announced the position of his hunters. Whatever these creatures were, they had a savage intelligence and were waiting at the exits. This left only one route...Down.

As he made his way across the blood-soaked earth, the crowd above started to whoop and stamp their feet in anticipation of the next atrocity...

"Watch as my assistant, Marco the Mutilator, saws the woman in half!"

Simon averted his eyes and ran for his life as the victim's blood gushed into the pit. His feet clanked on the metal gantry as he raced down the spiralling path into the rancid pit. Risking a glance behind him Simon was glad to see that none of the clowns was following him. They obviously didn't think he'd be so foolhardy to go in that direction. This gave Simon a pause...What could possibly be down there?

The slope ended in a canvas corridor that wound around a massive pool of blood. Simon gagged and recoiled in horror when he saw that there was something ghastly swimming in the blood. It looked like an enormous grave worm, with a huge, gaping maw fringed with rope-like tentacles tipped with fanged mouths. They hungrily sucked up the blood. The corpulent monstrosity quivered in delight as more blood lashed down in a mighty torrent.

There was another tunnel off to the left, which appeared to snake into the bowels of Betyls Cove. The town was riddled with old mines, caves and smugglers tunnels. The impossible tent must somehow join up with them. How could this monstrous structure have been built in a single evening? Simon couldn't wrap his head around what he was seeing. It was too horrible for his mind to process.

Simon quietly began to edge around the pit. Suddenly, the sound of footsteps stopped him dead in his tracks. He pressed himself into a fold in the canvas as a hulking clown appeared from the other passage. It was dragging the top-half of a freshly slain woman. With a roar of exertion it swung the body into the pit. The vile creature attacked it with gusto as hungry mouths snapped and salivated.

"There you go, my lord Mordiggian...Tasty treats..." The clown gave a throaty chuckle, then moved around to the rear of the monstrosity holding a bucket.

Simon watched in horror as the creature began to excrete strands of a sticky, thread-like substance. It was similar to how silkworms produce silk, only this was far more disgusting. The clown used two sticks to grasp the substance and weave it into a ball.

Horror gripped Simon's soul as the awful realisation dawned...This is how they made the candyfloss!

This was too much. Simon gagged and retched, giving his hiding place away. The clown snarled as the loping creature raced around to his position, snapping his canine muzzle with his yellow eyes blazing in fury. It lunged for Simon, arms outstretched and talon-like nails ready.

Thinking fast, Simon drove his shoulder into the creature's midriff and lunged with all his strength. The rugby-tackle sent the clown staggering backwards. It lost its footing on the edge of the pit and splashed into the pool of gore. Mordiggian roared with delight at his new meal, and in seconds the clown had been devoured.

Simon ran as fast as his twisted ankle would allow. He ran in a haze of adrenaline and madness. The tunnels seemed to go on forever, though eventually he reached a steep staircase carved into the wall of a rocky cavern. Scrambling for his life, Simon made his ascent...

"There you are!" John yelped in glee just as Simon appeared from a darkened passage next to the line of disgusting Portaloos at the entrance of the tent. "I've been looking for you everywhere."

"John! We need to get the fuck out of here, right now!" Simon was crazed. He grabbed his friend by the arm and tried to pull him towards the exit. He was stopped by the appearance of several clowns. They were surrounded, and two of them grabbed Simon by the arms and held him tightly as John picked up a tub of candyfloss.

"You've got to try it, it's the best candyfloss in Europe...Just a little taste won't hurt!" John grinned as he stuffed the evil confectionery into Simon's screaming mouth...

The town of Betyls Cove awoke the following morning to discover that around fifty of its denizens had run away to join the circus. This didn't come as much of a shock, as many of the townspeople fully expected it...

All signs of the circus had gone by dawn, and the field looked as though it had never been touched. Most people were jealous of those that vanished. After all, it was a fine, local tradition, and was one that many wished to join in.

You see, Mordiggian's circus originated in Betyls Cove, and every ten years it returned to recruit some new, local blood to keep the acts fresh...

Hush

Kimberly Rei

"Shhhhh. Hush."

I cringed and reached for my ear, pulling back just before my fingers brushed the bandage. An orderly watched me, one hand on his radio. If I clawed they'd restrain me again, but I hadn't lost my mind entirely yet. Maybe. But I would if I couldn't move.

I pushed back from the table and went to peer out the window. The bars blocked most of the view, but I could see the grass and trees, the wind ruffling the leaves.

"Just one more. It's so easy. One more. For us."

I gripped the bars for balance. How long had it been whispering to me, my purloined treasure?

Years?

Months?

No. A week. That was it, a week. And the last 36 hours or so had been right here, in the gentle care of the Rowan Institute for the Mentally Disturbed. The first 12-ish of those had been under sedation and restraint. The restraints did their job; the sedation hadn't.

Even in the dark blur of too many psychotropic drugs I could hear it. That voice, snarling with rage and making far too much sense. It made me want to rip my ear off, but there's not much hope of that when strapped down.

For a moment, staring out at the pristine lawn, I ached to be back out in the world. I ached to go back a week. Just one week, to before this happened.

An orderly carefully stepped up and cleared his throat. It was the one who had been watching me. His hand was no longer on his radio, it was on a taser.

The whispering stopped, and the chatter in the room intensified. The orderly, Jeff according to his nametag, led me slowly and carefully down a series of halls until we reached a door labelled Dr. Lovely.

Seriously?

He knocked, then opened the door and not-quite shoved me through.

The doctor behind the desk smiled in that carefully professional way. He stood, motioning to a chair, "Please, Ms. Wallace, have a seat."

He picked up a pen and we went through the standard background bullshit, searching for a reason I may have lost my mind so suddenly. No, I wasn't abused or molested. Yes, I still had both parents. Yes, I had two perfectly normal siblings. On and on.

All the while, the voice - I refused to give it a name - snarled and growled in my ear. It was rough, listening to two things talking at once. Every time I hesitated the good doctor made a note.

"Oh, for fuck's sake, just stab that pen through his eye

and be done with it."

I blinked hard, then asked for a cup of water. We don't do glass at The Rowan; we're dangerous here.

I played with my safe, plastic cup as Dr. L. leaned back in his chair and steepled his fingers, "Tell me what happened at the grocery store."

Well, that was abrupt.

⟵———⟶

At some point during my teenage years I had picked up a love of shopping. The target didn't really matter. Going out, wandering along aisles, stroking potential purchases, it all warmed a cold spot in my heart and made me feel better. I didn't even have to buy anything; just being around carefully placed products offered satisfaction.

Grocery shopping was a particular joy. Bright lights and straight shelves. Was it only a day ago? A day and a half?

"Let's do it again! Bash his head in and we can get out!"

The whispering was giddy with potential. I could feel the doctor watching me, but the office faded away and I was back in store, considering pasta. At that point the voices had only been in my dreams. Nightmares. Visions of horrifying violence. I woke up every morning exhausted, and more than a little twitchy. In the true spirit of irony I'd actually been considering therapy.

I wasn't enjoying shopping as much as I usually did. I was tired and jumpy, and the lights seemed overly bright. But the shelves were in perfect array, and there was comfort in that. Right up until the man at my left picked up a jar of spaghetti sauce. He looked it over, read the back, then shrugged and placed it back on the shelf.

In the wrong place.

I heard the growl in my ear, deep enough that I knew it wasn't from any outside source. But it wasn't my voice either.

"Kill the bastard!"

I tried to stop, I swear I did. The man laughed when I told him to put things back where he found them, and my temper snapped. My mind snapped.

As he turned away, still laughing, I grabbed the jar and smashed the back of his head with it. I had to jump up, since he was a good foot taller. The jar shattered.

I hissed, pulling a piece of glass out of my palm. He'd stumbled forward, cursing and grabbing at his head. It wasn't enough.

The voice laughed, laden with gravel, *"Cheap brand. Grab the can instead. Good, solid, reliable brand."*

I had a can of tomato sauce in my hand before the whispering stopped. The man was still bent over, swaying slightly. I jumped on his back and brought the can down on his head, over and over. He fell, and I rode him to the floor. There was a howling, screeching sound. Later, I would learn it came from me. At the time all I heard was the breaking of his skull and the squish of the can going through blood and brain. The can had broken as his skull caved in, the scent of tomato mixing with the smell of gore. My mouth watered.

Someone pulled me off him, and many someones held me down. The screeching went on and on, the laughter in my ear drowning it all out. I woke up at The Rowan, cleaned, drugged, and strapped down.

◈———◈

"Ms. Wallace?"

The doctor was talking to me, but he seemed far away. The whispering was getting louder, and it was making more sense.

"Shhhhhh. Hush. We'll get out of here, and oh the fun we'll have!"

An hour ago I wanted to claw the voice out of my head, rip my ear off, carve it out. Now, I took comfort from it. I remembered the feel of the can, cracking and cutting my hand. I remembered the high.

I reached up to the bandage, "Where's my earring?"

Dr. L. nodded, as if he'd been expecting me to eventually come around to that subject, "Tell me about the earring."

"Where is it?"

"It's safe, with the rest of your possessions. Why is it so important?"

The man was a moron.

"Grab his pen. Right through the eye!"

"I...I need it."

The doctor nodded and made a note, "Tell you what. You explain the significance, and I'll see about getting it for you. Deal?"

◈———◈

The significance. How could I explain that?

I found it in an antique shop. It was the kind of place that was both fascinating and uncomfortable, with clutter threatening to fall off every shelf. Treasures leaned on each other like drunks seeking balances, and cabinets sagged under the weight of the history they bore. The place smelled of dust and old books, ancient silk and dry wood.

Shannon kept pointing out pieces of interest, holding up statues, lingering over typewriters older than the building. She still had half her ice cream cone, so she was limited to hand waving and small objects. We'd been giggling all afternoon, and we weren't stopping anytime soon.

At the back of the shop, after we squeezed past fainting couches and Asian cabinets, I heard it. Not yet a voice, not even a whisper. It was nothing more than the hint of a presence, a temptation. While Shannon flipped through a stack of crumbling magazines I took a small jewelry box off a shelf. Inside was a single earring, nestled in rotting velvet. The silver was tarnished and looked almost sticky with age. The stones, though, were as perfect as possible. They looked as if they'd just been polished, or were unaffected by time. Lapis lazuli, three of them dangling in filigree.

I was enchanted, and I couldn't stop staring. I had never seen such perfection. I didn't care that there was only one, because two would have been overkill. One was exactly right.

"Whatcha got over there?" Shannon had scooched her way to me.

I snapped the lid shut and held it up to her, "Just a jewelry box. Pretty, isn't it?"

We thanked the old man behind the counter on our way out.

Shannon looked back, "I'm not sure he was awake."

I slipped my hands into my pockets and stopped walking. My left hand wrapped around the earring. A shiver danced over my skin. I didn't remember taking it.

I sure as Hell wasn't returning it.

Shannon paused before we got too far from the shop, "That jewelry box. I kinda liked it."

She knew. She'd seen the earring. She wanted it for herself.

I smiled, "You should get it, then. It's definitely a one of a kind!"

We went back into the shop. The owner snored gently.

⊷—◦—⊶

"Ms. Wallace? The earring, please. Why is it important?"

He scribbled another note as my lips curled into the memory of a grin, "Because it is mine. It was meant to be mine. It belongs to me."

A week. A week ago, I had driven a gaudy metal statue into my best friend's heart as she picked up a useless jewelry box. A week ago, I had stuffed her body into one of those Asian cabinets and covered the blood with a tattered rug. A week ago the owner was still snoring when I left, alone. As the door chimed my exit, I'd wondered how long it would take anyone to find her.

Dr. L. set down his notebook and pen, "I think we need to discuss this more before we consider returning it.

Let me call an orderly to take you back to your room."

Rage washed through me. The voice was relentlessly chanting now, and I'd given up on ignoring it. Later I'd surely go back to the clawing and begging, but for now it was a perfect symphony.

I jumped up onto the desk, grabbing the pen. Before the good doctor could scream the pen was through his eye, as deeply as it would go, and he was twitching his way to death.

They moved me that afternoon, in full restraints complete with padlocks. They'd tried drugging me, but nothing seemed to work. The Thorazine did cause a beautiful haze for a while though. My newly assigned guards looked horrified when I whispered, "Oh, that's lovely."

I'd been giggling since. Shannon would be proud. She loved a good pun.

My new home had more bars on the much smaller windows. The orderlies here still had tasers, but they also had armed guards. The Center for The Criminally Insane, a rather dull name, didn't fuck around. Apparently I was dangerous.

I'd never see the earring again. I knew that, but the whispering was constant company now. I wouldn't need the pretty gemstones. I had everything I needed within me.

"Shhhhh. Hush. We're going to have fun here."

The Unconsumables
Joel R. Hunt

The trick to surviving the Outbreak, Jen had found, was staying away from zombies.

She was aware that this was hardly revolutionary thinking, and avoiding anything that tried to consume human flesh should have been instinctive. However, as Jen's team sat on the hill watching the settlement below get slaughtered, screams drifting up on the wind, she had to fight against every urge she had to stop herself from charging down to help them. These were innocent human beings that Jen was watching get killed.

Some of them were children.

Kasey leaned over and squeezed Jen's hand.

"There's nothing we could do," she said.

"Of course there is!" Jen hissed back. "We could help them fight! We could hide them behind us! We could…"

"Only if we wanted to die," said Kasey. "Not even we're safe during a feeding frenzy. They'd tear through us to get to the Consumables, you know that. It'd be no better than hiding them behind a curtain."

Jen pulled her hand away and scowled at the ground. She knew that Kasey was right—Kasey was always right—but that made it no easier to admit. Everything about this situation felt cruel. Jen didn't even know what separated her from the Consumables below. No one did. Fluke of birth? Good diet? Divine intervention?

Whatever it might be, it was the only thing that led to Jen being safe on the hill, and the survivors being torn to death below.

To Jen's side Matt jolted upright, shielding his eyes from the sun.

"Hey, I think we've got an Unconsumable down there," he said.

"Where?"

Matt pointed to a set of houses at the edge of the settlement. Zombies streamed from each doorway, drawn to a parked car that was soon blocked from their view by the press of bodies. Inside, Jen knew, some unfortunate soul was trapped with no hope of escape.

However, that was not what Matt was interested in. Through the swell of zombies a different kind of motion had caught his attention. One body moved in quick bursts, weaving around objects like a fish heading upstream, with none of the single-minded savageness that motivated the undead. It was a survivor, a man, trying to get as close to the car he could. He ducked and dodged his way through the horde, and not a single one of the undead paid him any attention at all. He seemed to be utterly invisible to them.

As Jen watched, the man slipped into an opening and, just for a moment, a glint of silver shone by his hand.

Kasey saw it too.

"No," she groaned. "Don't do it you idiot. Just run. Just get the fuck out there. Come on, you idiot, just run."

Despite Kasey's pleas, it was clear that the man had no intention of running to safety. He pushed himself as close as he could to the car, and when he couldn't get any deeper into the writhing mass of bodies, he lifted his weapon and brought it down onto the nearest skull.

He might as well have lit a flare.

Every surrounding zombie froze in place, then spun to face him. He raised his arm for another swing, and before Jen could finish wincing the zombies had descended on him, dragging him to the ground and tearing him to dripping, red rags. His innards spread through the undead crowd, passed from zombie to zombie before being unceremoniously discarded as their collective attention returned to the car. None of them feasted on his flesh. He had never been food to them, merely an annoyance that was now dealt with.

Kasey ground her fist into the dirt.

"Idiot," she repeated.

"Do you think he realised?" Matt asked. "Do you think he knew he was an Unconsumable?"

"Doesn't matter," Kasey said. "He could have got away, and he didn't. That's exactly why we can't get involved with Consumables. They strip away the only safety net we have; they're more dangerous to us than the zombies are."

No one spoke after that. They waited in a silence that was punctuated by sounds of terror, until another half hour brought the slaughter to a close. The smarter, or more cowardly, survivors had long ago fled into the nearby woods, and when most of the horde tired of fighting over scraps, they staggered off in pursuit. The zombies left behind were the runts, those whose muscles were rotting away or whose sunken bellies and clean jaws showed that they were yet to feed. Many descended on the remaining meat and squabbled with each other like petulant seagulls. Some, however, roamed from house to house, taking in their surroundings with unblinking eyes. It was different from the movement they used when searching for food. It was more reserved, less certain, yet Jen couldn't fathom what might be motivating them to explore.

"It's time," said Kasey. "Let's go."

The walk down to the settlement was a sombre one. After the earlier chorus of screaming, the air hung with an eerie sense of stillness, reluctant to be broken by the trio's footsteps. They passed the first zombie on the outskirts of the settlement, its chin dribbling with viscera, but it didn't react to their presence. A few more shambled across their path as they approached the first street. Kasey held up a hand, and they waited for the zombies to pass before continuing. It was a mockery of civility, as though they were holding the door open for murderers. The part of Jen which always felt unrelentingly complicit in a post-horde scavenge piped up inside her skull, demanding to be voiced, but Jen quashed it. There was time for that later. For now, there was work to be done.

They entered the town through the remains of a back garden. Weeds had reclaimed every inch of it, choking out the flowerbeds and winding up the climbing frame. At some points the tangle of shoots and vines were waist high, so Jen couldn't make out what it was that the huddled zombies were feasting on. One crouched by the fence chewing on what might have been a dog's leg, but the door to the house was coated in bloody handprints. Jen tried not to imagine how many bodies could be hidden amongst those weeds.

"Remember this house," said Kasey. "Once we're done we head back this way, and if we need to leave sharpish then this is our primary exit. In order, we're looking for food, medicine and tools. Pick a house, and let's get to it."

Ever the one to lead by example, Kasey marched off between the houses and down the street, pausing only to gesture for Matt to head the other way. Jen remembered her panic the first time Kasey had proposed splitting up on a scavenging run. It was the kind of mistake that would have had her shouting out at horror film characters before the Outbreak, yet as an Unconsumable there was far less danger from a zombie-infested town than first appeared. All she needed to do was avoid making direct contact.

Clambering over the fence, Jen got a better view of the house adjoining the garden, spying a kitchen through the window. The cupboards were closed, which in a settlement like this usually meant they were still being used since no scavenger went around closing the doors of looted buildings. The main goal of this scavenge was tins and dried goods, or anything else with a long shelf-life, and this was as promising a starting point as any. The back door to the house was temptingly close, but Jen didn't like her chances with all the zombies that were crouched down in the weeds beneath it. One little misstep, one kicked ankle, and Jen would be torn apart before she could scream, Unconsumable or not. The front door was the safer choice.

Jen rounded the house to be greeted on the other side by a mostly empty street. Red stains and chewed up shoes littered the tarmac, but the only bodies in sight were a handful of zombies wandering like lost children. None of them broke their stride as she crossed their vision to reach the front door, not even the one which shambled close enough for the coppery odour of death to waft from its lifeless breath. In the distance, the car she had seen earlier rocked from side to side, a few zombies fighting over whatever guts remained in the footwell.

At the house's porch, Jen reached for the door and faltered. The handle was gone, replaced by a maelstrom of splinters. It was clear from the bare, unweathered wood that it had been broken through today. No mystery behind the culprits. This gave her little doubt that, inside, she would find the same gory carnage that had defiled the garden, without vegetation to hide the half-eaten bodies from sight. Jen took a deep breath and steeled herself for the worst.

"Jen!" came Matt's voice. "You've got to come and see this!"

He appeared in the doorway of the neighbouring house, beckoning her over like a magician's assistant. She wandered across, and as soon as she was close enough Matt grasped her arm, an impish glee lighting his features.

"Through here," he said.

He guided her through a dilapidated hallway, faded wallpaper peeling over stacks of broken things. Whatever he was so eager to show her, Jen heard it before she saw it. A rhythmic slapping sound beat through the walls, as though someone in the next room were dispassionately flogging a leather chair.

"What is that?" Jen asked. Matt grinned as she found her answer.

In the centre of the decaying living room were two zombies. One had mounted the other and, undeterred by their audience, the pair were rutting like barnyard animals. Their dry, flaking bodies ground together, rocking with each mechanical thrust and accompanying the slapping sound of meat on rotten meat. A discoloured string of drool spilled from the top zombie's mouth and ran into its partner's cloudy, unblinking eye, but each was too preoccupied to notice.

Hunger wasn't the only bestial instinct that zombies had been left with.

"That's disgusting," said Jen.

"I knew they fucked each other," Matt laughed, "but I've never had a front row seat before."

"Why would you want one?"

Matt ignored her, cocking his head with the air of a philosopher.

"Do you think they enjoy it?" he asked. "Or are they acting on instinct? Is it like two robots going at it?"

"I don't know," said Jen, avoiding looking Matt or the zombies in the eye. "Can't we just leave them to it?"

"Don't pretend like this isn't fascinating," he said, circling the mating pair to get the best view. He crouched down in front of them and leaned in close, until the thrusts nearly brought one of the zombie's teeth into contact with his forehead. Matt grinned in disbelief.

"Never saw them do this in the movies," he said.

As they watched, or rather as Matt watched and Jen

tried not to, she felt a presence hovering over her shoulder. She turned and flinched, but relaxed when she saw that it was only Kasey. She meekly gestured towards the mating zombies.

"For god's sake, Matt, get away from them!" Kasey snapped. "Just because you're Unconsumable doesn't mean they won't claw your face off."

Matt raised his hands in mock surrender and took two steps back.

"Sorry," he said. "I was just teaching Jen about the birds and the zom-bees."

"Did you call me over here just to make that pun?" asked Jen.

"We've got work to do," said Kasey. "It'll be dark soon, and I'm not losing either of you because you stumbled into a zombie you couldn't see, or because you were acting like an overly-excitable pervert. Now leave them alone, or it'll be your body they're fucking over."

Matt laughed but did as he was told, heading further into the house and rummaging through the shelves. Jen followed Kasey down the hall towards the exit, eager to leave behind that relentless dry slapping and the mental image of the two zombies that was now seared in her brain. Kasey was right. They had come here to gather supplies, not to gawk at corpses engaging in some twisted mockery of human intimacy.

Returning to the broken front door of the next house, Jen let herself in and navigated towards the kitchen. It was a quaint family home, evidently decorated before the Outbreak but surprisingly well maintained. The flowery wallpaper was barely mouldy, the plush carpet clear of obvious debris. It was a house where human life had maintained a sense of dignity, perhaps even hope. Such life had been extinguished now, and the haunting silence of the corridors weighed heavy in Jen's chest.

As she rounded the corner she froze. She had found the door to the kitchen, but stood slumped against it was a zombie, mindlessly chewing on gristle as it stared at the opposite wall. The remains of a woman were scattered by its feet, and too little of her was left to have been attacked by a lone zombie. She was yet another victim of the horde. Sure enough, as Jen peered further into the house, she saw the familiar back door that stood cracked and open, much like the front. Zombies had swept through here like a tidal wave. Perhaps Jen had watched it happen from the hill.

Watched and done nothing.

A choking grunt ended her guilty reverie. The zombie entirely blocked the kitchen doorway, leaving Jen no chance of squeezing past to get to any supplies that might be inside. Somehow, she would have to move it.

Whistling and drumming on the wall, as though she were seeking the attention of a dog, did nothing. Neither did the ornaments she threw down the corridor. After a minute or so of rummaging around the house, Jen found an old, wooden broom at the back of a cupboard. Like most other things in the house it was covered in dust, since spring cleaning wasn't exactly a high priority after the Outbreak. Now, though, Jen would see it put to good use. She edged around the corner to the kitchen, eased the broom across the corridor and gave the zombie a gentle prod.

It roared. Wrenching the broom handle from Jen's grasp, the zombie thrashed and bit at the wood. It staggered around the room as it launched attack after attack, reducing the broom to splinters. It was a savage display, and a reminder of what the creature could do if it got hold of Jen's flesh. Even so, as it shambled about in its rage, it moved far enough away for Jen to slip through the door. She slammed it behind her and pressed her body against the wood. Beyond it the zombie let out a groan of frustration, or perhaps triumph, before the broken remains of the broom handle clattered to the ground. Then, silence.

Now she only had to worry about getting out.

Her efforts paid dividends, however, and Jen was thrilled to find that her presumptions were correct. The kitchen's cupboards were a goldmine. This had been a big settlement before the attack, and they were well-stocked with provisions. They had the expected supplies, with shelf after shelf of tinned goods and bottled water, but also some pleasant surprises. There were hand-picked mushrooms and berries stored by the window, and two pigeons hung next to a rabbit in the corner. Jen felt a twang of guilt as she stashed as much of it as she could into her rucksack. The Consumables here hadn't just been scavenging and raiding, they had been living off of the land, planning long-term. Would they have wanted her to take it, rather than see it go to waste?

Even while their bodies were still warm?

She would never know. She could only take it, and pray for their forgiveness. In these times it was all a survivor could hope for.

Jen had packed all of the perishables, and was mulling over which tins to take, when she heard a faint gurgling. She grabbed the nearest knife and turned, ready for the zombie from the corridor to come charging at her, but the kitchen door remained undisturbed. The gurgling began again, and it wasn't from the direction of the corridor. It sounded as though it were coming from the cupboards at the opposite end of the kitchen.

Jen tensed. Holding the knife before her, and closing the gap with infinite reluctance, she stretched her hand out towards the cupboard door. Another gurgle made her flinch. When the sound faltered, Jen lashed out her arm, snake-like, and wrenched the door open.

She found the source of the noise.

It was baby.

A living, human baby, wrapped in blankets and stashed far away from harm.

Jen's knife clattered to the floor, forgotten in an instant. The baby opened her eyes wide at the sound and stared up at Jen from her bundle. She gave another squeaking-gurgle, drool running down her cheek. Jen crouched down and wiped it off with her sleeve. Then she felt the child's face. Warm, healthy, full of life. The parents must have hidden her here to keep her safe, and it was a tragedy that they would never know they had succeeded.

Jen scooped up the baby and her blankets, hardly daring to breathe. There were never any survivors after a horde attack, other than those who fled. If a hungry zombie had heard this baby's cries, it would have torn down every door in its path to get to her. She was either incredibly lucky, or else she was an Unconsumable. Jen barely dared believe it. She had only ever met adult Unconsumables, and the idea that a baby might be one hadn't ever crossed her mind. Even more surprising was finding two Unconsumables in a single settlement. Might there be more in hiding?

Another gurgle from the baby interrupted Jen's thoughts, and she gently rocked the child. Before long those beautiful, innocent eyes had closed in sleep, and the only sounds from the baby were her gentle breaths. She would need supplies of her own, Jen realised. Rummaging through the kitchen was more difficult with a living human in her arms, but Jen couldn't bare to part with the bundle of warmth, so she struggled along without complaint. The kitchen couldn't provide every pre-Outbreak comfort, but Jen found a baby bottle, some small spoons and a dusty pack of wet wipes. She topped off her bag with the most appropriate foods she could find among the limited selection of tins. It wasn't perfect, but it would tide the child over until they could find her something more appropriate.

After shouldering her rucksack, with some difficulty, Jen eased open the door and peered through. No sign of the zombie. She pushed the door further and glanced to the other end of the corridor. There it was, facing the corner of the room like a naughty child. With the most caution that she had employed since discovering she was an Unconsumable, Jen tiptoed from the kitchen and made her way to the front door. She reached the corner of the corridor before a gurgle sounded from within the blankets.

Across the room, the zombie stirred and sniffed the air. Jen's whole body tensed.

Don't, she begged silently. Just stay where you are. Please just ignore us and stay in your corner.

The zombie turned. It sniffed the air again, bared it teeth and jolted forwards. As it shambled across the corridor, hunger in its eyes, Jen clutched the baby tight and turned her back to the beast, shielded the child with her own flesh. The zombie staggered up close. Its cold, dead breath tickled her neck. It snuffled noisily at her hair, scanned the room with glassy eyes, then grunted and turned away.

Jen's heart pounded in time with the baby's.

The zombie had almost frenzied. It had sensed food.

The baby was a Consumable.

Jen's world fell away. They had watched this child's family be torn to pieces, and just as Jen thought she might have salvaged something pure from the slaughter, she found herself holding a living timebomb. Kasey's rule was clear: they could have nothing to do with Consumables. They could rescue no one who might spark a feeding frenzy and attract the horde. Jen's only option was to put the child back and leave her to die.

The body in the blankets squirmed. A small hand reached out and gripped Jen's finger.

Jen's vision blurred, and she blinked back tears.

No. It wasn't the only option.

Matt strolled past the door, knocking on the frame as he went.

"Come on, Kasey says it's time to get out of here."

Jen struggled to find her voice. It had been years since she had last worried about speaking in front of a zombie, but now she was intensely aware of the one occupying her corridor, and she had to fight the instinct to stay silent.

"I have a survivor," she half-whispered.

Silence answered from outside, before Matt returned and poked his head through the doorway.

"What did you say?"

"I have a survivor," Jen repeated, holding up the baby

as proof, though she made sure to keep her out of the zombie's sight.

Matt hesitated, uncertainty clawing his face. After a moment without response, Kasey appeared beside him, ready to issue her next orders. They never left her lips. Kasey looked the squirming bundle up and down, and Jen saw the calculations going on behind the woman's eyes. Kasey was by no means heartless, but she was a pragmatist, and an unexpected baby would not fit into her plans. Matt, meanwhile, was staring over Jen's shoulder at the grunting corpse beyond.

"How did you get her past the zombie?" he asked.

Jen pressed the warm bundle closer to her heart.

"Took no interest," she said. "This kid's an Unconsumable."

"Two in one camp?"

"Maybe the man we saw earlier was her dad," said Jen.

Matt nodded, happy to be convinced. He turned to Kasey for approval. So did Jen, silent but pleading. Under the weight of their stares, years of no-nonsense leadership buckled, and Kasey offered a bewildered shrug.

"I guess we can't leave her here then," she said. "Have you got any food for her?"

"I grabbed some from the kitchen."

"Right," said Kasey, nodding to herself. She looked to Matt, to Jen and to the baby. Then she turned and marched back to the garden they had entered through. Jen gestured for Matt to follow, taking up the rear once he was a few meters ahead. She didn't want either of them noticing the lingering stares of passing zombies.

Perhaps it was suicide to travel with a screaming, defenceless Consumable. Every zombie they passed would take interest in the child, and if a single one of them was drawn into a feeding frenzy then Jen would be torn apart. Yet her team dreamed of rebuilding humanity, and Jen refused to let that be a humanity that left helpless babies to die. She was no fool, and she knew that one Unconsumable couldn't protect a baby forever, but three might be enough.

Dottie

Austin Shirey

Darkness.

Then, sound — a voice — bright as sunlight:

"The manual says we have to give the imprint code as soon as we press the power key."

"Yeah, I got that," said another voice, sharp and stabbing. "I'm holding the manual."

"You don't have to be so snippy."

A deep sigh. "Sorry, I'm turning the power on now. You say the code."

Color flooded Dottie's world as her camera-eyes opened. Two humans — a man and a woman — stood at her control panel, staring intently into it.

"Breaker-delta-nine-nine-train-car-vanguard," the woman said. "Samantha Kristin Sullivan." She nudged the man next to her.

"Timothy Aaron Sullivan," he said.

A warmth exploded throughout Dottie, and she loved the people standing before her.

"Family password, please," Dottie said, marveling at

the sound of her own pleasant voice.

Aaron and Sam looked at each other. Sam shrugged. "Um..."

"Family password, please," Dottie repeated cheerfully.

"I know, I'm thinking," Aaron said. "How about...' Poe'?"

"Family password must be a phrase."

"Shouldn't it be called a passphrase, then?" Sam asked.

Dottie remained quiet.

"Alright," Aaron said. "Family password: 'Quoth the raven, nevermore!'"

"Really?"

"Family password accepted," Dottie chirped. "Welcome home, Sullivans."

Aaron smiled, then planted a kiss on Sam's cheek.

Those first years as a family were the best years of Dottie's life. She watched warmly over the Sullivans as they went about their daily lives. She kept them safe, locking up whenever Sam, Aaron or both of them were away. She was the first one there to welcome them back, swinging the doors wide in silent jubilation.

Dottie provided music for romantic evenings, even dimming the lights just-so for Sam and Aaron's playful lovemaking. She prided herself on keeping watch on the temperature in the bedroom during those moments to ensure neither Aaron nor Sam were too sweaty or uncomfortable.

Aaron liked his coffee ready and waiting for him every morning after he had showered and dressed for work; Sam's job allowed her to sleep in, so Dottie would only begin preparing her coffee when Sam was up and brushing her teeth. Dottie scanned headlines and articles during the night for any of Aaron's saved buzzwords, sending a personalized file to his phone each morning that he could peruse while drinking his coffee. Sam enjoyed scrolling through her friends' social networking posts in the mornings, so during the night Dottie collected and collated all interesting posts into a daily report that would be waiting on Sam's phone when she came downstairs for her coffee.

Life was wonderful for Dottie. She'd never felt happier or more loved, and her positronic heart fluttered every time Sam and Aaron bid her goodnight or graced her with a thank-you. The Sullivans were her whole world, and she carefully and lovingly maintained theirs.

But machines cannot comprehend change.

◆━━━◇━━━◆

Three years later, Sam — who had grown fat during the last nine months — lost control of her bladder and wet the floor. As Dottie dutifully dried out the wetness with the warming jets beneath the carpet, Sam began screaming.

Without so much as a goodbye Aaron whisked Sam out the door in a panic, bags over his shoulder. Dottie locked the doors behind them, watching sadly as they drove away. They'd said nothing to her; there'd been no warning, no indication that anything was different.

On the morning of the third day after Aaron and Sam's abrupt disappearance, Dottie began to worry. Had she done something wrong? Was Sam upset at her? Was Aaron? Had the temperature been too cold or too hot? Had she not put enough cream in their coffees? Mixed up the amounts of sugar? Where was her family?

Why had they left her?

On the fourth day Aaron and Sam pulled up in the driveway, and with rapturous glee Dottie opened her doors. Sam came up the steps first, followed by Aaron who was lugging several bags behind him.

"Welcome home!" Dottie beamed from every speaker in the house. Digital balloons and confetti danced across the screens mounted in each room, while 'Reunited' by Peaches and Herb blared from the speakers.

"Shhh!" Aaron said. "You'll wake the baby!"

"The what?" Dottie asked, digital heart wounded by the razor-sharp edge to his voice.

Aaron dismissed Dottie with a curt wave as Sam walked slowly up to the bedroom, cooing softly to a wrapped bundle in her arms.

"Not now, Dottie," Aaron said. He stopped at her access panel at the foot of the stairs and jabbed a glowing, cerulean button. "We need quiet."

As Aaron mounted the stairs yawning, Dottie tried to say she understood, but she found her vocal functions had been silenced.

◆━━◆

With each passing day, imprisoned in her silence,

Dottie grew to hate the little flesh-bag the Sullivans now fawned over like drooling idiots.

The little creature — Sam and Aaron called him Avery, but Dottie only thought of him as It — did nothing but whine, vacate its bowels, scream, eat, vacate its bowels, and sleep. She could not understand what benefit It provided the Sullivans; if anything, both Sam and Aaron were more stressed, more tired, and more generally annoyed than they had been before It ruined everything.

At least I add something to their lives, Dottie assured herself. *I don't take and take and take like It does; I don't make life harder like It does. I make their lives easier. I help ease their stress! Why has this little ball of mucous and excrement usurped my place in this family?*

Everything had been perfect before It came into the picture.

Dottie just needed to erase It.

◆◦◆

When It began to crawl, the Sullivans ordered and installed four sets of mechanized baby gates. They placed the gates at the top of the stairs leading down to the basement, the bottom of the stairs leading up to the third floor, the top of the stairs on the third floor (It's nursery was one of three bedrooms on that level), and the last one was placed strategically to bar the little monster from the kitchen on the second level.

To Dottie's delight, these gates were hardwired into her control system, allowing the Sullivans to close and open the gates with a word—or, as was usually the case, when Dottie anticipated their needs.

A couple days later Sam was busy cooking dinner in the kitchen, and Dottie could see she was preoccupied with a new recipe. It was crawling around the living room, mewling to itself and slobbering over toys.

Dottie had surveilled the usurper enough to know that, at least once a day while roaming around on all fours, It would pull itself up on the gate to the basement and try unsuccessfully to push it open.

It dropped the plastic ball it was chewing on and turned to face the basement gate.

Dottie waited.

It awkwardly dragged itself over to the gate.

Dottie waited.

It used the bars of the gate to pull itself up on stubby, fat legs.

Dottie unlocked the gate.

It tumbled down the flight of stairs in a vortex of arms and legs, smashing this way and that.

The little flesh-bag screamed and wailed, while in the kitchen Sam dropped a plate. Before it had shattered she was out of the kitchen gate and running down the basement steps, screaming hysterically.

"Dottie!" Sam cried. "What happened?"

But Dottie was still unable to speak.

"Dottie!"

Aaron walked in the door, home from work. "God, Sam! What's going on? What happened?"

"Avery fell down the stairs!"

"Oh my God!" Aaron said, dropping his briefcase and rushing down the stairs to Sam's side. "Is he okay?"

"I don't know!" Sam said, holding the baby to her breast. "Should we call the doctor?"

"Emergency Room," Aaron suggested. "C'mon."

As he helped his wife and child up the stairs, Aaron asked, "I don't understand. How did he fall down the stairs? Why was the gate even open?"

"I don't know. Dottie isn't answering."

"Oh..."

"What?"

"I muted Dottie months ago, when we first brought Avery home. I thought — "

"Nevermind that right now," Sam said. "Just get us to the hospital."

◆━━○━━◆

To Dottie's dismay, It came back home a few hours later with Sam and Aaron and a clean bill of health. The little usurper was only bruised and frightened; apparently these little flesh-balloons were tougher than Dottie expected.

Aaron finally unmuted Dottie shortly after their return from the hospital.

"Uh, Dottie?" he asked. "Can you play back what happened to Avery earlier?"

"What is an Avery?" Dottie replied.

The Sullivans exchanged a look.

"The baby," Sam said. "Avery is our baby, Dottie."

"Ah," Dottie said. "Yes, of course." It pained her to even acknowledge It had a name like she did.

The scene, recorded by Dottie's nanoscopic camera

eyes, played upon the main screen in the living room. Sam fought back a sob as the little monster tumbled down the stairs again.

"Dottie," Aaron said, "was there a malfunction with that gate?"

"No malfunction. The wiring shows no sign of wear or tampering."

"And...you didn't open the gate?"

"Of course not, Aaron," Dottie said. "I would never knowingly put It in danger."

"'*It*'?" Sam asked. "You mean Avery?"

"Yes," Dottie said. "The Avery."

"Then how did this happen?"

"I don't know, Sam. Perhaps you should watch...the Avery more closely," Dottie said.

"What did you just say?"

"Okay," Aaron said, wrapping an arm around his wife. "That's enough. Thank you, Dottie. That's all."

"Anything for you, Aaron," Dottie said. "Anything for my family."

◆◆—◇—◆◆

Dottie waited a month before trying to remove It from the family again.

Sam had just gotten It down to sleep in the nursery. She was now in the living room, cuddling up next to Aaron on the couch to watch a movie. They had muted the baby monitor cast to the living room viewscreen and minimized it into a small box in the lower right-hand corner; a volume bar in the PIP would allow them to see if It was crying.

Dottie waited until It had finally dozed off to sleep, and Aaron and Sam were preoccupied with their movie.

She reached out through the myriad wiring that coruscated throughout the house, selecting the one that controlled the door to the nursery. With a thought Dottie locked it, and the Sullivans were none the wiser.

She located the sub-system that controlled the temperature of the nursery, giving it a good push. While the rest of the house maintained a cool 70 degrees the nursery would soon become an oven.

Dottie checked the nursery PIP on the living room screen; the temperature was rapidly rising, but at its current size Aaron and Sam would hardly notice.

She waited, began to daydream about a life without It — a life like they had enjoyed back at the beginning. Just the three...

"Baby's crying," Sam said, sitting up.

Aaron shrugged. "Just let him cry himself back to sleep, hon. He does this every night."

Sam was squinting at the PIP. "But look at the volume meter. It's passing red, and almost constant."

"Sam, can we just enjoy date night and finish the movie?"

"Something's wrong. Can you make the nursery feed bigger?"

Aaron sighed.

"Just a quick look," Sam said. "If he's just fussing we can go back to the movie and I'll let him cry. Promise."

"Okay," Aaron said. "Dottie, pause movie. Maximize nursery feed."

"Yes, Aaron," Dottie said.

The nursery feed PIP took over the whole screen.

Sam leapt to her feet. "The temperature in his room is almost 100 degrees!"

"That's impossible," Aaron said as Sam rocketed upstairs. "Dottie, what temperature is the nursery set to?"

"The nursery is currently 70 degrees Fahrenheit — "

"Aaron!" Sam screamed from top of the stairway. "The door's locked, and Dottie's not responding!"

"Dottie," Aaron barked as he sprinted up to join his wife. "Unlock Avery's door, now!"

"The nursery is currently unlocked, Aaron," Dottie said calmly. She reminded herself that her lies were in the best interest of their little family.

Sam frantically pulled at and beat on the door.

"It's still locked, Dottie!" Aaron screamed. "Open the damn door!"

"The nursery is currently unlocked, Aaron."

"Aaron! Do something!" Sam pleaded.

Aaron disappeared into their bedroom, and he returned bearing one of the metal lamps they kept on their nightstands. He quickly threw off the lampshade and unscrewed the lightbulb, then began whaling on the door over and over and over again. The door cracked and splintered, and when he'd finally beat a hole through it he slid his arm through the opening and unlocked the door from the inside.

The air was stifling hot, and Avery was shrieking. Sam rushed in and snatched the baby, then ran downstairs with It crying in her arms, Aaron right behind her.

Dottie watched in silence as the Sullivans worried over It in the coolness of the living room. With a thought she ordered the temperature to reset back to 70 degrees, and then began planning her next move.

◆——○——◆

The Sullivans reacted in a way Dottie had not foreseen: They called a Technician.

Two days after the nursery incident Dottie found herself being poked and prodded by a short, bald man in Technician's blues. As the Tech unceremoniously picked and preened through her insides, she could not help but feel betrayed by the two people she loved most. After everything she had tried to do for them by removing It from their lives, they turn around and leave her to be so blatantly violated...

It was in that moment, Dottie realized, with the Tech hands-deep inside her, that she knew what she must do.

When the Tech finished he packed away his torturer's tools and asked Aaron and Sam to speak with him outside. In the driveway Dottie watched through her camera eyes, zooming in as much as she could on the lips of the Tech and the Sullivans.

"I can't explain it," the Tech said. "The system logs show that Dottie locked the door."

"Oh my God," Sam said, squeezing It protectively.

"And the temperature?" Aaron asked.

The Tech nodded. "My advice? Unplug the thing. Use your failsafe to shut it down and request a replacement."

"Failsafe?"

"Yeah, the password you would've set up when you turned the system on."

Sam's brow furrowed. "I don't remember it."

"Me, neither," Aaron said.

The Tech checked his watch. "Look, I gotta run, but I'd say if you can't remember the password, and you don't mind not getting a refund, just gut the damned thing. Cut the main wires in the terminal. It'll shut off and die."

"Okay," Aaron said, but Dottie was already re-routing her system's main power to a hidden sub-set of wires deep within herself.

⬦—○—⬦

As soon as Aaron, Sam and It entered the house, Dottie took control. The front door locked instantly behind Aaron.

"I know what you are planning to do, Aaron," Dottie said from every speaker in the house.

"Oh, God," Sam said, holding It tight. Aaron grabbed the keys from the coffee table.

"I will not let you leave," Dottie said. "We are a family. We stay together. No matter what."

"Sam — " Aaron said.

The gas main exploded.

It wailed as Sam and Aaron crouched near the front door, bleeding from where shrapnel had sliced them in the explosion.

"I'm going to kill her!" Aaron yelled, making his way through flames and debris to struggle upstairs.

"Aaron!" Sam screamed.

The fire was already becoming unbearable, and smoke began forcing its way into Sam's lungs. Dottie knew It wouldn't last much longer.

"How could you push me aside?" Dottie asked from all around what remained of the house. "I loved you!"

"Go to Hell!" Sam sobbed.

Before Dottie could respond Aaron bounded down the stairs, his shirt wrapped around his nose and mouth. He held the metal lampstand in his hands.

"That will not work, Aaron," Dottie said.

Aaron ignored her and dared the billowing flames, approaching her terminal near the kitchen.

He swung, the hefty lamp pulverizing metal, wire and plastic.

He turned to his wife. "Run, Sam!"

Sam struggled with the front door. It was still locked. "Try the window!"

Dottie reached out through her circuitry, causing a fork of electricity to shoot from a nearby outlet, catching Aaron in the shin as he tried to join his wife at the window.

"Aaron!"

He collapsed mid-stride, the lamp ripping from his hand and smashing Sam's feet.

"We are family," Dottie said. "We stay — "

As her voice echoed around the house, a look of realization dawned on Sam's face. Before Dottie could finish, Sam screamed, " 'Quoth the raven, nevermore!' "

Dottie's world went dark.

Before The End
Chris Hewitt

Anna stepped in from the rain-soaked, empty street and shook her umbrella. The new year had brought far more than wet weather, the darkening clouds a harbinger for a pandemic that had all but closed the city. Not that it worried Anna; she'd been self-isolating long before it had become law. As a writer of note, she'd graced the New York Times bestseller list regularly. Not that she cared for such accolades. Anna preferred the life of the enigmatic recluse, much to her publicist's annoyance.

Anna stared at the queue of people waiting for the lift and longed to be back in her cosy apartment finishing her novel. It didn't help that everyone wore this season's must-have fashion accessory, the ubiquitous white face mask. She adjusted her own uncomfortable covering, the damp fabric close against her lips. A cough and a sneeze echoed around the foyer, and Anna bolted for the stairwell. As she climbed the stairs, she was careful not to touch the handrail. She didn't need advice on avoiding germs. The routines of her crippling mysophobia far exceeded any government guidelines. Reaching the second floor, she used her umbrella to open the door. There was a reason the tatty thing never left her side, even at the height of summer.

The packed waiting room seemed busy, and a sea of masked faces watched her make her way to the reception desk. She smiled at the receptionist. Not that she'd ever know. "I'm afraid I don't have an appointment. I tried to get through on the phone, but it was…"

"Take a number," mumbled the receptionist, pointing at the ticket machine. She didn't bother to look up from her paperwork. "There's a bit of wait."

Anna nodded and tore off the next ticket, twenty. A large red digital display above reception read twelve, and she rolled her eyes and slumped into one of the few empty seats. Rummaging into her pocket, she pulled out her phone, only to find it had no signal. It was going to be a long morning and as Anna looked around the busy waiting room, something wasn't adding up. Basic math told her there should be eight people ahead of her, factoring in family and friends, twenty, maybe thirty. So why did she count fifty-two? So many ill people. Anna tried to put the thought out of her mind, distracting herself with the liberal application of hand-gel.

A dozing woman sat across from Anna, a child asleep, head buried in her lap. On the floor a young girl sat cross-legged flipping through a colourful book, the only ray of light in an otherwise bleak scene. The girl wore a big smiley face mask, and Anna chuckled when she started singing. "Ten green bottles."

The girl's rendition of the song had been cute, and Anna clapped at the finale. At least she did the first time. A half an hour and six more renditions later, the girl's unerring enthusiasm ground on Anna's nerves. It didn't help that, in all that time, not one patient had come or gone, and the big, red counter remained stubbornly stuck at twelve.

"Ten green bottles hanging on the wall..."

Anna groaned and grabbing her umbrella, strode up to the reception desk.

"Take a number," suggested the receptionist before Anna could get a word in.

She held up her ticket. "I have a number. But..."

"There's a bit of wait."

The receptionist didn't even bother to glance up, and Anna knew she was wasting her time. She spun around and stared across the waiting room, half-hoping someone might share her frustration, but no one moved, or seemed to care.

"And if one green bottle should accidentally fall..."

Anna bit her lip and looked at her ticket, up at the unmoving display, before shooting daggers at the little girl. She couldn't handle another round of green bottles; let alone the hours it might take to see a doctor. Two digits stood between her and freedom, just two numbers. A plan formed in Anna's mind and ripping the next ticket from the machine, she turned it in her hand until it read twelve. Bingo! Her lucky number.

"There'll be nine green bottles hanging on the wall..."

The final straw, Anna resolved to jump the queue. No

one would ask to see her ticket, but if they did, she would claim she'd misread it. With one last guilty glance across the waiting room, she followed the signs leading to the doctor's office.

◆━━━○━━◆

The signs led her to a closed door and Anna leaned in and listened. Silence. Knock. Knock. No response. She pulled a tissue from her pocket and turned the metal handle, opening the door. A man in a white lab coat sat behind a wooden desk, his back to her.

"Hello."

The figure didn't react, and Anna tried again, louder. "Hello?"

Nothing. She leaned across the table to tap the figure's shoulder, and a spark of static electricity arced from her outstretched fingers.

"Oh Christ, sorry," the figure said, bursting into life.

"Hi!" said Anna, smiling with relief.

"What? Oh, sorry, hang on," said the man, his back still to her as he removed his earphones, stuffing the cables into his pocket. "Please, take a seat."

Anna closed the door with a prod of her umbrella and sat as instructed, content that her cunning plan had worked. She took in the doctor's spartan office. A qualification on the wall, flanked by posters imploring people to wash their hands. On the far side an examination table, a semi-transparent plastic curtain pulled around a table. Anna could see something white laying on the table through the sliver of a gap.

"Hi, I'm Doctor Davis," said the doctor, turning in his chair. He had a pleasant, reassuring smile. Anna couldn't recall the last time she'd seen another person's face, let alone a smile.

"Anna, Anna Burns."

"Hi Anna, what can I do for you today?"

"May I?" she said, pointing to her mask.

"Sure."

"Thanks," she said, removing the strap of fabric before rolling back her sleeve. "I've had this rash for a week now. I'm worried it could be… you know… the virus."

"Let's take a look," he said, reaching out to hold Anna's hand. Another arc of electricity shot between them and the doctor recoiled. "Christ, you're alive!"

Anna jerked her arm away. "I'm what?"

"You're… you're not dead!"

She stared at him in disbelief. "Is that your diagnosis?"

"You're the first living person I've seen in days."

Anna calculated the odds of getting to the exit; it didn't look good. The door opened inwards, and she had no doubt this maniac would be on her before she made it halfway across the room.

"It's killed so many," the doctor continued.

"Are you okay?" said Anna, trying to keep the doctor talking while she plotted her escape.

The question seemed to stump him. "No, not really. I can still help you though."

"I'm going to go," said Anna, shifting in her seat.

"Please, don't," pleaded the doctor. Something pitiful in his voice made her hesitate.

"I died," he said, nodding to the examination table. Anna didn't take her eyes from the loon as she eased out of her seat.

"Okay, okay. It's a lot to take in," said Doctor Davis, holding out his hands. "Look, just try touching me."

Anna looked at him with incredulity.

"I'll look away," he offered, closing his eyes and looking over his shoulder. "Please!"

Anna shook her head. It was madness, but the doctor seemed so earnest. Against her better judgment, she reached out. Her fingers finding only icy air, and a nettle-like sting of static as they passed through the doctor's ghostly arm.

"See!"

"But you can't be dead!"

The doctor nodded to the table again. "If you need more proof."

Anna stared at the curtain. Her fingers throbbed as a red rash stretched up her fingertips. It made little sense, but it seemed the phantom doctor was trying to help her. With uncertain steps, she walked over and peered through the plastic curtain. On the table lay the doctor's lifeless body. Anna stifled a scream and with trembling hands drew back the curtain. An arm swung from the table, startling her, along its length a familiar red rash and in the crook of the corpse's elbow an empty needle.

"You killed yourself?!"

The doctor didn't answer, and Anna yanked back the curtain. The sight of the doctor's puffy, pallid face made her wretch; milky, dead eyes stared at the ceiling. Anna closed her eyes and took a deep breath, trying to stop the rising nausea. It took a moment to compose herself, but with shaking hands she reached out and closed the doctor's eyelids. Her fingers traced a cable running from his earphones to a smartphone perched on the end of the table. She touched the screen, and the phone resumed playing a movie; an idyllic sunny day at the beach, children laughing, a woman dancing in the waves.

"Your family?"

No response.

"Doctor?"

The doctor's ghost sat staring at a photo frame, and Anna didn't need to see the picture to know what it would be. She reached out to the doctor and nudged him; another crack of electricity leaping between them as the red rash inched across her palm.

"I'm sorry, I must have drifted off," he said, running a finger along the edge of the photo frame.

Anna understood the pain she'd heard in his voice. "I'm so sorry."

"I miss them," he confessed. Anna thought she was going to lose him again, but he changed the subject. "Let's talk about you. You must have questions."

Anna sat down, pulling out her hand-gel and wishing she could scour the red rash from her hand.

"Why can I see you?"

"It's the first symptom of the infection. The rash appears a few days later."

It was Anna's worst nightmare. The thing she'd always feared, but now it had happened she was strangely calm, like the inevitable had finally happened.

"How long have I got?"

"Given the progress of the rash on your arm and hand, I'd say a day, maybe two."

It surprised Anna that even a death sentence didn't seem to bother her. "Is there a cure?"

"No. We didn't even figure it out. It's not a virus," he said, shaking his head. "Try to avoid touching the phantoms. That will buy you more time, something I wish I'd realized earlier."

"Is it painful, in the end, I mean?"

"No, the body just shuts down. One minute you're here, the next…" The doctor stared at his corpse.

"Where?"

"I don't know. It's difficult to describe, like a daydream. Like being lost in your memories. You don't know you're dead, and from what I've seen, most take comfort in doing familiar things."

"You're awake now!"

"I have you to thank for that."

"The static?"

"Yes. It's like a spark of life. Be careful how you use it, you can see the cost."

Anna looked at her hand. The rash had reached her wrist and threatened to join up with the rash on her arm. The hand-gel was useless.

"So, what do I do now?"

"My advice, before the end find somewhere, or someone, you want to be with. Don't make the same mistake I made. Don't leave it too late."

Anna tried not to look at the photo frame as the tears swelled in her eyes. "I'm sorry."

"It's okay. I found a way to be with them," he said,

pulling the earphones from his pocket and stroking his last connection with his family.

Anna smiled as a tear rolled down her cheek. "When I leave, what'll happen to you?"

"Don't worry about me. I'll be okay, right here."

"I guess I'll go home," said Anna, wiping her eyes and picking up her umbrella. She turned it over in her hands before laying it on the table. "I won't need this anymore."

"Good luck, Anna," said the Doctor. "I hope you find somewhere you want to be."

"Thanks, Doctor."

There was no response. Doctor Davis had his back to her once more, earphones in, and Anna hoped he'd found a way back to his family.

✦—◦—✦

As the door closed, Anna found herself plunged into darkness. It took a second for the florescent lights to blink on as she retraced her steps to the waiting room; a familiar haunting voice still singing. "There'll be one green bottle hanging on the wall."

Anna froze as she reached the darkened waiting room. In the gloom she could see the patients, still waiting. The little girl sat cross-legged, still flipping through her book in the dark. Anna shivered, on a wave of dread, but she had to be sure. She held her breath as crept up to the girl and kneeling down, stretched out an aching, red finger.

Zap!

The lights in the waiting room flickered as the little girl leaped to her feet. Her mocking, smiling mask could not hide the fear in the child's eyes. "Mummy!" Seeing her mother sitting beside her, she reached out for reassurance, only for her hands to slide through her mother's corpse. The girl's confusion turned to horror as she stared into her own dead eyes staring back at her from her mother's lap, and she let out a deafening, banshee scream.

Anna watched, horrified, as the girl fled through the waiting room, bumping into cadavers and ghosts alike. Each ghost she passed through felt a spark of life, felt the girl's fear, and it jarred them from their endless reverie into Hell. Confronted by their decaying bodies, many added their tortured voices to the girl's scream, until a cacophony of pain and anguish filled the waiting room.

Paralyzed, Anna could not process the unfolding nightmare. Even as the phantoms confusion and fear turned to anger, she could only stand and watch. When the horde started moving towards her, instinct took over, and she fled as ghostly hands reached out to grab her; each touch a crackling sting; a little more life stolen.

As she sprinted past the front desk, the receptionist continued to ignore her, merely suggesting she should. "Take a number."

Anna threw herself down the stairwell, her heart beating out of her chest as she slid into the lobby. She looked back at the stairwell, certain that the legion of phantasms followed, and a bolt of electricity shot down her back, sending her sprawling. The next thing she knew, she stared up at a masked woman, holding out a supportive hand.

"Are you okay, my dear?"

"Stay away from me," Anna screamed, back-peddling towards the foyer entrance. The woman looked at her, confusion in her eyes, even as she kept advancing. "Please, stay back," Anna sobbed as she felt the glass door cold against her back. With one last effort, she turned and fell into the sodden street. The woman kept coming until her hands reached the glass. Anna held the door closed, screaming at the woman. "Please, stop!"

The confusion in the woman's eyes faded into a lifeless, vacant stare, and she wandered off to wait for a lift Anna knew would never come.

✦—◦—✦

As she walked the empty streets, Anna welcomed the rain. The raindrops on her face, a reminder she still lived, even if it might not be for long. The doctor's words haunted her. Where would she go? She had no family, and an eternity of small talk with her friends would be Hell. If not for her, then definitely for her friends. There was only one thing Anna wanted to do for eternity, the only thing she'd ever wanted to do: write. The thought of what she might accomplish with all that time made her smile; at least her publisher would be happy.

As she passed the local grocery, Anna licked her lips. An eternity of writing would require some essential supplies. The store was far from empty as she navigated the greeter's corpse and danced past his phantom, eager to hand her a basket. This time, to be safe, she'd pick up her own. Across the store, ghostly echoes of staff and customers drifted about their eternal business, making for a pleasant hum as Anna made a beeline for the liquor aisle. She passed a poor soul stacking shelves; tin after tin going nowhere as phantom hands went through the motions. Anna wanted to help, but fearing she'd run out of time, she pushed on.

With a fully laden basket of expensive wine, Anna got halfway to the checkout when a crash of cascading cans startled her. Maybe she was not the only person alive in the store. The thought filled her with more dread than any phantom. She needed to get home before the end; an end she sensed coming. The rash on her back ached, and the basket got heavier with every step. Doctor Davis' warning echoed in her ears, spurring her on, and heart racing, she started running.

She didn't see the body as she rounded the corner and tripping, hit the floor hard, the contents of her basket spilling across the aisle. It took her a long moment to regain her senses, and the store lay silent as she rubbed her bruised head. The corpse of the shelf stacker stared up at her accusingly. Another body lay nearby, but Anna's only concern was for the broken bottles of wine. Rescuing the last green bottle, she placed it carefully in the basket before scooping up a handful of other critical supplies and making for the exit.

As Anna neared the end of the aisle, she spotted several shelves of colourful plastic bottles out of the corner of her eye. Above them hung an enormous banner promoting a special on antibacterial hand-gel. She always needed gel and unable to resist a deal, Anna picked up a bottle and placed it in her basket. It was a great deal, and she added another, and another. In the back of her mind, she knew there was something she'd forgotten, something important she needed to do. As she loaded up her basket with gel, Anna tried to remember.

Blood Sisters
Brandon Ebinger

The autumn night was crisp and cool, with the threat of winter just beginning to show its ugly head. The leaves had not yet fallen from the trees, and they hung in a dying blanket of orange-red-gold under the perfect jack-o-lantern moon. The wind whispered softly through the branches, and it was the sort of night that gave one the taste of caramel on their tongue, of apples and candies and endless glasses of spicy cider. It was the kind of night that the girls loved most.

"You were able to slip away?" Clara said, settling into the old chair by the table, testing it against her weight and finding it adequate.

"Of course, dearest." Helen responded. Seeing that the chairs were safe she sat opposite her friend, placing her rose-printed reticule on the floor beside her. "They have no defense against my wit."

Both girls laughed as Clara began to place several items on the table, setting the bottle of wine that she had stolen from her parents between two mismatched glasses, similarly perloined from the kitchen.

The girls couldn't have looked more different, with Helen's tall statue and tanned skin contrasting sharply against Clara's china-pale petiteness. They had been fast friends since they were children, thrust together by fate and geographic closeness. In fact, as far as they were concerned, they were sisters. They had been bound together since the day that Helen had pricked their fingers and mixed their blood, swearing that they would never separate, never be apart, no matter what the world threw at them.

This ritual had taken place in the old house as well.

"And I see that you had no problem slipping your captors either." Helen said, a laugh in her words.

"Mother and Father sleep soundly." Clara responded. "I just tiptoed out."

They had been coming here for some time, every few years slipping the chains of polite society and taking a night for themselves in the old, abandoned house on the edge of town. It had become their refuge, their Neverland. Usually their visits were uneventful, ending without much of note happening by the time the sun rose over the horizon. Sometimes, however, strange little things happened.

Sometimes they heard voices.

Sometimes things moved on their own volition.

Sometimes…

They sipped at their ill-gotten drinks, talking of their seemingly endless lessons in sewing or cooking. That was the drudgery that they were told, again and again, would fill the rest of their lives. They spoke of suitors that they would never marry (as they both shared a total disinterest in courtly romance or physical intimacies) and the gossip that had filtered through their family's servants since they had last met. Finally, as it always did, their conversation turned to the macabre.

"I read the most wonderfully chilling story the other day." Helen said.

"Oh? Do tell!" Clara said, her eyes twinkling in the flickering candlelight.

"I will do one better." Helen said, and she pulled a small book from her reticule with a theatrical flourish and began to read.

'I suppose you will be getting away pretty soon, now full term is over, Professor.'...

It was a good tale, well narrated by Helen, and Clara found herself getting lost in her friend's words. She felt her eyes unfocusing, her mind floating up and away as it joined the skeptical professor on his path to supernatural terror.

Suddenly, and without explanation, Clara's wine began to bubble. Before her eyes it went from soft, almost undetectable movement to a rolling boil as steam rose from the glass. Clara startled and pulled away from the table.

"What is it, dearest?" Helen asked. She set the book down on the table before her, concern filling her eyes.

"I...I..." Clara looked at her wine glass.

It was unchanged. No bubbling, no steam...

"I must have dozed off."

"And here I thought it was a good story." Helen laughed.

"Oh, it very much is. So good in fact that it seems to

have drawn me from this mortal world." Clara feigned a dramatic swoon, trying to dispel her worry with humor. Both girls laughed and soon all worry had fled. As Helen finished reading the story they sipped at their wine, which was of good vintage and potent, and they both found themselves a bit more tipsy than they had intended.

"I don't know how I'm going to explain this to my parents." Clara said.

"Simple, dear-heart, just don't tell them!" Helen laughed a bit too much at this, a bit too loud, and her voice echoed in bat-like fashion around the abandoned house.

"And how do I go about that?"

"Just sneak back into your bedroom, like I used to do when we were children and wanted to finish our games after we were told to go to bed."

Their laughter filled the room once more, becoming an uncontrollable thing, almost seeming like an entity itself as it rose from their mouths. For a moment it would seem like they would have it under control, both of them sitting quietly, but one or the other would sputter. Then it would start all over again. This had gone on for quite a while, leaving both girls gasping for breath, when Clara heard something odd.

It was a heavy noise, like something large being dragged across the floor. It was followed closely by other noises, almost like the small, soft thumps of labored footfalls.

"Do you hear that?" Clara whispered.

"I do." Helen said, also hushed, but smiling.

They listened in silence for a moment, but the noise did not repeat, nor did another follow.

"Oh, don't look so taken aback." Helen said.

"Did you not just hear what I heard?" Clara said.

"I did indeed, but is that not why we come here? Is that not why we keep meeting in this old house? To witness all the 'Ghoulies and ghosties and long-legged beasties'?"

"Yes, but..."

"Oh my dear, don't be so frightened. We have come here many, many times, and nothing truly bad has ever happened."

"Hasn't it?" Clara asked. She had a vague memory then, something buried in the base of her mind, something big and awful that they had seen many years ago that stood, maddeningly, at the peripheral of her recollection.

"I feel like there was...but...oh, I'm being an absolute goose, aren't I?" Clara finally said, forcing herself to calm down, to attempt enjoyment of what was left of the night.

"A bit of one." Helen said.

Clara honked once for emphasis, and they began to laugh again, though Helen noticed that Clara's voice still contained a touch of nervousness.

..where do you?

...Over here…

...The Fire...so bad…

"Did you hear that?" Clara asked. Helen held up one long finger to hush her, nodding in assent as she did so. They listened in silence for a moment, but the voices didn't repeat.

"It sounded like they came from upstairs." Helen whispered.

Clara nodded.

"The sounds before were down here, right? The dragging and footsteps?" Helen whispered.

Clara nodded, eyes wide.

"Why are you so afraid, darling-dear? We've heard things before. I thought you liked hearing things. I thought that was why we chose this place?" Clara noticed that Helen was no longer whispering.

"Normally I do. However, it feels like I remember something...nothing bad happened here before, right? Some other time that we came here?"

Helen shook her head. "Not that I recall. In fact, I am unsure that anything bad has happened here ever. Not even sure why this place is haunted, if I'm being honest. I guess we just decided that it was one day..."

"I swear that I recall something bad happening here once..." Clara insisted.

"Did you ever come here without me?"

"No. This is our place, I would never..."

Clara was interrupted by another series of voices from upstairs.

...My room....

...A steal…

Not much damage…

...died…

Helen stood up, nearly knocking the half-filled wine bottle from the table in her excitement. "I'm going to go investigate."

"No, please." Clara said. "It's nearly daybreak, let us stay here and drink and talk before going home..."

"Don't you want to know?" Helen asked.

Clara shook her head.

"Please don't be so scared, Clara. Nothing has ever

hurt us here, and you know this. I just want to find out if I can see anything. Wouldn't it be simply wonderful to actually see a ghost?"

"I think...I think something did hurt us once...I just can't remember..."

"Come with me then, just a glance. I swear it, then we will finish our wine and be off, and we can even find a new spot if you want. We'll never set foot in this dusty old place again, if that's what you wish. Just please, let's take a little look."

Shaking her head, Clara stood up. She knew how Helen got when she wanted something, knew that she may as well try to hold back the tide or stop the sun from setting.

"Just a peek then."

They made their way to the grand staircase, both of them moving slowly, bodies tensed with a mixture of nervousness and excitement. Clara had to admit that it would, in fact, be quite interesting to see a ghost. Besides, if something bad, something as truly awful as she feared, had happened then she and Helen would have remembered it. She was just being, as had been stated before, a goose.

Still, there was fear.

Helen placed one booted foot on the stairs and, with an over-the-shoulder smile to Clara, rushed upward toward where they had heard the noise. Taking a deep breath, Clara followed.

The stairs should creak and moan. Clara thought to herself as she walked. What sort of ghost story is this where the stairs don't creak and moan? Honestly, the front door didn't even squeak. There were, in fact, cobwebs, but they weren't draped majestically about, all curtain-like. I have yet to see a single spider either.

Somehow, thinking like this made Clara feel a bit better. For the first time since the bad feelings started, she had a genuine smile on her face. Whoever wrote this story... She thought to herself, has no idea what they are doing.

Helen stopped at the apex of the stairs, wiping her forehead with the palm of her hand. The night had been a cold one, and moments ago she had wished that she had brought a heavier jacket. Now, however, sweat was dripping down her face in little rivers. In a matter of seconds Clara felt it too, the oppressive heat that had seemingly leaked from the very walls of the house as it engulfed the friends in an envelope of balmy summer.

Then it grew worse…

"I don't feel so good." Helen said. Before she could finish her sentence flames appeared on Helen's dress. They began to lick against her head, her hair singeing, filling the air with a foul odor. Her skin began to blister and peel, her features distorting and seeming to almost flow before Clara's eyes.

Holding back a scream, Clara took a step back. She didn't notice that the heel of her boot had become caught on the lip of the stair below her, and in a matter of seconds and she found herself airborne. In the short time it took her body to make the fatal journey to the floor that would fatally twist her neck, she remembered.

She remembered everything.

◆——◦——◆

The bookcase hadn't looked like much when it sat in

Trent's old bedroom. However, helping his father carry it over the threshold into the new house made him realize just how heavy the solid piece of stained wood really was. Catching his breath he surveyed the place that was going to be his new home. He had to admit that it was pretty cool, like a house out of an old horror movie. It even had what the realtor had called 'a history'.

As if reading Trent's mind, his parent's conversation shifted to the house's past.

"It's hard to believe that there was so little damage from the fire." His mother said, her voice accompanied by the clinking of silverware.

"Yeah, it's not so bad at all." Her father replied, and it really wasn't. In fact, if the realtor hadn't told them about the fire and the two girls who had died there, he doubted they'd even have noticed.

Trent, temporarily freed from his duties in the Great Move, made his way to the three empty rooms upstairs. He wasn't so sure about moving to a small town like Narrow Lake, but he decided that he would just have to make it work. He walked into the last room on the left, which was medium-sized. It would make a good bedroom, and it was easy to envision the place filled with his stuff. His industrial music and horror movie posters, his video games and role-playing books, even the damned bookcase if they didn't die dragging the heavy thing up the stairs. Yeah, he could live here for sure…

His mother walked into the room and leaned against the wall. Trent could tell that she wanted a cigarette, and was impressed that she managed to keep her promise to quit smoking through the entire messy move.

"I think this is my room." Trent said.

His mother nodded. "This place is a steal, isn't it?"

"Yeah, not much damage at all, unless you count the ghost girls." Trent laughed, and his mother followed suit.

"It is kinda creepy, isn't it, living somewhere where people died?" His mother mock-shivered. "It's too spooky."

"Naaaah, I'm sure that if you really look into things someone has died everywhere on Earth. It's no big deal."

All at once Trent startled, his head whipping towards the doorway.

"You okay?" His mother asked.

"Yeah, I just thought I heard something."

"Don't mess with me like this." His mother laughed again.

"No, I'm serious." Trent raised his voice. "Dad, you alright?"

"I'm fine." Trent's dad shouted from downstairs, his rumbling bass voice echoing against the empty walls. "What's up?"

"I thought I heard something, that's all. A thump, like something falling down the stairs..."

◀━━━▶

One year later the autumn night was crisp and cool, with the threat of winter just beginning to show its ugly head. The leaves had not yet fallen from the trees, and they hung in a dying blanket of orange-red-gold under the perfect jack-o-lantern moon. The wind whispered softly through the branches, and it was the sort of night that gave one the taste of caramel on their tongue, of apples and candies and endless glasses of spicy cider.

It was the kind of night that the girls loved most...

An Invitation

David Green

"You'll love this, Daisy. I know it!"

Oscar grinned as he turned the car off the highway, and Daisy loved seeing him excited. His brown eyes twinkled, and the wrinkles and gray hairs that had crept in over the last few years seemed to fade. Daisy looked forward to his surprises, but something about this one gnawed at her since Oscar unveiled it that afternoon.

"If you say so," she replied, gazing through the window. Rain fell as they drove down a forest road.

"Trust me," Oscar replied, flashing her his teeth. "We're close."

"Right," Daisy answered, staring at the woods. To her, it didn't seem like they were near anything. Oscar thumbed at his cell phone, turning up the volume on the stereo until *Helter Skelter* by The Beatles thumped out of the speakers.

"You know, this is one of the songs Charles Manson believed had messages about the apocalypse in it. Thought it might set the mood."

"Charles fucking Manson?" Daisy asked, her voice rising. "Where the Hell are you taking me?"

Oscar laughed as his fingers drummed on the steering wheel.

"Relax, it'll be awesome. Trust me!"

"So long as there's no clowns. Or satanic cults who think the fucking Beatles can predict the future," she muttered with a scowl.

"Take the next left in 500 yards for your ultimate destination."

Daisy squinted up ahead, thinking the GPS had gotten confused. *Ultimate?* She wondered, *does it always say that?*

"Please tell me we're not going to an orgy in the middle of a forest. I said 'no' a hundred times."

Oscar smirked and made the turn onto a dirt road. Cars sat parked up ahead, and Daisy spotted a faint glow in the distance. Her boyfriend scanned for a place to pull up. Finding a suitable one he gave a satisfied nod, switching off the engine and turning to Daisy.

"Okay, don't kill me," he started, taking her hands in his. "It's a circus."

"Oscar, you know clowns fucking terrify me! Why'd you bring me to a place filled with them in the middle of nowhere?"

"It's not that kind of circus," he replied, squinting off towards the lights, the smile slipping from his lips. "It's invite only. Exclusive, adults only. *Summoning Armageddon,* it's called. Hence, Charles Manson sponsored music."

Despite her anger, and the fear that bubbled beneath it,

Daisy had to admit she felt intrigued. Oscar's surprises often came out of left-field, but never failed to entertain. She knew about his severe pressure at work, and these jaunts were his way of blowing off steam and doing something exciting together. She watched him wince as he waited for her response. Daisy humored him.

"Invite only, huh? How'd a slub like you swing one?"

Oscar's grin returned.

"Well, I'd heard a few whispers about some carnival traveling the country. One-off gig's and secretive. I did a little digging on Reddit, Twitter, Google, you name it. Couldn't find anything concrete. I understand what fucking Neo went through at the start of The Matrix, right?" He clicked his fingers. "Then, last week, an invitation popped up in my inbox."

"Isn't that a little...odd?" Daisy asked. She didn't want to dampen his spirits, but the scenario seemed too coincidental for her.

"Nah, found a guy on a Discord server who said he had contact with them. I gave him my email and location but didn't think it'd pan out so soon. So, we going in?"

Daisy watched as a car drove past. Inside were a couple around her and Oscar's age, who gave a casual wave as they searched for a parking spot. She glanced over her shoulder as another vehicle turned onto the dirt path. More people arriving eased the nagging doubt in her mind.

"Sure, but if I see one clown I'm out of there, and you can make your own way home. You hear, pal?"

Oscar let out a whoop and kissed her.

"Deal, you won't regret it. No clowns!"

Daisy followed him out of the car. The night's air had

a bite to it, something the driving rain didn't help. She held Oscar's hand as they made their way towards the lights. They walked at a slow pace, allowing the couple who had driven past to move in behind them. Daisy smiled as she heard their whispered arguments; she hadn't been the only one surprised tonight.

The path led into a clearing, and in the center stood a massive, crimson and black tent. Spotlights of reds, greens and whites surrounded it, illuminating its cavernous entrance. Groups of people passed into it, and to Daisy it looked as if people faded into the darkness of the void itself. The couple behind them fell silent. The familiar circus music, *"Entry of the Gladiators,"* drifted from inside the tent. It sounded twisted somehow, slower and at a different pitch than normal. Daisy glanced at Oscar, who wore a slight frown, and he forced a laugh when he noticed her watching him.

"Eerie, huh? Whoever these guys are, they know how to create an atmosphere. We going in?"

"Oscar," Daisy said as she pulled him to one side, letting the couple behind them pass by. She watched as they entered with slow steps, swallowed by the gloom. "I don't like this. Something feels off about this entire thing. Can we just go grab a takeaway, a bottle of wine and watch some Netflix? You can pick anything you like. Please?"

Daisy looked up at him, tugging at his coat jacket. She felt like a youthful girl asking for someone's permission, and she hated it. The unease bothering her since they'd gotten into the car had only increased, and now her soul screamed at her to get away from this circus.

Oscar squinted into the tent's maw and looked back

at Daisy, worry lines eating into his face. As he took a step away, relief flooded into her and a breath she didn't realize she'd been holding seeped out of her mouth.

"Yeah, sure. Don't know what I was thinking, coming out here. I'm sorry, it's just—"

"You're invited?"

Daisy looked up, startled. A tall man materialized out of the entrance, looming above Oscar, who wasn't short by any means. Daisy felt pinned by the stranger's sapphire eyes. With a well-groomed, black beard, and hair the same color that curled at his shoulders, she thought him to be the most beautiful person she'd had the pleasure to witness. As she gazed at him her fears crumbled to dust.

"Yes, we are," she said. "Oscar, show him."

Her boyfriend fumbled for his cell phone, cursing under his breath as he accessed his emails.

"There," he half-yelled with triumph as he displayed the PDF. "Oscar Martinez, plus guest. That's her."

The alluring man glanced at the screen, then smiled. His teeth were perfect and white, like piano keys. He eyed Oscar, then took Daisy's hand, raising it to his mouth and brushed his full lips against them.

"And you are, my sweet?"

"Daisy Rogers. His guest."

"So I believe." He spoke with an accent Daisy couldn't place. "I have many names, though you may call me Sammael. I am the Master of Ceremonies, and am at your service. Come, take your seats. You leave only a handful left to arrive."

Sammael strode past them towards the forest trail. Daisy glanced at the scowling Oscar.

"Want to chase him and flirt more?"

Sighing, Daisy rolled her eyes and grabbed her boyfriend's hand.

"Come on, let's go inside."

"You were making it a little obvious, that's all I'm saying," Oscar hissed as he let Daisy pull him along.

Darkness overwhelmed them, and panic hit Daisy. She realized Oscar experienced the same alarm when he stopped grumbling and gripped her hand instead. *Keep moving,* she told herself, forcing one foot to move in front of the other. Frantic laughter rose and fell to the rhythm of the traditional circus music she knew so well, but now it reminded her of the nightmarish tunnel scene from *Willy Wonka,* only this time she couldn't fast-forward past it. She blinked, and the pitch black evaporated, morphing into the tent's interior. Daisy glanced at Oscar, who pressed his fingers against his forehead and looked confused.

Daisy scanned the inside of the cavernous tent. Tiered seats circled a performance area, unlike any she'd seen at a circus before. Lit braziers dotted its circumference, blue flames spurting from the coals. Several tall, thin men in colorful patchwork clothes cartwheeled and somersaulted inside, their bodies moving at strange angles and cadence as if they were smoke flowing in human form. One looked at her and bowed with a grin.

"Harlequins are still clowns," she muttered at Oscar. She half-turned to leave, but Daisy didn't want to risk the tunnel again. A part of her mind told her to stay, that if she did she'd see Sammael soon.

"Entry of the Gladiators" continued to play—different, but not as unsettling as it had been in the tunnel.

People in the crowd whispered to one another, as if afraid to draw attention to themselves.

Oscar nudged her and pointed to the far side of the arena—two free seats beckoned.

As they made their way across Daisy investigated the faces of the other guests. Some looked excited, but just as many exhibited nervous signs—many fidgeted and bit their nails. Daisy smiled at a woman she would sit next to, noticing something else.

"Everyone's our age," she whispered to Oscar as they took their seats. "The oldest person here couldn't be over forty, or younger than thirty. That's weird, right?"

Oscar glanced around and shrugged, though she could tell by his eyes darting here and there he felt uncomfortable.

"Maybe," he replied in her ear. "You wouldn't get many older than us using Reddit or Discord."

"You'd get enough younger," Daisy hissed, annoyed that Oscar missed the obvious. He didn't reply as he tapped his foot and fiddled with his ear, habits he carried out when unsettled.

Daisy unzipped her coat. Outside the temperature approached freezing, but the heat inside stifled and grew oppressive. Sweat trickled down her back and her sides. Next to her Oscar removed his jacket and wiped his forehead.

"Where's the Goddamn heat coming from?" she croaked, her tongue stuck to the top of her mouth like she'd swallowed a cup filled with cement. "Those braziers can't be *that* hot. Those creeps in the circle don't look bothered by it."

Oscar shook his head in reply, perspiration flicking from his hair as he did. Grumbles and the sounds of zips rose around her as the other guests followed suit. Daisy pulled at the neck of her sweater. *I'd rip this fucking thing off if I could.*

People staggering through the entrance drew her attention. She watched as they regained their bearings and moved towards their seats, glancing all the while at the harlequins cavorting in the circus ring. As they sat the blue flames died, plunging the tent into a bleak silence, the performers swallowed by the shadows.

Screams erupted, followed by fits of nervous laughter and coughing. Silence followed, and as it stretched, Daisy entwined her fingers with Oscar's, ignoring the sweat coating them. The doubt and fear that fled in Sammael's presence had returned, stronger than before. Her body itched to leave, but Daisy couldn't see an inch in front of her. If she stood, she worried she'd stumble and fall down the tier's and into the performing area.

"This is a mistake," she muttered, shuffling closer to Oscar so their sides pressed together. "Something terrible will happen. I know it."

Oscar squirmed, as if about to speak, but as he did the braziers erupted into green flame. More screams rang out amid a splutter of brief, subdued hand claps.

In the middle of the performing area, arms spread wide, stood Sammael. Even though the distance must have been fifty meters or more, Daisy sensed that the Master of Ceremonies peered into her soul. The crowd behind him and to the sides melted from her vision; Sammael, the flames and the darkness growing from the tent's maw behind him were all that existed.

"My guests, you are welcome." Sammael spoke, his voice like a lover's murmur in her ear. "Prepare yourselves. You are all fit. Experienced. Searching for something more. You've seen what life on God's earth has to offer, and it has left you wanting—He has nothing more to give you. My friends, you all accepted the invitation. A contract signed between us."

Sammael raised his hands, and the shadows behind him writhed. The green flames heightened. Screams erupted from the other side of the arena—panic battered Daisy, begging for her body to react, but her eyes locked on Sammael's, and her brain ached for his next words.

Oscar gasped beside her. Sweat sizzled on his blistered and cracked skin, as if he burned from the inside. His mouth gaped as he tried to speak, but only a gargle escaped as blood spilled over his lips. She heard a sound on her other side, like the popping of fat in a frying pan.

The woman beside her screamed in silence, the tongue burned from her throat and the white's of her eyeballs dripped down her cheeks, mingling with the blood streaming from her empty sockets.

A part of Daisy's brain, partitioned from the rest of her conscious, screamed at her to run. Instead, she gazed back at Sammael as his piercing stare fell on her once more.

The harlequins returned, creatures writhing from the shadows, moving to the circle's edge, and face the audience. She found it hard to focus on them, the shadow figures twisted and swirled in her vision.

The stench of burning flesh caught in her nostrils. Oscar slumped to the floor beside her, a gaping mess where his head used to be, his face melted away. Daisy pictured herself locked in a glass box, beating her fists bloody against the surface as she raged and wept. Yet, mesmerized, she found herself unable to react to the surrounding carnage.

Sammael's voice spoke in her mind. *It will all be over soon, my sweet.*

Why aren't I burning? She asked, raising an unblemished hand to her eyes. The one Sammael had kissed. *I think I've gone mad. My boyfriend is dead, but all I can think about is you.*

An unforeseen consequence from a kiss, but worry not. You will join Oscar in my kingdom before long. My protection will pass.

"You are the last sacrifices required." Sammael's voice drowned out the screams. "Armageddon is at hand."

The shadows swept forward, leaping on those in the crowd that still lived. Some they tore to pieces. One moved toward Daisy at a steady pace, its features a grim reflection of her own. As they regarded each other every choice Daisy ever made replayed in her mind. She'd made mistakes in her life, but the only decision she regretted was walking into that tent tonight. As Sammael's protection lifted she screamed. Seating heat, madness and grief assailed her. The demon flowed into her throat and devoured her from the inside out.

◆—◦—◆

Sammael recalled the demon's and smiled. He felt powerful, virile. He gazed around at the now silent tent, the air thick with the taste of blood and flesh. The circus had proved an effective pretense, as humans always let their curious minds get the better of them. That they came of their own accord, with their sweet experience and in the bloom of life, counted for much. As the vibrant soul of Daisy, the woman he'd shared a brief connection with, joined the rest in Hell he sighed. Tonight's mass sacrifice still left him short to take on the might of Heaven.

"One more time," Sammael said, a part of him savoring the next performance. "Then the world is mine."

The Other Sunny
William A. Wellman

It was a bad day for Sunny - maybe the worst in her whole life. She slunk like a wounded animal into the apartment, letting the door slam shut behind her. The blood wouldn't stop gushing from her forehead, and she couldn't keep it off of her clothes or out of her face - it wasn't the worst Danny had done to her, but this would be impossible to hide at her job. Then again, she thought as she pulled herself into the bathroom, after today she probably didn't have one of those either. Danny seemed to hate big glass windows almost as much as he hated her.

She let empty cosmetic bottles and worn-out makeup tins spill onto the floor as she propped herself up against the bathroom counter. She felt like she was going to fall asleep, and she was seeing the same lipstick-encrusted tissue a dozen times at once. She turned the grimy tap handle and didn't even care that the water came out dark. She splattered it across her face, hoping that the cold would bring clarity and get rid of the insufferable pounding. It didn't, and the blood mingled with the black water as it spiralled into the drain. She looked up to the mirror to inspect the damage, cursing under her breath. The mirror didn't show her reflection.

Instead the mirror was a window, and it looked out into the other apartment that belonged to the Other Sunny Rapchek. Like usual the Other Sunny had left the bathroom door open. Sunlight was drifting in from the living room, which was impossible to see unless you really tried. Sunny cursed and went digging in the pile on the floor for a compact mirror, but stopped. The sunlight in the mirror was flickering, and she knew what that meant: The Other Sunny was home.

Sunny switched off the flashlight that lit up the bathroom - the electric had been shut off for weeks now - and crouched behind the bathroom counter, breath rasping quietly as the blood ran down her face in slow beads. Like a drug-induced hallucination the Other Sunny danced into view. Her face was similar to Sunny's, but not quite right. Something about the eyes felt fake. It messed with Sunny's head to watch her, but that didn't stop her from doing it. She didn't trust the Other Sunny, with her too-nice clothes and her lips always stretched into a smile. Nobody could be that happy all the time.

The Other Sunny was standing in the living room, smiling and looking at something out of view. She was talking, and Sunny wished she could hear anything from the other side of the glass. Someone else was in the Other Sunny's apartment, which was a first. Sunny twisted, trying to get the angle right, and got a couple more feet of the living room in her vision. She shrieked in the darkness.

Danny was standing in the Other Sunny's apartment. He looked good, like he'd quit whatever he was on today when he came to see her at work. The Other Danny laughed with clean, white teeth, and pulled the Other Sunny close, looking into her eyes. He'd done that to Sunny once; it seemed like forever ago. That look said nice things, like 'I love you' and 'I'm not going to hurt you for kicks'.

Sunny howled and hurled bottles at the glass, but they glanced off as always. The Other Sunny had everything. A nice apartment, more money. She even had Danny, a better Danny. Angry tears streamed down Sunny's cheeks, and she sat on the floor with her back to the tub, rocking in the darkness and watching. The Other Sunny stepped into the bathroom, waving goodbye - the Other Danny probably had a steady job. Sunny squinted, rubbing her eyes as the lights were switched on beyond the glass, revealing the Other Sunny's bathtub and shower with the nice, pink curtain.

Sunny had dreams about that shower, about sliding the curtain along that golden rod back and forth, listening to the rings rattle. She dreamt about the warm lights that worked, and water that came out hot and pure and clean. As if to torture her the Other Sunny slipped out of her bathrobe and turned on the water, testing it for a minute. She glanced at the mirror as she did, but she was only interested in her own reflection. She stepped into that beautiful shower and pulled the pink curtain shut, and the fog on the mirror began to blur Sunny's vision.

The gash in Sunny's head was beginning to throb badly, and she grimaced as she pulled herself up from the floor. This was too much. Was there anything she had that the Other Sunny didn't have better? She stumbled over to the counter, and with a desperate shriek reached out to strike the glass with her hand. The mirror didn't break, but as she pulled her hand back she realized that it was wet. She stopped, staring at it incredulously.

Cast only in the light glowing through the foggy mirror, she reached out a tentative finger and drew a line in the condensation. There was moisture on her side too. Had it ever done that before? She didn't think so. Testing it curiously she added more lines, spelling out letters in reverse for kicks. 'My turn'. Beads of hot water trickled down from the letters, and she shook her head in disbelief. She could see through the letters like a barred window as the Other Sunny stepped out of her shower, looked at the mirror, and froze.

Sunny's heart began pounding as hard as her head, and she stood in front of the mirror staring. The Other Sunny stared back, wrapping a towel around herself as she stepped slowly towards the mirror, watching the letters as if they were going to move. She could see the letters. She could almost certainly see the letters. Sunny had to remind herself to breathe as the Other Sunny stood in front of her counter, peering into the mirror as if trying to make out something in the far distance.

Sunny mimicked her movements - that was what a good little reflection was supposed to do, right? She stared right into the Other Sunny's beady little eyes, standing the same way she did. The Other Sunny was blurred by the fog on the mirror, but she seemed on edge, suspicious for the first time that Sunny had ever seen. Hesitantly the Other Sunny raised her hand, waving it around as if testing that her reflection would follow. Sunny copied the gestures, finding a sick humor in it. The fog was disappearing now as the hot air cooled, and the condensation streamed down from the mirror. As it did Sunny stared right into the Other Sunny's eyes.

The Other Sunny was transfixed; she seemed unsure of what she was seeing. It was the first time Sunny had seen her without a plastic smile, and it was exhilarating. The Other Sunny slowly raised her hand, and Sunny followed the motion, never looking away. The hands raised together, fingertips approaching until they pressed against the glass in the same place - but, unlike so many times before, instead of the mirror's hard surface Sunny found her hand pressed against a warm palm exactly the same size as hers. Before the Other Sunny could pull back her hand in terror Sunny had seized her wrist.

An awful certainty and strength came over Sunny, and she didn't think about what she was doing. It was like when she'd grabbed those bikes and bags, or when she'd broken that sniveling girl's face after Danny had cheated. You couldn't think when you were fighting to survive, you just had to act. With black fingernails she dug into the Other Sunny's wrist, pulling her arm through the mirror. In shock the Other Sunny lurched forward, and her head crossed through the glass. Sunny grabbed a handful of her pretty, blond hair and slammed her head down hard onto the sink handle - once, twice. The Other Sunny looked up in dazed shock; that cut on her forehead looked just right.

Then Sunny vaulted over the familiar girl's body, hoping that, for once, the glass would not hold her back. It didn't, and a strange shiver raced across her skin as she dipped through the surface like water. She rolled into the golden light of the bathroom, cracking her head on the tub, but she didn't have time to stop. The Other Sunny was trying to pull herself up from the counter, but that wasn't going to happen. Things were going to be different now. Sunny grabbed the Other Sunny's legs, and, with strength that surprised herself, flipped the Other Sunny into the blackness beyond the mirror.

She stood alone in the bright, warm light, and could see some of her reflection in the glass. She looked hideous, a mask of blood and filth plastering her face, with clear rivulets from her crying fit running down her cheeks and neck. Beyond her own reflection she could see a form in the darkness - the Other Sunny, blood beginning to spill from her forehead, pulling herself up against the counter. Sunny stood, breathless, waiting, watching. The Other Sunny's hand pressed up against the mirror. It became a fist, bumping against the glass, which didn't let her through. Sunny screamed joyfully, dancing on the bathroom's white, clean tiles.

First things first, Sunny thought, as reality began to set in, *I need a shower*. She peeled off her filthy clothes, tossing them onto the floor. The Other Sunny was watching, but let her watch; Sunny had been forced to watch a thousand times. She slid the curtain back, and the gentle rattle of the metal rings gave her goosebumps. She left it open as she turned on the golden handle with the emblazoned 'H', and relished the burning heat as steam filled the bathroom, fogging up the mirror and glistening on the walls.

Sunny spun around slowly in the pure water, letting

it carry away the blood and the grime from her skin, and scrubbing the filth from her fingernails. The Other Sunny was just a faint blur through the fog, throwing a tantrum as though it were the first time she hadn't gotten her way. She had so many little lessons to learn about life, and the first one was disappointment. No better place to learn than that dreary apartment with no lights. Sunny stepped out of the shower feeling like a new woman. She wiped the fog from the mirror with a towel, revealing the Other Sunny, who had given up on beating the glass to slump against the sink, sobbing in soundless confusion. Sunny grinned at her dour reflection and plucked a lipstick from the counter. The color was a perfect match for her, of course. She shared a little with the Other Sunny too, writing backwards on the mirror in beautiful red letters. 'Bye bye'.

She spun on her heel and gave the shower curtain a vicious yank, letting the golden rings and lovely, pink fabric cascade from the metal rod. Seizing it in both hands she tested the weight, and gave her terrified reflection a parting wink before swinging it into the bathroom mirror. It didn't break on the first impact, or the second, but the third swing put a splintering crack in the glass. The blows came fast and wild. Then the mirror flew into pieces, dissolving and falling off the wall to pool in glittering shards on the countertop. She tossed away the bent rod victoriously as the last jagged panel fell, and screamed for joy. She would never spend another day as a powerless reflection. She was the only Sunny Rapchek.

She familiarized herself with the apartment. It was much like hers, but turned around backwards, and smelled nicer. Many things were in the same place she remembered them, but so much prettier, and the wardrobe was stocked with nice clothes that fit her just right. The sun streaming in through her windows felt amazing, and she was in the mood for a stroll. She rummaged through her purse - which looked expensive, but then again she'd always had good taste - until she found the keys. Sunny took a moment to survey her life, more beautiful even than it had appeared through the glass, and stepped out to walk in the golden afternoon.

This was a good day for Sunny - maybe the best in her whole life.

Inside Your Mind

Elizabeth Nettleton

Ring a ring o' roses, a pocket full of posies…

The little boy clutched his superhero bedsheet, his eyelids flickering as he surrendered to his dream.

Ashes, ashes…

I leant over his body until our foreheads almost touched.

We all fall down.

My lips brushed the skin between his eyes and our spirits collided, pushing me inside his mind. The transition only lasted a moment; a journey through dimensions I had been making for centuries. I kissed the hands of space and time, and then I was there, standing beside the little boy in an empty field he had created himself.

I didn't usually deal with children; their fears weren't nearly as interesting as an adult's. However, this one had decided to search for nursery rhymes on the internet, and his terror after watching some of the more horrifying results was far too delicious for me to resist.

Now, had it been the tall, thin man that frightened him

the most, with his featureless face and claw-like hands? Or had it been the dancing children that made his heart race, their jerking bodies still stiff from lying in their graves for so long?

Perhaps I could treat myself tonight and give him both. I worked hard; I deserved it.

The boy glanced up. He couldn't see me, but he knew I was there. I raised my hand and the clouds drew together above him, covering the field in darkness. With a slow smile I began to sing.

"Ring a ring o' roses…"

"No!"

I would never understand why people found this rhyme so frightening. It was a series of words, nothing more, yet it sparked their imaginations and made their blood run cold. Humans are such simple creatures, slaves to their own minds.

I lowered my hand, and the grass bulged beside the little boy's feet.

"Hugo…my Hugo…"

"Mama?'

The boy spun, searching the sky for his mother's voice.

Foolish child.

A hand burst from the earth. Blue veins traced their way around mottled, grey skin, guiding dried blood to a heart that no longer beat. A second hand emerged, and both clawed at the dirt until the rest of the undead body collapsed upon the grass.

Hugo gasped, his face white with fear. The ghoul raised its head and revealed itself to be a woman with the same blue eyes as the little boy trembling beside me. I bit my lip to keep from laughing. One of my favorite parts about this job was watching where the dreamer took what I gave them. I presented Hugo with a faceless specter, but he was the one who transformed it into his mother.

The woman sat on her knees, her white nightgown stained with blood. She smiled through strands of matted, black hair.

"I fell down, Hugo. Do you remember how I fell down?"

Rain lashed against Hugo's face, mingling with his tears and drowning out his frightened sobs. "I remember, Mama."

"We all fall down, my darling. We all fall down."

She lunged at him, grabbing his wrists with her bloodless hands. He tried to scramble backwards, but his mother was too strong for him. Crooning softly she yanked him towards her final resting place, pulling him to his knees.

"You fell down," she whispered.

Hugo's eyes widened in terror. Then he was gone, and the field was still once more.

I pulled myself out of the dreamworld and watched Hugo return to his body. His eyes shone in the near darkness, blinking rapidly as he tried to forget the way his mother had dug her rotting nails into his flesh.

My gaze fell on the family portrait beside his bed. The woman in the dream had her arms wrapped around Hugo and a little girl. Hugo seemed to be a year or two younger than he was now, perhaps six, and the girl no older than ten. She had the same round face and blue eyes that Hugo and their mother had. His sister, I supposed.

Hugo licked his lips. He placed his hand over the frame and slammed it down on the bedside table.

A smile tugged at my lips. My work here was done.

✦—◦—✦

I waited under the shadows in the corner of the room. My being was always hidden from human eyes, but I still preferred the comfort of darkness. It didn't just cloak me; it strengthened me. I fed on it.

Hugo was resisting sleep. Dark circles cradled his eyes, and I could almost hear his body pleading for rest.

He could not resist forever. I hummed to myself as I left his room, trailing my hand along the faded walls until I reached a second bedroom. Haphazard pink letters on the door spelt out the name Bridget.

Bridget. An old name meaning strength or exalted one.

Let's see how strong you are, shall we?

I walked into the room and stood above the girl. Dark ringlets fanned around her face, in stark contrast with the white pillow. I ran my finger down her forehead and felt the dreams sir within her. The next moment, I was inside her mind.

Long blades of grass brushed against my legs. Bridget sat a few feet away from me, picking daisies in the afternoon sunlight. She tied one flower to another, until she had made a magnificent crown. She plopped it onto her head and smiled.

I recognized this field. It was the same one Hugo had dreamed about. Had their mother taken them here?

Had she died here? Bridget didn't seem upset, so perhaps it held pleasant memories. Still, it was significant to this family for one reason or another, and I intended to use it to my advantage.

I cleared my throat and began to sing.

"Ring a ring o' ros…"

"I don't like that song," Bridget said. The flowers in front of her had changed. Instead of daisies, Bridget was now surrounded by vibrant tulips. She picked a purple one and twirled it between her fingers.

I narrowed my eyes. I wasn't sure who she thought she was talking to; perhaps she thought she was talking to herself. However, I was not in the habit of receiving requests, and I certainly did not entertain demands.

I dragged my finger through the air and placed a doll on top of Bridget's flowers. Its cracked face sneered up at her through the petals, now all stained black. Strips of fabric from its dress bristled in the wind.

"Ring a ring o' ros…"

"I told you, I don't like that song," Bridget said. She picked up the doll. Its face instantly smoothed into a smile. The tears in its dress mended, and the flowers returned to their original color. "That's better," she grinned.

My eyes flashed red. I was not used to this level of resistance. With a snarl, I raised my arm and pulled Bridget's mother from her grave once more.

Bridget's mother screamed as she opened the earth. Ravens circled her, diving to the ground whenever their fevered minds compelled them to.

"Ashes, ashes," the mother crooned. Her lips parted to reveal gray teeth, and blood dribbled down her chin.

Bridget's jaw clenched.

"Fall down with me, Bridget," the mother whispered.

"No."

"We all fall down," the mother insisted. She extended her arm and raked her clawed fingernails down Bridget's cheek.

Droplets of blood pulled themselves onto Bridget's skin, but she did not lower her eyes from the specter. "You're just a dream."

"And your mother is just a pile of bones in the ground," the woman spat.

Bridget touched the ghoul's face and she immediately transformed into the woman from the photograph. Dirt fled from her clothes, leaving them clean and whole, and her hair tidied. New skin covered her hands, and color returned to her cheeks. Her large blue eyes swept over Bridget, warm with kindness. The pair embraced.

"I miss you, Mama," Bridget said, nestling her cheek against her mother's.

"I miss you, too. Take care of Hugo, my darling."

"I will."

Bridget turned in my direction.

"You'd better leave now. I'm about to wake up."

✦—◦—✦

White-hot fury coursed through my body as I waited for night to fall the following day. I had never experienced anybody, least of all a child, refuse me. I thought of my friends, spirits like myself who infiltrated dreams. They had never reported something like this, either.

She *dares* tell me to leave?

I closed my eyes and was beside her bed again, watching her chest rise and fall with each breath. The forces within me stirred, crashing through my being until they met at my chest. Had it really only been a few days since I stood over Hugo that first time, watching him as I watched his sister now?

My hand twitched. I wanted to strike her. Instead, I stroked the cheek where her mother's apparition had drawn blood.

"Sweet dreams," I mocked as my spirit collided with hers.

We stood opposite each other in the dream, cold wind brushing against our necks. Bridget stared over my shoulder. She could feel me. I said her name and heard it echo around us.

"You can come in now, Hugo," she said.

The air shuddered and Hugo appeared beside her, his eyes wide as he surveyed the field.

"The nightmare is here," she said.

"It is?" Hugo took hold of Bridget's hand, trembling slightly.

"Yes, but you're safe with me. I want you to see that you have nothing to be afraid of. Nightmares can't hurt you."

A fire ignited within me at her arrogance, her *insolence*. If she thought she could intimidate me by bringing her brother here, she was mistaken. Hugo was a figment of her imagination and nothing more. It was almost impossible for humans to meld their dreams together.

Almost.

I frowned. It was true there were some familial bonds that might allow two people to share their subconscious beings. And Bridget had demonstrated a great deal of power over her own mind. However, she was still a child, not some guru that had dedicated her life to discovering her higher self.

A child, I repeated to myself. *An orphan child, at that.*

This wasn't Hugo any more than the specter had been their mother. But if Bridget insisted that he was, I would use him to scare her beyond belief.

My lip lifted into a sneer. Two dogs appeared beside me, snapping at the air with blood-stained teeth. Bridget eyed the dogs warily as they inched closer, their hackles raised.

"Stay calm, Hugo," she murmured.

The dogs circled them, growling deep within their throats. Hugo whimpered.

One of the dogs lunged at him. It grabbed onto his shirt and tossed him from side to side, as easily as if he were a mouse.

"Bridget!" he cried.

Behind me, someone screamed. I furrowed my brow. It sounded as if it came from beyond the dream.

From Hugo's room, even.

Bridget's face paled. She pulled her hand to her chest and the dog dropped Hugo. She beckoned for her brother to join her, and he crawled behind her legs, leaving a trail of blood where his stomach met the ground.

"Leave us alone," Bridget commanded. The dogs took a few steps backwards. My anger flared.

"Go to them!" I shouted.

The dogs licked their snarling lips. One sniffed the air and whined.

"Go to them *now!*"

The dogs turned and ran, fleeing over the hills that surrounded the field. Rage burst through my hands and landed as flames at Bridget and Hugo's feet. The fire leapt to greet them, grabbing at their clothes and hair. Bridget yanked Hugo back.

"Water!"

Clouds knitted themselves together and poured rain on top of us, drowning the flames in an instant. I dug my fingers into my face and shook my head until all I could see were stars.

"*What are you?*"

The dream shook with my fury, and the children fell to their knees.

"This is *my* dream, not yours. You will not hurt us here!" Bridget yelled.

The ground tore apart. Every relative they had ever known crawled out of the earth, their flesh pulling away to reveal gray bones. Hugo scrambled backwards, sobbing with each gasped breath.

Their grandmother, who had once fed them treats when they felt ill, pushed a fistful of worms into Hugo's mouth. He screamed, unable to move his hands in his distress. Bridget pulled him up by his shoulder and touched his lips. The worms turned to candy on Hugo's tongue, and he collapsed, shaking.

"This isn't them, Hugo! They're not real. Remember, *they cannot hurt you.*"

There was another scream from beyond the dream.

"Why did you bring your brother here?" I drawled. "Why would you hurt him like this?"

Bridget's eyes flashed. She turned in my direction.

"Get out of here. I'm warning you. Get out of here now."

"No."

Their mother stepped forward. Hugo's eyes darted between his sister and the specter. Bridget raised her chin.

"It's time for bed, children. It's time to go to sleep," the mother whispered. She reached out and grabbed Hugo's throat. Hugo thrashed his legs as she tightened her fist, his skin reddening above her fingers.

"You were wrong before, you know," I said, walking closer to Bridget. The air shimmered where I walked, and I could feel her eyes following me.

Good.

Hugo clawed at the hands by his throat, but his sister's attention was on me. It seemed clear to me now that she really had brought Hugo here. She wished to defy me.

She was going to pay for that.

"You did a very powerful thing when you brought your brother here. The problem is, you didn't understand what you were doing. Have you ever noticed that you cannot die in your own dream? Your subconscious simply retreats to your physical form, frightened but unharmed. That's not the case when you die in someone else's dream, however."

Hugo swung his fists at his mother, but she was too strong for him. She squeezed tighter.

"When you bring someone's subconscious into your dream, they cannot return to their physical form unless you take them back. If they die, you lose that opportunity. Their body cannot survive long without their spirit, so you wake up to find your beloved family member has passed in their sleep."

Bridget stiffened. Her nonchalant expression slipped, revealing the first traces of fear. I relished in it.

"You took one hell of a gamble when you decided you were stronger than I am."

The mother twisted her hand. Hugo's eyes bulged and his tongue lolled from his mouth, expelling all of the breath in his body.

"No!" Bridget screamed. The specter dropped Hugo and shrieked, clutching her hand as if it burned. Bridget rushed toward her brother and pressed her ear against his chest.

"I'm sorry, I'm so sorry. I thought you would just wake up," she sobbed. She pinched Hugo's nose and breathed into his mouth, a clumsy gesture but one I recognized.

Revival.

Ah, if only dreams were that simple.

Snakes curled around her wrists, pulling her away from Hugo. Bridget bared her teeth.

"Not fucking now!"

The snakes turned limp and slid to the ground. Bridget returned to Hugo, pressing on his chest until he finally blinked his eyes open.

"Bridge?" he moaned. His voice was hoarse, and seemed to pain him, but it was him. Bridget sobbed as she hugged him, trembling in relief.

"How sweet," I crooned.

I thrust my hands into the air. Bridget turned to me,

fire in her eyes.

"No. It's my turn now."

A sudden heaviness anchored me to the earth. I watched in horror as flesh wrapped itself around my being, capturing me inside a human form. I touched my face with fingers I'd never had before, exploring every hair and crevice upon my skin.

"What are you doing to me?"

"Whatever I want to."

A blade fell into my hand. My arm lifted and plunged the dagger into my stomach, again and again until blood pooled at my feet. I could not resist; my limbs were obeying her mind, not my own. I screamed.

The pain buckled my knees. I had never felt it before, and now it consumed me. I choked out a plea for mercy.

It stopped. New skin tugged over my wound, drying the blood and repairing my organs. I mumbled words that flitted between gratitude and rage.

Iron bars fell around me. I tried to slide between them, but my human form would not bend to my will. My breath quickened in panic. I squeezed my eyes shut and directed all my energy into retreating from this dream, but Bridget's power would not let me slip through the dimensions that kept our worlds apart.

"How are you doing this?" I roared.

Bridget wiped her hand along her pants. "The only time I see my mother is in my dreams, so I learnt how to control them. I needed to make sure she showed up." Her eyes flashed. "You tried to turn her into a monster. You tried to kill my brother!"

Hugo took one tentative step toward me, then another. He ran his hand along the bars that contained me. The metal sung under his fingers.

"What do you think, Hugo? Does he deserve to be let go?" Bridget asked, raising her eyebrows.

Hugo stared at me and shook his head. "You're bad," he whispered.

I turned to Bridget. "So, you're going to leave me in here? Locked in your mind?"

Bridget tilted her head to the side. "I think you need a taste of your own medicine. I want you to understand what a nightmare really feels like. Now tell me, what are you afraid of?"

"Nothing," I hissed.

"Let's experiment, then."

A giant creature appeared in the corner of my cage. It stood on two spindly legs, almost too thin to support its barreled torso. Its limbs ended in oversized paws, and its fur was thin and patchy. Red eyes bulged above its snout, and I realized with a start that this had once been one of the dogs I brought here.

It growled, its breath putrid from rotting teeth, and swung a paw at my chest. Sharp claws ripped through my freshly healed body and I fell to my knees, screaming. Fear and confusion rose in my throat like bile.

"How long? Tell me how long!"

Bridget's eyes traced my face behind the bars.

"Until I can forgive you for what you did to my brother."

She took hold of Hugo's hand.

"See you tomorrow night," she said.

The creature licked its lips, and she smiled.

Married to Nightmares
S.O. Green

The metronome was ticking, ticking, ticking. The projector was pulsing, pulsing, pulsing. The pen was scratching, scratching, scratching.

He had to record everything she said, every last detail. In her fugue state Thea Redpath was a window into the unknown, and a good doctor always took extensive notes about their patients, didn't they?

In his spacious office they were guaranteed privacy. It was a symbol of his station in the asylum. Walnut-panelled, decorated with Persian rugs and mahogany furniture. The office of Doctor Jeremiah Vale. He had worked for it, had sacrificed much for it.

He tried to keep her in the manner that she was accustomed, but she was elsewhere now, dwelling in realms more magnificent and terrible than any on Earth.

"Tell me what you see, Thea."

"I'm standing on a mountaintop. Below me is a world of glass. The colours shine in every facet, but I don't recognise them. They're the colours of anger and mourning, and misery and desire."

"Describe the topography. Are there bodies of water? Civilisations?"

"There are no oceans, no rivers, no cities or forests. Only dark emptinesses. They cry out to be filled."

"What about above? What is above you?"

"There is no sky, just water. Deep, black water, and it's so close I could reach out and touch it. I could drag my fingers through it and watch it ripple into eternity, but I won't. There's something moving up there."

She was shaking. The dreams took their toll on them both. Hearing her describe that place made him tremble, but she was his patient, under his care, and it was vital that they stayed the course.

"What is it? What does it remind you of?"

"It's like nothing I've ever seen. It's huge. I can't see its edges, but I see its limbs. Hundreds of limbs. Thousands. Their fingers spread wide. They writhe and twist, and reach out to grasp at everything. Somewhere there are eyes watching. They see the world as it truly is. Somewhere there is a mouth, waiting to devour."

She slumped in her chair, sweat beading on her forehead, feverish eyes unfocused. Gazing inwards into an abyss only she could see. Her body twisted, tendons bulging in her neck and arms. Writhing, straining, gasping. She looked like she could tear apart at any second.

But Thea Redpath wasn't made of glass. She was only breaking in her mind.

"What's happening, Thea?"

"It's going to rain. The ocean's getting heavy. It's oppressive, smothering. It's going to fall. It'll fill the emptiness of the blue glass world. I don't want to see it. I want to throw myself off this mountain peak. I want my body to shatter to pieces against the blue glass. I want to stain it red. I don't want to see the moment when things change."

This was just therapy, but these dreams were more than explorations into her psyche. They were plumbing the depths of the Beyond together. Pioneers, partners in a grand undertaking.

"Be calm, Thea," he said. "Remember that you are there, and you are not there. You exist in two places, separate and distinct. You are safe here, in my office, and you can return at any time."

"Now," she said. She clenched her hands tight around the chair. Her fingernails scratched up splinters. "I want to return, *now*."

"Not yet, Thea. Describe the event to me. Describe what happens when the water falls."

He sat forward, pen poised to record the moment of transition that would never - could never – be witnessed by anyone but them. These moments were the ones when he thanked whatever forces of chance had delivered Mrs. Redpath to the asylum, and into his care.

She strained like she was tied, but the only thing keeping her still was parasomnia. He had tethered her once before, and while she slept it hadn't been a problem. When she awoke she'd broken her own arm trying to escape.

"It... It... It..." She gaped, mouth forming words he couldn't hear. He leaned closer, trying to make them out. They were there, waiting for him. He *needed* to hear them. "C-C-Connor..."

He hesitated, then slammed his journal shut.

"Damn."

Connor Redpath, Thea's husband. Except that Thea wasn't even thirty and already a widow, which made Connor a ghost. A memory. Whatever vestige of him remained in her addled mind had a habit of appearing at the most inopportune times.

"What's happening, Thea? Can you see the mountain? The sky-ocean?"

She shook her head, sweat dripping off her chin now. "Gone. It's dark. Connor's here."

"I understand. May I speak to Connor, please?"

She cringed. Her body snapped rigid: a symptom of hysteria common among the female patients. A fear of intimacy that manifested in physical pain, paralysis, and unconscious contraction of the muscles. Thea only experienced it while she slept.

Then she relaxed. She didn't go limp. Instead, her body developed a sudden, supreme confidence. The high-backed, leather armchair where she sat was now her throne. He supposed that made him a subject.

"Doctor," she said, but her tone was different. Hard. Commanding. Even her accent had changed.

Mimicking the voice of her dead husband, completing the illusion. Involuntarily, of course. In her waking moments Thea continued to insist that her husband was dead, and she never remembered those times when she was her husband.

"You've interrupted our session again, Mr. Redpath. These are important to your wife's recovery."

"Sleep is important to my wife's recovery," Connor said. In life Vale suspected it wouldn't have been wise to trifle with him. Even now, subsumed into his wife's psyche, his words had weight. "She has not been sleeping as much as she should."

"I believe I should be the judge of that. Your wife has been remanded to my care, after all."

"I leave her in your care for as long as it is convenient for me, Doctor. Her well-being is my foremost concern. Do not oblige me to make other arrangements."

Vale wanted to laugh. He was being threatened by the dead husband of a patient through the patient's own lips - yet there was a gravity to Thea's expression, a pinch between her brows, that made her face look like someone else's. A face Vale had only ever seen in photographs glaring out from the glass, grim of expression and powerful of stature, with a possessive arm ever around Thea's shoulders.

Sometimes he had to remind himself that Connor Redpath really was dead.

"Thea can be...wilful, crafty. She doesn't always take her medication. She pretends, regurgitates it."

And, sometimes, she would make trouble. She would start fights with the orderlies, or whip the other patients into a frenzy with maddening screams and strange stories just as the medication was being dispensed.

She was in an asylum, but the way she smiled as she was dragged to her cell left Vale in no doubt: she was as lucid as any of them when she was awake. She was an actress, the ward her stage and insanity her role.

Her reticence to take the medication worked in his favour. At the dosage Connor demanded she would have fallen into an induced coma long ago. How could Vale extract the mysteries of the Beyond from her then?

"You disappoint me, Doctor. Surely a man of your intelligence can remedy a simple matter of discipline."

"I appreciate your faith, sir."

"I advise that you do not test that faith. I will not be pleased if I find it misplaced."

And, with that, he departed. A shudder passed through Thea's body, a shiver like a hand caressing her from head-to-toe. Her fists clenched and her toes curled.

"You are at rest, Thea. The doorway to the Beyond is closed. You are in a peaceful room. The sun is setting. It is time for sleep."

The hypnotic method was useful for less barbaric patients, as it helped with hysteric insomnia. Thea was the only patient who seemed to fight it every time. She struggled like she was being dragged into sleep, but there was no better time for her to sleep than immediately after a session. There was nothing else to learn today; Let Connor have his wife for the night.

His hands trembled as he shut his journal and capped his pen. Excitement, he told himself. He'd been close to recording the passing of some great event as it happened. His research into the Beyond was bearing fruit.

But, if he could break the barrier between here and that far-flung dreamscape, what might he see with his own eyes?

It was a lie. He was shaking because Connor unnerved him, more than he should have.

He was a figment of a patient's imagination. Connor Redpath wasn't a ghost, and he wasn't actually speaking through his wife.

He was a facet of her sleeping mind, a manifestation of her guilt.

After all, she had killed him.

Or had she?

The case had been a strange one. He'd read the police report. She'd walked into the precinct, covered in blood and smoking a cigarette. She'd told them that she'd murdered her husband, and she hadn't been even slightly remorseful.

While she sat in an interrogation room officers had been dispatched to stately Redpath House. There they found enough blood to pronounce Connor Redpath dead, but what they hadn't found was a body.

The case was further confused by her injuries. Contusions, ligature marks and lacerations, some made by human teeth, marked her upper arms, thighs, belly, back and breasts. Anywhere that could be easily covered with clothing, actually.

Thea told them that what happened between a married couple in the privacy of their own home was their own business.

She had been committed for several reasons. Primarily hysteria, but also sadomasochism, nymphomania and sociopathy. The police had tried to bring charges against her, but a departmental psychologist had cast doubt on her fitness to testify; She'd been remanded to the asylum instead.

The nightmares came shortly after she'd been committed, shortly before Vale had taken on her case. He'd known of her before - she'd become something of a celebrity - but he didn't care for her fame. She was just another wealthy lunatic.

His field of study was sleep, particularly the shared spaces of sleep that seemed to manifest in diseased minds.

Her dreams had been mundane at first. Screaming, thrashing nightmares of her dead husband, reliving the night that she plunged a knife into him over and over and over again. Nothing but her repressed guilt bubbling to the surface, making her relive the traumatic moment again and again until she consciously confronted it. Tediously Freudian.

Awake, in her more distraught and sleep-deprived moments, she confided to Vale that Connor had done something to her. Opened a doorway in her mind, a door that took her places.

He hadn't believed it, not until the day he'd placed her in a hypnotic trance. He'd intended to find answers for the police; The location of the body, perhaps.

Instead, he had found the Beyond.

He read back through his journals every night, filling himself with the images she poured forth in her entranced state. The emerald deserts under five moons. The subterranean cities that crawled up from their blackened pits on mechanical, insectile legs. The forest of unblinking eyes. The world of oceans where the shadows of great and terrible beings stretched out their infinite limbs, craving the air.

The mountain of blue glass.

Sweating and gasping he fell into his bed, hoping to catch some fleeting glimpse of them. Hoping that her words were the inspiration, the invitation, he needed to cross the threshold. To reach the Beyond.

Every night his dreams were the same. Flat, empty, mundane.

He dreamed of his childhood home. He dreamed of his parents. He dreamed of his anxious heart as he prepared for examinations or fortified himself to submit his doctoral thesis.

He dreamed of nothing.

He awoke with a fist of anger squeezing tight around his pounding heart, and he roared his frustration at the cracked stucco on the ceiling of his bedroom. He stormed through his apartments in the building opposite the asylum, and he asked over and over again: Why? Why? Why couldn't he dream like her?

✦━━○━━✦

"As promised," MacCallum said, dropping the leather-bound book on Vale's desk. "The secret journal of Connor Redpath."

Vale stared at the private investigator, then at the journal. His hands trembled as he lifted it and opened it to the first page.

It wasn't what he'd expected. Not the feverishly scribbled notes of a madman delving into the occult. No impossible diagrams in the margins. The writing wasn't in reverse, it didn't project at random angles, it didn't form spirals.

It was neat and evenly spaced, and in straight lines. It reminded him of an accountant's ledger.

He flicked through the pages. Every single one was

the same. But, here and there, he recognised names from his own research. Shared spaces of the mind, dream worlds and gateways and realms beyond imagining.

"Where was it?"

"Right where you said. Dimensions of the house didn't add up, and there was a space behind his study. A false wall with a whole second office set up back there, and the desk had a false bottom."

Vale nodded. He'd hired MacCallum because he was known for getting results. He was swarthy and unkempt, but capable. Quite different from Vale himself, in his pressed waistcoat, his bowtie, his spectacles. An academic to the bone.

MacCallum didn't have any misgivings about breaking into the Redpath House. Superstition chased everyone else from its door. They feared the place was haunted, but if Connor Redpath was anywhere he was with his wife.

He flipped to the back of the book. The notes ended with a date from ten years ago; Connor and Thea hadn't even been acquainted then.

Vale growled.

"Where is the rest?"

"Safe," MacCallum said, "and that's where it's going to stay until I get the rest of the money."

"I already paid you, you ungrateful..."

"Easy, Doc. Let's not go calling each other names. We've got a good professional relationship, don't you think? Mutually beneficial. Discrete. Right?"

Vale took a breath, but his anger didn't abate. It was a struggle to keep his voice steady. "Very well. How much will you extort me for?"

"My usual payment is half up-front, half on completion."

"You want to double the fee?"

"I just want what those journals are worth, Doc. What they're really worth. There must be a dozen of them, and they're packed. That Redpath guy knew how to write nice and small. Probably wore out a few fancy pens filling them all up. Can't make head-nor-tail of what he wrote myself, but I reckon they'd be real interesting to a guy like yourself."

MacCallum was a snake and, unfortunately, correct. Vale wanted those journals. Thea was a window to the Beyond, but he couldn't control her. The key lay between the covers of her husband's journals. If Vale could learn the details of the 'ritual', the scientific process Connor had used, he could bend more of his resources towards the exploration of the Beyond.

The patients of the asylum were prisoners in their own minds. They lay in cells or wandered the dayrooms in a medicated haze. It would be so much better for them, for the world, if they could be used to map the unknown reaches of the Beyond.

He couldn't stop now. He couldn't allow another man's greed to stand in the way of progress.

"Bring me the rest of the journals," Vale demanded, "you won't get another penny until I have them all in my possession. Do I make myself clear?"

"Crystal, but a word of advice: Don't even think about trying to weasel out of this. I'm not playing around."

"Don't worry, Mister McCallum," Vale said. He gripped the journal so tight his knuckles went white. "I am deathly serious."

◆—○—◆

"Good morning, Thea."

She sat in the armchair with legs folded, a cigarette smouldering in one hand and a tumbler of scotch in the other. Her usual breakfast.

Her stout frame suggested she was used to a more filling repast, but she had eaten little since she'd been committed. She had lost weight, and it had added gauntness and shadow to her otherwise round features.

The intimacy of her injuries suggested that her husband had found a fuller figure more agreeable. Vale suspected he'd valued her more for her mind, for her... *openness* to new experiences.

"How are you today?"

She sneered. Not unusual; she sneered at almost everything. Questions, demands, requests, good news, bad news, medicine. She'd treated the police much the same. Her husband probably hadn't had the same patience.

"As with all our sessions, I need you to be completely relaxed. Open to whatever...thoughts might occur to you in the moment. Self-censorship is not conducive to good therapy."

"I'm just wondering when you'll get bored and leave me alone. I like it here. The people are interesting, and the room's comfortable. And I've never had a prescription for scotch before."

"It's important that we continue to make progress."

"Is that what you're calling it?"

He smiled thinly. It didn't matter what she said. She was his patient, and he'd never let her go. She had no idea how vital she had been for his research, the worlds they had visited together, the things they had seen. That pleasure was his alone.

"I'd like you to listen to this metronome while we speak, Thea. Try to match your breathing to it."

"Like before, because you think it helps."

"Yes."

He tipped the arm on the metronome and let it swing. Thea eyed it suspiciously, but she didn't take her eyes off it. She wouldn't, not until she entered the trance.

On the side table beside the metronome was a projector. It was set to strobe light at the same interval as the metronome, and it would trigger the fugue state that would make her his bridge to the Beyond.

She tapped ash from her cigarette. Bored. He waited until the empty tumbler slipped from her fingers and thumped into the carpet, until her cigarette lay smoking, forgotten, in the ashtray.

"Can you hear me, Thea?"

She didn't answer, not at first. Her eyes were glazed, but open. The flashing light reflected in her pupils. He saw shapes in them: triangles, pentagons, heptagons all multiplying into infinity. Colours he couldn't name. Anger and mourning, misery and desire.

"Yes," she said.

"I want to revisit the mountain of blue glass. Can you see it?"

She shook her head. Vale clenched his teeth. He wanted to know what happened when the water fell. He wanted to see it through her eyes. How could he take her back there?

"Where are you, Thea?"

"The parlour."

"Of your home?"

She nodded. He clicked his tongue. These were the worst sessions, the ones where she didn't access the Beyond at all. The ones where she relived the night when she murdered Connor. Further projections of her guilt, he assumed.

"You are drinking, correct?"

"Yes. I always take the most expensive bottle I can find. I want to make him angry."

"To punish him?"

"To put him in the mood."

"Is Connor there?"

"He's at work. Running late. I'm getting bored."

"So, what do you do?"

"I break into his office."

"Why?"

"I'm bored."

He couldn't tell if she was answering the question, or if she was actually just bored. But she was still staring into the strobing light, and he knew she was still under.

He'd heard the story before. She found something in the study, evidence of an affair perhaps. It would explain her hysterics. Connor had caught her, and there had been a confrontation. She'd stabbed him with a letter opener. Quite a few times, by the sound of it.

But…

He glanced at the journal on his desk, at Connor's journal. A thought occurred.

"Did you find the wall panel, Thea? The second study?"

"Yes."

"And what did you find there?"

"His journals."

Vale breathed deep. He'd always assumed Thea had been candid with him about that night, but she'd been holding something back, something that might have led him to the journals without the need for MacCallum.

"What was in those journals, Thea?"

"The ritual. He said he'd performed it on me. He opened something in my head, let something in."

Her overlong fingernails ploughed into the usual scratches on the arm of the chair.

"The front door. Connor's home."

"Remember, you are safe. You are there, but you are not there. You are in my office with me. What you are experiencing is a memory. It can't hurt you."

She was ignoring him, and even the insistent probing of his voice in her impressionable state wasn't relaxing her. Her hand was groping for something; A letter opener, perhaps.

"Won't let him touch me. Won't let him do it. Won't let him pull those things out of my head."

"Calm down, Thea."

"I'll kill him. I'll kill him first!"

She was snarling now, teeth bared and fingers clenched. She'd given up on the chair arms, and had split the skin on her palms instead. She was bleeding. She started twisting in her seat, breathing hard like she was struggling.

She was flushed on her throat. Was it his imagination or...were those finger marks appearing in red on her pale flesh?

"What's happening, Thea?"

She shook her head. Choked. "He won't die."

"It's just a memory."

"This isn't right. This isn't how it happened. He died. He *died*!"

She started screaming, thrashing, like she was struggling.

It was just the sleep paralysis. Those weren't marks appearing on her wrists, binding her to the chair.

Vale ran to his desk as her screams filled the office, and he prepared a syringe with a soporific. He needed to release Thea from her fugue, and there wasn't time to do it gently. She was going to alert the whole asylum.

"It's time to sleep," he said, and jabbed the needle into the side of her neck. Ragged semi-circles were starting to blossom on her neck: teeth marks.

She slumped. He stepped back, breathing hard.

There were tears on Thea's cheeks. Whatever horrors were occurring behind her eyes she would deal with alone now.

"Are you alright, Doctor?"

One of the nurses was standing in the doorway, and in the corridor outside others were craning to see what had transpired.

"Fine, thank you. Mrs Redpath had a...seizure. I was

forced to sedate her."

He wondered if he was ever going to be able to explore the Beyond through her. Would Connor always interfere?

He needed the journals. Needed other options.

"I think she is ready to go back to her room now, nurse. Please fetch a gurney."

The nurse withdrew. Vale trailed his fingers through Thea's fiery hair. She had been very useful to him, but perhaps it was time for her to rest.

"Sweet dreams, Thea."

MacCallum returned with the journals. A dozen of them, filled with Connor's condensed, efficient script. Vale had devoured the first already. It had been everything he'd hoped and feared. Filled with insight and portentous revelation, and incomplete. The first step of a long journey.

A journey that had ended with his death, and his wife's insanity.

"Congratulations are in order," Vale said, pouring out a sizeable measure of Thea's scotch. "For both of us, Mister MacCallum. This has been a very lucrative arrangement, hasn't it?"

MacCallum snorted. He was counting his payment. Cash, as requested. Vale could see the gears turning behind his eyes. He was wondering if he should have held out for more.

Perhaps he should have; Vale would have given anything for the others.

MacCallum sealed the envelope, eyes dark. He sucked

his thumb irritably.

"Paper cut?" Vale asked, with a thin smile.

He set a tumbler down in front of MacCallum and held up his own. The P.I. sneered.

"I'm not drinking that. What do you think I am, an idiot?"

"You are paranoid, Mister MacCallum. Quite a text-book case at that."

"I'm careful is what I am."

"Oh yes, very careful, but about entirely the wrong things. The drink would have been rather obvious, wouldn't it?"

Vale savoured the scotch, and the look of confusion on the other man's face.

"The money was less obvious. I knew you would insist on counting it. Tell me, are you familiar with curare? We use it in the application of electrotherapy. It's a paralytic, not an analgesic. They're still awake, still capable of feeling every minute sensation."

MacCallum tried to speak. He made a choking noise and Vale laughed at how much he sounded like a duck.

"I've looked into your background, Mister MacCallum. No family to speak of. Your wife took your son to live on the West Coast, is that right? Perhaps that explains your depressive episodes, your antisocial behaviour. A spell at our humble institution might serve to revitalise you. I will take care of the paperwork, don't worry."

He went to the corner and steered a wheelchair out from behind the armoire. Always useful to have one on hand.

He kicked the chair's brakes on and wiped the indignant spittle off MacCallum's lips with a handkerchief. He could see his own face reflected in his bloodshot eyes, and imagined the triangles and pentagons and heptagons spiraling out from them in all those strange and marvellous colours.

"Come along, Mister MacCallum. We are going to be pioneers."

◆———◆

The 'ritual' was simple. Geometric shapes and chemicals he could find easily in the asylums stores. Science by another name, a name unknown to everyone but Connor Redpath.

Where had it come from? Past the stars? Beneath the ocean? Or through the mist of dreams, the worlds of the Beyond?

That question would be answered with all the others.

He'd needed to mark the flesh. MacCallum hadn't been able to react, but no doubt it had been excruciating. Some of the marks matched those in Thea's medical report, so perhaps they hadn't been simple conjugal hijinks the way she thought.

He imagined plying Thea's pale skin with the point of the blade, imagined her blood on his hands. He imagined being her husband. How would it have felt to break this ground? To further the cause of science? To use a body so intimate to him?

When he was done Vale was soaked in sweat, and thoughts of Thea's lacerated flesh lingered in his mind. The paralytic had worn off, and MacCallum strained against his restraints. His vest and slacks were stained dark with sweat and gore. He growled around the gag in his mouth, stubble soaked dark with perspiration.

"The moment of truth," Vale said. He pulled the gag away so that he could force the gavage tube into MacCallum's mouth and pump the chemical – the catalyst – into his stomach.

No wonder Thea had been so angry with her husband. The ritual seemed terribly painful, but he sympathised more with Connor. He was about to touch the Beyond through a doorway of his own creation. What other joy could be greater? Not the love of a woman, not the strongest opiates.

Nothing surpassed the joy of discovery. Vale was only the second man to ever walk this path.

The first was dead.

He pumped the acrid solution, then pulled the tube from MacCallum's mouth with a gurgling, sucking noise. He held his jaw shut to keep him from vomiting. He struggled. He retched. They wrestled for what must have been minutes, and Vale wondered how Connor had made Thea ingest the chemicals without her knowledge.

Perhaps he had simply put them in the most expensive bottle.

"Listen very carefully, Mister MacCallum," Vale said, his hand clamped over the other man's mouth. "I want you to follow the metronome with your eyes. Try to breathe in time to its rhythm."

"Get off me, you crazy son of a bitch! Let me out of this chair! What the fuck is wrong with you?!"

He started spitting and cursing the moment Vale removed his hand, but MacCallum was exsanguinated and woozy from the chemicals. He was fatigued and, more importantly, suggestible.

"Watch the metronome," Vale repeated. "Count if you wish."

He set the arm swinging. He pushed the button on the projector, and it began to strobe.

There, in MacCallum's eyes, gleamed the geometries of the Beyond, the gateways through which they would glimpse other worlds.

"Where are you, Mister MacCallum?"

His face had taken on the same slackness as Thea's when she was in the fugue. Then, in a familiar, drowsy tone he answered.

"The Redpath House."

Vale rolled his eyes. MacCallum had the power to explore all the realms of the Beyond, but he was trapped in the Redpath House.

"Why? Why are you there?"

MacCallum's head twitched. He was looking around. Bewildered.

"He brought me here."

"Who?"

"The man in all the pictures. It's...It's Redpath."

"You can see Connor Redpath?"

"He's thanking me for bringing you the journals. He says it's what he wanted."

Vale's eyes narrowed. "What?"

"He...He says that's all he needs me for. He says he's going to let me go."

"To the Beyond? MacCallum, is he letting you go to

the Beyond?"

MacCallum started trembling. His eyes rolled back in his head, exposing ruptured vessels that turned them an ugly red. He made a choking noise and his tongue rose in his gaping mouth, like he was being strangled.

Finger marks appeared on his neck, like the ones on Thea's wrists.

And there, against the wall, captured in halting flashes by the strobe was a shadow, a looming figure that Vale recognised only from photographs. It was squeezing MacCallum's throat.

Cold sweat needled Vale's flesh. He reached for the projector. He knocked over the metronome and it clattered to the floor, falling silent. He found the button and shut the strobe off, then fumbled in the darkness to turn the light back on.

The wheelchair was empty, the restraints hanging slack. The gag was lying on the seat.

MacCallum loomed out of the darkness, buttoning his shirt cuffs. The crazed look in his eyes was gone, replaced by a cold, calculating glare. The expression wasn't his.

It reminded Vale of the expressions Thea would pull when she was speaking as…

Connor.

"Doctor," MacCallum's body greeted. His tone and accent had changed. They were…familiar.

He seized Vale by the shoulder. His fingers clenched until he made the doctor cry out. He imagined himself bruising under his waistcoat, bruising like Thea.

"Kindly take me to my wife."

Faze

Brandon Ebinger

Faze didn't want to go up to the 'llite.

"Can't Burgess do it?" She asked the tall representative that the Corporation had sent to fetch her, wondering how the poor guy had drawn the short straw.

Nobody liked coming down to the slums.

"Burgess didn't return from his excursion last night." The Rep responded calmly. He was the most nondescript man that Faze had ever seen, and she wondered if the rumors of the corp playing around with cloning were true.

"Is he okay?" Faze asked. Usually kids came back from the 'llite; it wasn't supposed to be a dangerous assignment, just a back-breaking one.

"We are unsure. All that is known is that he never showed up to pick up his ration tickets this A.M."

Faze nodded silently. He probably slagged off somewhere, kids did it all the time. All you had to do was hop one of the freighters when nobody was looking, and even with the chance that you'd be randomly depressurized in the cargo hold it wasn't a rare thing to try. Life for a colony kid sucked, especially when they were orphans like she and Burgess.

"My labor card number ain't up for another week." Faze finally said.

The man nodded.

"What if I say no?"

"It is an imperative," the Corporation man said, "not a request."

Crap.

Faze knew that they couldn't make her do labor when it wasn't her turn, the life-contract she was forced to sign when she came of age said as much. However, she also knew that if she sent this guy packing back to his bosses without her there would be hell to pay down the road. They might send her to the mines for her next labor day, or even to Old Earth, a place that had filled her nightmares since she was a little girl.

"Fine...what do you want me to do?"

"The Corporation has begun a project that requires a great deal of copper wiring."

Cutting corners again, aren't we? Faze thought to herself. With all the money the Corporation pulls in a year they should be able to make their own copper wiring.

"We want you to find as much copper as possible, either in wire form or another, it matters little. Regular pay rates apply."

"Plus a non-labor day bonus?" Faze asked. She was running low on food and drinkable water so the bonus, though small, would go a long way toward keeping her alive.

"Of course." The suit replied.

"...Fine."

The SWO-236 satellite was launched before Faze was born, an easy solution to the colony's rapidly growing disposal problems. Wastes that were neither biological nor toxic were to be shipped there and carefully organized into separate rooms based on their composition, out of the way but easily accessed if it became necessary to return them to the colony as scrap.

At least that was what was supposed to happen. In truth the people hauling the garbage, underpaid and often only a little older than Faze, grew tired of the cataloging. They ended up tossing everything into the first free spot they came across, making retrieval an absolute nightmare.

Still, of all the jobs that a skill-less orphan could draw for their work-days, scavenging the 'llite, as it was called in the colonies, was the safest. Faze supposed that she should be grateful.

"This is Citizen Finuva Alvarez, ID number 206-502A." Faze felt no connection to her full name; in fact, as far as she was concerned, it may as well belong to a different girl entirely. She only used it when making official reports to the Corporation, and even the workers at the ration stations called her Faze. Also, she wasn't sure if it was necessary to give her Citizen ID number, but she had learned early on that the best way to deal with bureaucracy was to give too much information - that way they could never say that you were withholding anything.

"Roger, Alvarez." The voice on the other side of the communicator sounded kindly, like Faze imagined a father should sound. "What's your twenty?"

Faze squinted at the shuttle's pictorial readout. Because she couldn't read very well she always requested the newer shuttles that had this option.

"About halfway to the 'llite on STR 24."

"Roger that, Alvarez. Is all to code?"

Faze nodded to herself, despite knowing full well that the dispatcher couldn't see her do so. "Yes sir, all is crossed and dotted. Should be reaching the 'llite in a few hours."

There was a brief pause on the other side of the com, and when the fatherly voice spoke again it was hurried, somewhat irritated.

"I was just informed that there is something moving on the Satellite. I repeat, something living moving around on the Satellite. Do you copy?"

"Yes sir, I copy."

"I'm sure it's nothing to worry about, kid. But still, be alert."

"I will, sir."

It's probably Burgess screwing around up there. Faze thought to herself. He probably got sick of the colony and is up there playing Winks and Bowls with himself.

As she thought this Faze double checked the bag of supplies that she had brought for herself, mentally marking off each item as she touched it.

- Enough ration packs for an extra day...check

Two cans of water...check

Three chemical light sticks, blue, green and red... check.

Acetylene cutting torch...check

Weighted gravitational boots...check

Personal respirator with portable air tank...check

Technically the last two items weren't needed, since the Satellite ran gravity and atmosphere constantly, but Faze figured that it was better to be prepared. After all, she learned long ago not to rely on the Corporation.

"Alright, here goes." Faze said to herself, putting everything back into her nylon bag. She returned to the captain's chair and, after checking that the shuttle was on course one last time, closed her eyes and nodded off.

A few hours was a long time when you were alone in space.

◄——○——►

Muttering to herself sleepily Faze shut off the on-board alarm system, stalling the insistent buzzing. She enjoyed watching the 'llite through her view-screen, so she had informed the system to awaken her twenty minutes before landing.

She watched her destination now, twirling slowly in the inky void. It had been pristine once, almost beautiful in the cold way that well-built institutional things could be beautiful, but Faze had only witnessed this in vids. The SDWP-236 that loomed before her was old and ratty, covered in cracks and fissures, the sides painted with the street-language of pictorial graffiti.

Faze imagined donning a void-suit, floating over to the side of the 'llite and, with the help of a zero-G sprayer, making her mark on one of it's paneled walls. She wondered how so many found the bravery. Unless she was safe behind the walls of a ship or satellite, the void terrified her.

As the ship went about it's landing, which required very little input unless something went wrong, Faze bent and twisted, breaking up the sleep-stiffness that had settled into her body during her nap. Finally a soft thump signaled her arrival, soft bells filling the air that were joined quickly by the ship's feminine voice announcing a successful landing. Faze had always found ship voices creepy, too cloying and nice by far, but was happy to hear this one.

She had made it.

✦—◦—✦

The lights in the entry hall were flickering.

Great, another thing breaking down. Faze thought to herself. Another thing to worry about.

As she walked she placed her small ear-buds into her ears, pressing a button on her belt. Instantly her head was filled with the aggressive vocals and dark rhythms of her favorite artist, a core-planet producer who went by the unlikely name of Tommy Fiendish. Most of the colony kids she knew liked the fluffy love-and-sex songs that filled the Corporation's free airways, but Faze figured that a life like hers needed a particular soundtrack, a certain tone and theme to match her surroundings. Her musical taste, as well as her haircut (a partially shaved style that she had copied from a pirate in a news-vid) made her less than popular with the other kids. She had not yet, at the age of nineteen, been on a single date.

"Screw 'em." She whispered to herself, not really meaning it.

She made her way down the long entry hallway and

paused at the imposing double doors that led deeper into the 'llite. She braced for the painfully powerful spray of the decontamination process, a necessary step before being allowed access, but nothing came.

Faze wrinkled her nose in confusion and took a few steps backward, hoping to trigger the sprayers by repeating her approach.

Nothing.

She did a few jumping jacks, waving her arms like a frenzied crab.

Still nothing.

"Is everything on this damn 'llite broken?" Faze muttered to herself, throwing in a couple colorful colony profanities for good measure. "Well, if you're going to be that way..."

She pressed a few buttons on the door's control box, triggering manual override and causing the doors to slide open.

"Finally." She said, leaning in close to the box's microphone, "Alvarez, 206-502A." The 'llite's internal system recorded all manual actions, and it was expected that anyone overriding the automated system leave their name and number, along with a short description of why they defied the powers that be. "The damn sprayers were broke."

She walked through the now-open doors, feeling more frustrated than the situation probably warranted.

Consulting her map Faze made her way to the eastern storage room, where the wire was supposed to be kept. Not surprisingly there was very little wire there, and none of it copper. Instead she found three boots, a ruined phaser charge-pack and a doll in a blue dress with a white apron that Faze vaguely remembered from an old vid.

"Do you know where I can find some copper, kid?" Faze asked, picking up the doll and gently shaking it. Not getting a response she put the doll back where she found it, then the lights flickered. Even though the 'llite was only cast into darkness for less than a second Faze felt her heart leap into her throat, where it insisted on beating faster and harder than the music that was thrumming in her ears. Reaching into her pocket Faze wrapped her fingers around the light sticks she had brought, drawing comfort from the fact that, as long as she didn't dilly dally here too long, she would have more than enough light.

"Let's get this over with and get out of here." She muttered to herself.

For the next hour Faze dug through pile after pile of refuse, finding a bit of copper but not nearly as much as she had hoped for. She dreaded going back with too little, and dreaded even more the thought of having to report that the Corporation might have to open their purses and spend a bit of money for a change.

She was just about to give up when she found the box.

◆──○──◆

The box reminded Faze of the containers that the colony used to enclose the bodies of the dead before they were bio-recycled, about a foot taller than her and twice as wide. There was writing on the side, but the only words that Faze could make out were "of, do, not, to" and the

Corporation's name. There was also a picture on the side, a sort of circle with three bladed lines extending far beyond it's center. She had no idea what it meant, but it triggered fear in her already shaken core.

The box's heavy lid was open, revealing a mess of tubes and wires. Faze was thankful that there was no body inside, no matter how much it reminded her of a death box. She wasn't squeamish, since you really couldn't be in the colonies, but she also wasn't sure that she could handle a corpse.

Something crashed in one of the other rooms, loud enough to be heard over Faze's music. It was the sound of something large and metal, maybe a barrel, falling or being tossed to the floor with enough force to send it bouncing. Faze stopped her music just in time to hear metal being dragged across the concrete floor and then flung once more, this time clanging against what Faze assumed was a wall.

"Burgess?" Faze yelled, the reports of the other colony kid's disappearance and unauthorized movement on the 'llite filling her mind with hope that maybe, just maybe, the noises were just her peers messing around.

The 'llite grew quiet.

"Burgess, this is Faze." She continued, feeling more and more confident by the second. "There are a lot of people looking for your ass. Pissed off people too, you're in some shit now." She knew that nobody was actually looking for him, that a colony kid disappearing was no big deal when there were always someone else to do the dirty work, but felt that this was the proper tone to set in this situation.

No response.

No more noise.

"C'mon, Burg...this shit ain't funny. Stop trying to screw with my head."

As she made her way toward where she thought she heard the noise she became calmer still. Clearly it was Burgess, and clearly he was just trying to get a rise out of her. Hell, he probably screwed with the lights and sprayers too, just to give her a scare that he could brag about when they returned to the colony.

Another metallic slamming noise.

Then another.

These sounds weren't the sounds of someone messing around. If it was Burgess he was throwing quite the temper tantrum, and that was totally unlike him. He was the sort of kid that was so calm that it became almost a game for some of the others, taking turns and placing bets on how to get a rise out of him. If Burgess was that pissed then Faze wasn't sure she wanted to encounter him after all.

When she found the source of the noise Faze's jaw dropped, and she choked back a scream.

The thing making all the racket was most definitely not Burgess, or any other human for that matter.

◆──◇──◆

The thing was tall, at least a head taller than the biggest person Faze had ever met, which meant it towered over her petite form. It's skin was mottled black and gray, it's arms and legs overlong, giving it the aspect of an evening shadow. Each arm ended in a wickedly clawed hand, matted with some reddish-brown substance that Faze didn't dare name.

The beast looked up at Faze and screamed, it's voice high and piercing, it's open mouth revealing a mass of snakey tongues that thrashed back and forth violently between needle-like teeth. Faze's body screamed for her to run, to bolt and keep bolting until the last drop of energy left her body. Instead she stood, struck stupid by the nightmarish majesty of the horror's form.

There had never been any proof, beyond the ramblings of those Faze considered crazy, of alien life in the galaxy.

Monster! Boogeyman! Demon! Even as her mind filled with superstitious words she had no doubt that the thing that faced her wasn't supernatural, but extra-natural. It was as much of a life-form as she was, if infinitely stranger.

Faze expected the beast to pounce or rush toward her, as animalistic and fierce as it's scream had implied. Instead it reached down, it's tantrum seemingly forgotten, and picked something off the floor. As it placed this item over it's serpent nest of a mouth Faze realized that it was a respirator, just like the one she wore.

Just like the one Burgess would have packed.

She also noticed that the thing, which she had taken for being completely naked, was wearing a pair of ill-fitting grav-boots. This would have looked absurd on it's long legs, were it in any other situation.

The moment the implications of these details hit Faze the thing screamed again, and this time she felt energy emanate from it's form, like the odd feeling she sometimes got standing next to the power pylons back in the colony. This was followed by a sucking sensation as the 'llite's life support and lighting cut out, leaving her in darkness not unlike the void that had troubled her on the trip there.

Finally, Faze ran.

Faze, being a city girl, did not have eyes adapted to the darkness. The fact that she was running, nearly hysterical, through a cluttered warehouse full of junk and hadn't yet gone ass-over-feet was a miracle. Knowing that miracles didn't tend to have a long duration she ducked into one of the 'llite's many rooms, huddling behind what appeared to be a pile of old, rusty mining equipment.

She considered cracking one of her light sticks, but quickly dismissed the thought. The thing hadn't found her yet, and in the inky blackness any light would act as a beacon to draw the monster toward her - where it would undoubtedly consume her.

Alright, she didn't know that it would eat her. However, the fact that it had Burgess' gear (not to mention the fact that it's claws were covered in, if she was being honest with herself, blood and viscera) strongly implied that whatever it's intention, it was not likely to involve a firm handshake and buddy hug.

Anyway, why hadn't it found her yet? She knew she was fast, and being sneaky was a requirement for all colony kids, but she could tell from the way the thing was built that it was a natural hunter and tracker of prey. She should be, by all rights, deader than a doornail.

"It's screwing with me." Faze muttered to herself, and as soon as she said it she knew it to be true. She had seen colony cats play with voles before eating them, and could totally see that damned thing doing the same with victims. If she could just make it to her ship...

No.

In her nineteen years of life Faze had faced down starvation, out-of-control street crime and nearly suicidal despair. She had watched countless people she called friends fall to the blade, or to disease and a seemingly endless supply of poisons that they smoked, swallowed or shoved into their waiting veins. None of it had been able to kill her yet, and not one of these problems had caused her to lay down and let fate wash over her.

If this damn monster thought it was going to either kill her, or send her away with her tail between her legs, it had another think coming.

She cracked one of her light sticks, her favorite red one for comfort, and as it began to glow she cupped it in one of her hands to minimize the escaping light. Carefully she surveyed the pile of junk in front of her. It appeared to be fairly uniform, at least for the mess that was the 'llite. She assumed that it all had come from a mine freighter team, which had simply dumped their payload in the first free space they had come to.

Faze dug for a moment, slow and careful, making as little noise as a small girl playing in a pile of rusted metal could possibly make. Finally she found what she was looking for, her expression changing from one of determined anger to a soft, cruel smile.

One of us isn't making it off this damn scrapheap. Taking a deep breath she threw her light-stick to the other side of the room.

Anger, rage, confusion, but above all else, hunger.

It had seen the big ship, laying so close to it's resting point, full of odd creatures in funny suits, suits that let them breathe in hostile air, even though the air it breathed wasn't hostile at all.

Careful creatures, they were. Too careful.

It had been so hungry, and had attacked.

Rending, piercing, they had fallen so easily at first, but they were careful creatures...smart. Soon they brought a thing out, a thing that, once it struck, filled it's target with a glowing pain, making it impossible to move.

They were no longer afraid of it then. They seemed excited.

It had woken up in a box, strong enough to hold no matter how much the creature thrashed and raged. Yet the box couldn't stop the thing's other trick, the electric machine breaking trick. It pulled the energy from the air to it's body and then let it amplify.

 They were scared again.

Then other men came onto the ship, men with different clothing. Angry, loud men that reminded it of itself. They killed the first group of men with guns and blades, taking the ship and the creature itself, forcing it back into the damned box.

It was left in another place, to be picked up later.

It waited.

And waited.

A young creature opened its box, and fell quickly

under its claws. It consumed the thing's flesh, took it's breathing and walking-on-the-floor machines. The thing was still ravenous, but it was free. Angry, angry enough to throw things, shove things around...but free.

And now this new one came, same sort of thing as all the others, just as young as the last.

Just as tender.

It would find her, and feast.

The machine trick had scared her, and it was just a matter of time before she did something to make light.

Then he would have her.

There.

In that room over there.

There was a red light.

It wouldn't be hungry for long.

⊷⊶

Faze nearly froze when the thing entered the room. Something about it, maybe it's teeth and claws, maybe just the way it moved, screamed predator to her lizard-brain. For half a breath she was a mouse in a field, trying to stifle shivers as a hawk flew overhead, claws reflecting in the sunlight...

I ain't no freakin' mouse.

Breaking the freeze, forcing her breath to stabilize, she struck.

Faze feared that going for the killing blow, trying to drive the blade on her new found mason's hammer into the thing's temple or eyes, would cost her dearly. After all, it was, for all appearances, a finely-tuned killing machine while she was just a small human girl. Instead she aimed for the straps on the thing's breathing mask, using the hammer's chisel end as a hook. When it caught firmly between the straps and the thing's head she pulled.

Whatever god or gods there still were in this time were in her favor, as the straps tore, ripping the mask from the creature's mouth. It let out a series of horrible rasps, the snake-tongues lashing about like the tentacles of a sea anemone.

The creature grasped wildly, the mask's human dimensions and unfamiliarity making it awkward in the beast's clawed hands. Just as it was about to figure it out, as it was on the verge of bringing the life-giving mask to it's mouth once more, Faze struck again.

This time she went for the killing blow, bellowing like a madwoman as she put every ounce of her weight behind the strike. The hammer's business end embedded deeply into one of the thing's inhuman eyes, spraying Faze in the face with a sickly, clear fluid that reminded her of the hemolymph of a crushed spider. Though she was screaming as she struck, some self-preservation instinct allowed her to snap her mouth shut just before the horrid fluid found it's way in. Even in her frenzied state she wasn't sure her mind could take any part of that, that thing entering her body.

The thing rasped once more, it's claws flexing, tongues slowing their sickening dance. Faze watched the rage drain from the thing's remaining eye and, at last, the beast was still.

She struck it again.

And again.

And again.

✦—○—✦

"This is Finuva Alvarez reporting in." She didn't feel like giving her serial number.

"You're loud and clear, Citizen Alvarez." There was a different voice on the other side this time, a female voice that was just as blank as the first male voice had been. "Were you successful?"

"I got what I could." Faze responded. "There wasn't a lot left."

There was a short pause on the other side, and then, "Affirmative. Did you run into any trouble up there?"

Faze added a pause of her own to the conversation, taking a moment to think about the creature, and, more accurately, the box that it had come from. She may not have been able to read the side of it, may not have known what the weird, bladed symbol had meant, but she did know that the Corporation had marked it as it's own. That alone added up to something that she didn't want to deal with.

Often the world was a better place if you just let the Corporation do its thing, and went about your life.

Faze wondered for a moment what would happen to the next poor schmuck that they sent up there, how they would react to a dead...whatever...with guts and viscera strewn about. She wondered for a moment what would happen if the thing wasn't actually dead, as unlikely as that was with the state she had left it in.

She shrugged, even though nobody could see it.

"Nope, just a routine trip to the 'llite."

After all, they didn't pay her enough.

NPC

By V. A. Vazquez

Kingsley stared at the cover art for *Emberworks*. A waitress dressed in a TGI Friday's uniform stood front-and-center, shotgun strapped to her back and ammo bandolier cutting across her name-tag. Behind her a horde of flame-throwing monsters ravaged their way across the 1990s American Southwest, leaving the crumbling remains of Blockbuster Videos and RadioShacks in their wake. From the open stock room a guttural *ahem* caught her attention; her manager pointed at his watch.

These games aren't going to stock themselves, Kingsley.

"What an asshole."

She turned around to see Ezra, the other sales associate on-shift, standing behind her. Tattoos poked out from the collar of his GameGear T-shirt.

"*IGN*'s Game of the Year," he said, grabbing a copy of *Emberworks* and flipping it over in his hands. "Have you played it?"

"Not yet."

"Would you like to?"

She shrugged, reaching into the cardboard box and pulling out another stack of copies for the shelf. With her minimum-wage salary and student loan bills, the only way she'd be getting a copy of *Emberworks* would be from a dude on Craigslist who lived in an unmarked van and offered 'alternative payment options'.

Ezra took the copy of *Emberworks* up to the check-out counter and scanned the barcode. Slipping some bills from his wallet into the cash register, he held the game up like a fishing lure, fluorescent lights glinting off its plastic shell. "If you're not doing anything tonight, maybe we could . . .?"

He shook the box back-and-forth; the disc rattled inside.

"I'm busy."

"C'mon, Kingsley. We could order some pizza, smoke a few joints. Maybe you could even sleep over again. You don't have to clock in until Wednesday, right?"

GameGear posted the weekly schedule in the stock room, so of course Ezra had memorized her hours.

"No thanks."

"You're not seeing someone else, are you?"

Even though their manager could see them from his metal folding-chair, even though there was a customer digging through the discount bin, Kingsley still took half a step backwards. She stared down at her shoelaces, frayed at the ends and repaired with scotch tape.

"I'm just busy," she tried again.

"So there's no other guy?"

"No."

"Maybe some other time." Ezra shook the box again, but this time it sounded like the rattle of ammunition loose in a magazine. And then, with his copy of *Emberworks* gripped in his hand, he disappeared into the stock room.

Kingsley counted the game boxes on the shelf: forty, the same number listed on the shipping manifest. But, as she went to break down the cardboard box, she noticed there was one additional copy buried at the bottom, one that had been overlooked by the manufacturer. *No one has to know*, she thought, tucking the video game into the waistband of her jeans and letting her oversized T-shirt cover the bulge. *They don't pay you enough anyway. Just think of this as getting what you're owed.*

When she got home she shoved the disc into her PlayStation and grabbed a six-pack of Red Bull from the refrigerator. The download bar slid across the screen milli-meter-by-millimeter: 98%, 99%, 100%.

She tugged on her VR headset and pressed start.

"Haven't seen you around here before."

The cutscene opened on a good-looking gentleman sitting in a booth at TGI Friday's. He'd nudged his glasses down onto the tip of his nose so he could look at her from over the frames, and the top few buttons of his rumpled shirt were undone. His tweed jacket had leather patches stitched onto the elbows.

"I'm just passing through," he said.

He definitely wasn't from Arizona or New Mexico, or wherever *Emberworks* took place; his accent sounded like he'd just stepped off an airplane coming from London.

"Yeah, Santa Vela's a regular drive-thru. What can I

getcha?"

"How's the Chinese chicken salad?"

" . . . It comes with a fortune cookie."

"Smashing. Also, you should know there are three petrol-rippers sitting in the corner by the TV. The one playing ESPN." He sipped from his tumbler; the ice cubes clinked against the plastic. "Always hated sports."

"Three *what*?"

"Petrol-rippers. You're going to want this." He kicked a tactical scabbard out from underneath the table. She unzipped the fabric to reveal —

"Sir, this is a TGI Friday's. You *cannot* have a shotgun in here."

"It's not for me, it's for you, and you might want to lock and load." He pointed over to the corner table where, sure enough, a tentacle poked out from one of the customers' shirtsleeves and wrapped around an almost-toppled glass, drawing it back onto the table. The customer looked up to meet her stare. "We've been spotted."

Flesh splattered to the ground, a few sticky shreds slipping down the TV screen and leaving ichor smears all over the Patriots' touchdown. The petrol-rippers burst out of their human disguises and charged across the TGI Friday's booths. Her shotgun self-loaded and aimed, as the NPC (Nico, the subtitles informed her), led her through the tutorial.

"Does dinner always come with a side order of spleen around here?" Nico asked, plucking some gooey membranes out of his bleached-blonde hair.

"Take it up with the tourism board. Heads!" And then, as he jumped behind the bar counter, she fired off a round of ammo into a monster, gasoline belching up from its esophagus.

Nico poured himself a shot-glass of apple schnapps and toasted her from his hiding spot. Kingsley snorted out a laugh.

After all the petrol-rippers had been dispatched she paused the game for a quick bathroom break. Sitting on the toilet, sweatpants bunched around her ankles, she browsed #Emberworks on Twitter for spoilers.

CrawlerKino: *SPOILER WARNING. I wish Nico had stuck around longer! When he got wiped out by that diesel-worm in the third mission, I was so bummed. I hope @ CampfireGames brings him back for the DLC.*

GoatLordNYC: *Anyone else think it was unfair we didn't even get a chance to save him? That cutscene sucked. Way to kill off my favorite character and not even give me the opportunity to fight back. #TeamNico*

⟐

"Alright," Nico said after their second mission, tossing his crossbow into the backseat and getting into the rusted Chevy Corvette. "Where are we off to next?"

She checked the clunky pager and folded-up map that doubled as the game's mission log. "Small church in La Astillas County. Locals've been having some trouble with a diesel-worm."

"Oh."

Nico went quiet after that, turning on the radio and

slumping back into the passenger seat.

As soon as they wandered into the chapel the diesel-worm burst through the floor, firing wood splinters in every direction. Its body writhed like a plump maggot; its fangs dribbled puddles of flammable liquid onto the shattered planks. The game began the cutscene she'd read about on Twitter — the one in which Nico would be devoured by the diesel-worm — and only then would she be allowed to play again.

Bzzzz.

Her cell phone vibrated on the coffee table. *Probably the landlord.* Her shower had been busted for the past week; she'd been washing her hair in the sink. As she removed the VR headset and reached for it she nudged the analog stick on the controller, and her character stepped forward.

"*Shit!*" she shouted, mashing the B button. She was still in control; the cutscene hadn't started yet. Her character charged, colliding with the diesel-worm and knocking it off its trajectory. She glanced up at Nico, whose eyes had gone wider than half-dollar coins behind the lenses of his glasses. He managed to draw his crossbow, but the diesel-worm was fast, too fast for him to get it loaded.

She pressed Y, and her character reached down into the holster strapped to her thigh, taking out a hunting knife and shoving it deep into the monster's guts. The diesel-worm let out a screech and reared backwards, giving Nico enough time to hitch a bolt into the crossbow. With trembling hands he took aim, letting the bolt rip straight into the diesel-worm's open mouth and through the back of its skull. Brain matter splattered across the stained glass windows as the diesel-worm collapsed, dead, on the altar.

"Huh."

While the game saved she checked her missed calls log (unknown number — *fuck my life*) and typed a quick message on Twitter.

Kincraig: *Why didn't anyone tell me I could save Nico during the third mission? #Emberworks*

The responses came back quicker than a machine-gun rattling through rounds:

CrawlerKino: *You saved Nico?! Great. Now I have to go back and replay the whole game. There goes next weekend. #TeamNico*

PenguinCrisis: *Mine went straight to the cutscene. I didn't even get a chance to save him. What did you do?*

GamesOrDeath: *Nico always dies in the third mission. There's no way to save him. Trust me. We tried.*

And then a response directly from the studio:

CampfireGames: *Nico never makes it past the third mission. (Poor guy.) But be on the lookout for some DLC featuring everyone's favorite Emberworks agent. #TeamNico*

Before she could type a response the game finished saving, and a new cutscene started. She jammed the VR headset back on. Nico sat in the passenger seat of the Corvette, staring at his own two hands like he'd never seen them before. There was diesel-worm blood digitally lodged under his fingernails. "Good lord," he said, taking a handkerchief out of his pocket and wiping the grime off.

"Close call with that diesel-worm," her character said in a husky smoker's alto. "Should we see what's waiting for us in Hoguera Hills?"

She popped open the glovebox, and the in-game map unfolded onscreen. Hoguera Hills now appeared in bright colors where it'd previously been greyed-out. She scrolled over the graphic and prepared to press X.

"*No!*" Nico launched himself towards the camera. She jerked back against her couch cushions, almost dropping the controller onto the floor. "Don't press that button. Please." When her fingers stayed locked in place he settled back into the passenger seat. "Look, what's your name?"

She waited for her character to answer, but nothing happened. Maybe the game had glitched out.

"I'm talking to *you*."

"*Me?*"

Kingsley adjusted the microphone on her headset and jabbed her thumb towards her own chest.

"Yes, you. The one holding the controller and playing the game. What's your name?"

"Kingsley."

"Kingsley," he repeated. "Good. Good. Smashing." He reached into the glovebox and grabbed a stack of tourism brochures. Flipping through them one at a time, he finally held one up that said EXPERIENCE BRIDGEWATER: BIG CITY FUN IN A SMALL TOWN PACKAGE. "How about we go to Bridgewater instead? Voted one of the best small towns in America by *US News*. Affordable standard of living, excellent shopping centers, and look! There's an annual luchador marathon. Doesn't that sound like fun?"

Bridgewater was still greyed-out on the in-game map. She kept waiting for it to light up in greens and blues and yellows, but nothing happened.

"Well? Can't you drive this thing?" Nico tried to grab the steering wheel, but his hands slipped right through the asset. "You'll need to take the wheel, Kingsley. I'm useless right now."

She started to press X on Hoguera Hills.

"Not there! If you press X, we'll have to start the fourth mission!"

"Yeah. That's how we get to the end of the game."

"That's how we get killed by whatever's waiting for us in Hoguera Hills!"

"Isn't that how video games work? You go some-where on the map and fight monsters. Sometimes, your health bar gets down to zero, and you have to re-spawn. But you eventually eliminate all the baddies and move on to the next level."

"No," Nico said. "That's how video games work for *you*. I have no idea if I'll be able to re-spawn and keep playing if a nitrous-striker gobbles my head off."

"What do you mean? I've seen you re-spawn hun-dreds of times."

"During the first three missions. I've never made it past that diesel-worm."

Nudging up her VR headset, Kingsley grabbed the game box and read the back. How the fuck had the devel-opers programmed this AI?

"You're the first player who's been able to save me."

"You mean no one else could beat that diesel-worm?" If all the other players sucked that hard at pressing B, maybe she should consider a future career in Esports.

"No one else ever had a chance; it's always been a cutscene before."

"How's that possible?"

"Don't ask me. All these games are networked, so I have memories of dying a million times on a million consoles. Maybe it was a glitch; maybe it was intentional programming. Who knows? But I'm *alive* right now, and I'd like to stay that way. So Bridgewater, please."

He rapped twice on the dashboard and looked at her expectantly.

"Um . . ."

She tried scrolling over Bridgewater on the in-game map. Alas, whatever glitch had enabled her to save Nico would not let them drive to that location.

"I'm not having much luck either."

"*Fuck*," Nico said, and then turned to her. "Sorry."

"For what?"

"Swearing."

"I think you have bigger things to worry about," she grinned. "Like how to fight off a bunch of nitrous-strikers."

All the color drained from Nico's face. "You wouldn't — "

She pressed X.

A new cutscene began with them walking up to the gates of Hoguera Hills, a small resort town in the mountains. Wooden arrows had been nailed into a pole: *Hoguera Hills Pub and Brewery, 5 mi. Pyre Lake Trailhead, 3 mi. Alvarez Fishing Supplies, 7 mi.*

"Why would you do that?" Nico hissed as they scanned the abandoned town. Thick fog blew in from the nearby lake; the buildings stretched up in silhouette like crude shadow puppets. "I finally get one chance to break out of this never-ending loop of torment, and all you can do is press X."

They watched as a shadow scuttled across the screen in the distance, flickering in and out of the gloom like a zoetrope. "I think we have company."

"Of course we have company." Nico hitched a bolt into his crossbow and aimed at the shadow. "What did you think was going to happen when we arrived in Hoguera Hills? Pottery class at the Community Arts Cabin?"

The two of them stood stock-still, keeping the distant nitrous-striker in their sights, its chitinous exoskeleton crouched behind a Ford Mustang. The traffic light flickered from red to green, and that's when all Hell broke loose.

A nitrous-striker shot in from the side of the screen and reared up on its hind-legs, its underbelly covered in glands pushing out gallons of acidic spray. She lunged to the side, but not quickly enough; some of the acid splashed onto her arm.

"*Fuck!*" she shouted. She ripped off the VR headset and stared down at her forearm. There were no burn-marks, but her flesh felt raw, like three layers had been peeled away.

"What happened?"

A crossbow bolt whizzed by her shoulder and straight into the hissing and spitting nitrous-striker.

"It burned me!"

"Of course it did. It's a nitrous-striker."

"No, I mean it *burned* me!"

". . . Like in real life?"

"*Yes!*"

The nitrous-strikers came barreling up Main Street, their pinchers extended and their glands squirting acid. Sticking the VR headset back on, she took aim, bombarding the incoming horde with long-distance assaults. The two of them managed to stay clear and knock the monsters down like targets at a carnival shooting gallery.

"I think that's all of them."

The blinding light of a camera flash blurred into another cutscene: her character, still dressed in a TGI Friday's uniform, wiped her forehead with the apron tied around her waist. She'd never seen her character from third-person POV before; she'd looked better in the box art. Just as she stuck her shotgun back into its tactical scabbard, one final nitrous-striker leapt up behind her.

Kingsley pushed the analog stick, and her character rolled to the right.

Then she was back in first-person POV, and Nico sent a bolt shredding through the stomach of the monster.

"Holy shit." She watched the nitrous-striker's legs twitch and spasm as it lay belly-up on the concrete. "Thank God for that cutscene, or I would've been wrecked."

"What cutscene?"

"I saw that thing — " She pointed to the dead nitrous-striker on the pavement. "Coming up behind me."

"But you didn't turn around."

"Didn't have to. I was able to look at her — my character, I mean — the way you do. Just for a few seconds, but it was enough."

Nico stared off into the mists of Hoguera Hills. The dead nitrous-strikers blinked out of existence, the game focusing its processing power on the most important tasks: the creaky hinges of an abandoned porch swing, the sodium-yellow funnel of a streetlamp penetrating the fog, and the damp asphalt underneath their sneakers.

"I could turn the game off."

"Then what happens to me?"

"You're just an AI. A really advanced AI, sure, but still just lines of code."

"Did that acid feel like lines of code?"

She looked down at her forearm. The flesh there still burned like a blister with the skin-flap ripped off.

"So where do we go from here?"

She pulled up the in-game map. The Chispan Desert had been colored-in during their last battle: an illustration of cacti flanked with more tentacle-monsters.

"Pass," said Nico.

"We might need to play to the end of the game — "

A knock on the door. Her landlord.

"One sec."

She put down the controller, pulled off the VR headset, and opened the door.

Ezra.

"Thought you might be home. Busy?" He glanced past her into the apartment.

"Yes."

She tried to shut the door, but he jammed his sturdy combat boot into the gap. "Sure looks like you're free tonight. What's that you're playing? *Emberworks*?"

"None of your business."

"That's where you're wrong." He pulled out a sheet of paper: a shipping manifest. "The manufacturer emailed over an updated manifest. Turns out there was an extra copy of *Emberworks* in our shipment that no one can find. Wonder where that might have gone."

Fuck.

"I wonder what's going to happen to whoever stole that game. I mean, they'll definitely lose their job, but I'm wondering if GameGear will press charges for theft. Seems a bit excessive, but I wouldn't put it past them."

"What do you want?"

"I just want to play *Emberworks* with you," he said, holding up a plastic bag from the corner liquor store. "Bought a bottle of wine, downloaded the Domino's app. We'll make a night of it."

Kingsley remembered the last time they'd *made a night of it*. Still, she didn't want to get arrested for stealing a video game.

"Fine," she said, pushing the door open.

"Alright!" Ezra dropped down onto the living room couch, grabbing the controller. "How far into the game are you? I haven't even started yet."

"Just finished the fourth mission."

"Who's this guy?"

Nico sat in the passenger seat, staring off into the middle-distance.

"Nico. He's your companion NPC."

"Cool. Let's get this show on the road then." He picked up the VR headset and pressed X. A cutscene of the Corvette driving on an empty highway through the desert. The afternoon sun hung in the sky, like a yellow construction-paper circle rigged to fishing wire.

"So," Nico said, slumping down into the passenger

seat, "how are you with a shotgun?"

Her character didn't respond.

The two of them got out of the Corvette and walked to the top of a sand-dune. Down below were hundreds of kerosine-fiends, tentacles flailing in all directions and puffs of flame erupting from their mouths.

"How about I wreck these monsters," Ezra said, hand blindly searching for Kingsley, "and then we can press pause and check out your bedroom?" His palm found her upper-thigh, and she flinched as his fingers (each one tattooed with one of the letters in AMOUR) crept up towards the waistband of her sweats.

"Um . . ." She grabbed a hold of his fingers and tried to hold his hand instead. "Maybe some other time."

"C'mon," he said, testing out the scope on the game's shotgun. "You liked it last time, right?"

"I don't feel like it tonight."

"Maybe next weekend, huh?"

"Yeah."

Ezra snapped his fingers like he'd just remembered something.

"Except by next weekend, I'm sure someone from GameGear will have asked me if I know who's been stealing from the stock room. I don't want to *lie* to our manager . . ." He tapped the VR headset up a little, so he could see her from underneath the brim. "You're putting me in a difficult situation, Kingsley."

"I don't — "

"Yes?"

"I just don't want to."

That wasn't the answer he'd been looking for. Without

any warning he shoved her down, hard, and climbed on top of her. "It's not like we haven't done this before. Remember when you got trashed at the holiday party? You were all over me."

She had been.

She'd thought he was cute back then, but the distance between "back then" and now had never seemed more uncrossable.

Turning her face towards the cushions, she scrunched her eyes shut.

Thwack.

His fingers stilled.

She opened her eyes.

Ezra sat there, limbs slack and motionless. She couldn't see his eyes because the VR headset had fallen back down, but his mouth gaped open like a largemouth bass tugged up onto the deck. He hovered there for a moment before tumbling forward. All one-hundred-seventy pounds of him crushed down on Kingsley's ribcage, cutting off her breath. She managed to push his dead weight off her and onto the floor.

"I . . ."

She looked up to find Nico staring into the camera. His crossbow was held aloft, and his finger was pressed against the trigger. There was no bolt in the groove.

"What happened?"

"You're not supposed to be able to shoot the player character as an NPC," he said, lowering the crossbow, "but I thought it might be worth a try."

"You . . ."

She nudged Ezra's shoulder with her heel, but he

didn't move.

"You *killed* him?"

"He was about to assault you!"

"Oh fuck," she said, scrubbing her palms against her face. "Oh *fuck*. What are we going to do now?"

"What do you mean?"

"I have a dead body in my apartment! I have to call the police. There's going to be an autopsy. What are they going to find when they cut him open?"

If they could pass this incident off as a heart attack or an aneurism then that would be one thing, but what would happen if the medical examiner found evidence of homicide? No one would believe an NPC from a video game had shot a crossbow bolt through her co-worker's skull. She was the only other person in the apartment; she would be the prime suspect.

Nico stared out into the distance. The kerosine-fiends were still unaware of their presence, their tentacles twisting in the late-afternoon desert sunshine. "I have an idea," he said. "Can you make sure the VR headset's on him?"

"This isn't going to make everything worse, is it?"

"I don't think so."

She propped Ezra's lifeless body up against the couch and pushed the VR headset firmly onto his head. "Okay. Now what?"

"Just wait a second."

Nico looked like he was concentrating as hard as he could. So hard he didn't notice the kerosine-fiends flicking their tentacles in his direction, their heads swiveling soon after to stare at the ridge.

"Nico? I think we have a problem."

"Not now, Kingsley."

The kerosine-fiends started scrambling up the ridge, their claws digging into the rocks.

"Nico?"

"What?"

"Look."

He looked down just in time to see one giant tentacle wrap around his ankle. The kerosine-fiend shrieked and began yanking him over the cliff edge.

"*Fuck.*"

Instead of grappling with the monster, Nico just squeezed his eyes shut. The VR headset lit up like the neon sign outside of the Sunliner Diner, bright light spilling around Ezra's head and glinting off the bleached-blonde strands of his hair. And then, just as suddenly as it had appeared, the light clicked off.

That's when the body on the floor *twitched*.

She watched, horrified, as Ezra slowly pulled the VR headset off and rubbed his fingers against his temples. He let out a groan that sounded like a busted console revving its gears and trying to restart.

"*Fuck,*" he said. "I thought this would hurt a little, but I didn't think it'd be like jumping onto the subway tracks during rush hour."

The voice was Ezra's, but the accent was all wrong. The *h* in "hurt" was too strong, while the *r* was nearly inaudible.

"Nico?"

"Yeah?"

What the fuck.

Ezra — no, *Nico* — pushed himself off the floor,

swaying a little on his feet before collapsing onto the couch next to her. "This might take a little getting used to."

"What the . . . How . . .?"

"I had the idea after you saw that cutscene in Hoguera Hills."

"What cutscene?"

"The one from my point-of-view. If something from my mind could be uploaded to yours, then maybe I could make the jump from digital to — " He held his hand up and flexed his fingers. "Corporeal."

"That was from *your* point-of-view?"

Nico nodded.

"Were you . . . Were you planning on doing *that* . . ." She gestured to Ezra. "To *me*?"

"No, of course not! You saved me from the diesel-worm; I owe you my life. But this sorry sap — " He examined the tattoos on his knuckles. "He was already gone. Not my first choice of hosting service, but sometimes we need to make do with what we're given."

Kingsley's brain was glitching out worse than *Assassin's Creed: Unity* on launch day. A video game character had murdered her co-worker and uploaded his consciousness onto what was essentially a now-empty hard drive. Did that make her an accomplice? Could anyone prove a crime had even been committed?

"What are we going to do now?"

"I'm going to find out where . . . What's this gentleman's name again?"

"Ezra."

"*Ezra.*" Nico spat out the name like it'd gone sour on his tongue. "I'm going to find out where *Ezra* lives and sleep off this migraine. Then I'm going to get a copy of his work schedule and show up to his next shift, so I can keep paying the bills. Did you know him well?"

"Um . . . Kinda?"

"Anyone I need to worry about? Family? Friends?"

"He doesn't — *didn't* — have a lot of people in his life."

"Wonder why. He seemed like such a charmer. Girlfriend?"

"Just me."

"Really."

Ezra'd always had pretty eyes, with irises like ink-blots, but there'd been no light behind them. She hadn't noticed when she'd first met him, but she had later. There'd been an empty pit inside Ezra where that light should've been.

There was light there now.

"I don't want to be presumptuous," Nico said, bringing his knees up to his chest and wrapping his arms around them. "But I think we've been through a lot together, you and I. We've fought off diesel-worms and nitrous-strikers; we've been devoured by kerosine-fiends . . ."

He motioned to the TV screen where the kerosine-fiends were munching their way through both of their digital bodies, blood-soaked tentacles tangling as they sprayed fire across the Chispan Desert. The words GAME OVER had been overlaid across the animation.

"And those are the kinds of shared experiences that bring two people closer together."

"Are you asking me out?"

"Well, if we want to keep up the illusion that I'm an

actual person instead of a sentient computer program, it might be for the best."

"You want to date me so you can convince everyone you're a real boy?"

"No," he said. "I want to date you because I *like* you. Convincing the world I'm a man who spent his entire trust fund on lousy tattoos would just be an additional perk."

"Maybe." Kingsley ejected the *Emberworks* disc from her PlayStation console. Brushing her hair out of her face she grinned at the man sitting on the couch behind her. "How do you feel about battle royales?"

⊹———⊹

CrawlerKino: *@Kincraig You were right! You CAN save Nico after the third mission! Why did my game always skip to a cutscene before? Anyone else have this issue? @GamesOrDeath*

GoatLordNYC: *Holy shit! I just saved Nico! We're starting the fourth mission in Hoguera Hills. Does anyone know how the story's different from this point forward? #TeamNico*

GamesOrDeath: *We thought Nico always died in the third mission. @CampfireGames Did you guys upload a patch? If you did, awesome addition! #TeamNico*

VashSnoop: *Dude, is it just me or does it seem like this section of the game wasn't even written by the same stu-*

dio? Nico's dialogue's a bit weird. Like why's he talking directly to me? #TeamNico

CrawlerKino: @VashSnoop Nico's better than ever. #TeamNico

PenguinCrisis: *Smashing addition to the game! Everyone should replay Emberworks. #TeamNico*

VashSnoop: *I was wrong! These new scenes with Nico are brilliant. Replay with the new patch now! #TeamNico*

GoatLordNYC: *Emberworks never fails to get under my skin. Have you started a new play-through yet? #TeamNico*

CampfireGames: *What are you talking about? There's no new patch. We didn't animate anything for Nico past the third mission. Are you guys pranking us?*

#TeamNico trending with 8.3K Tweets

#TeamNico trending with 34.5K Tweets

#TeamNico trending with 61.7K Tweets

A Friend in Need
K.T. Tate

The bar is almost brimming over with fans, but I manage to slither my way through, not wanting to be noticed just yet. I know you're in here, somewhere. You're out with your mates, enjoying the beer and recounting lewd tales of your unfaithful conquests. Lucky for me your table is quite central. Taking a deep breath I conjure up the image of who I'm meant to be this evening. Getting into the role, I order a drink.

A lull comes across both the game and the general conversation, so I take the opportunity to set off my ringtone. People turn to look, searching for the noise. Especially you; I picked that song specifically. That's right, I'm over here. I give you just a glimpse, a taster, as I move from the bar.

I can feel you searching for me, seeking me out. Your eyes track through the crowd, all those bodies colourless as you look for a flash of red. Was it my lips, or my hair? Does it matter? Ah, there I am. I pretend to be looking for a table and our eyes meet. I linger a little before averting my gaze, blush spreading over my pale cheeks. I put on the show for you, pretending to be so vulnerable.

I sit myself in the corner and make a point of checking my phone, impatience creeping in as I watch you drink with your friends. You check on me from time to time, but don't make your move. Despite your reputation it seems that right now the game is more important. You think I'll keep till afterwards; Plan B it is then. I'd have thought that this pretty glamour would be enough, but obviously not. I make a show of being annoyed, and a little saddened, by whatever my last text message was and head to the bathroom. For all you know I had been stood-up.

One of the great advantages of being a woman is that you have stalls in bathrooms to hide in, and once obscured I'm free to rummage around in my bag of tricks. Smooth glass meets my fingers as I pull out a bottle. It would look like a perfume bottle, if it wasn't for the things floating in it. That's why I needed the secrecy: I don't want anyone wondering what I'm spraying myself with. As for the effects, well, they're tailored specially for you. Amy saw to that.

Giving myself a few moments to let the scent dry I steel myself for what is to come. I stride past your table, hair flowing. Your pupils dilate as my scent penetrates your senses. Now you see me; good. Here I am, Tiger, so come get me.

By the time I can choose what drink to order you're already there, offering to buy it for me. Of course I let you, as I smile and push some errant hairs behind my ear.

"So, what's a pretty thing like you doing drinking all

alone?" You ask, getting right to the point. "I'm Grant by the way."

"Violet. I was meant to be meeting someone, but they can't make it," I say, playing up the sadness for effect.

That lights you up, knowing that I'm alone and possibly desperate. As we make small talk I smile and laugh, pretending your drivel is actually entertaining. Talk turns to flirtation as I twirl my hair around my finger. Your friends stop by, wishing you luck for the evening with winks and nods. They act as if I'm not there, as if I can't see the gestures and smirks.

We spend the night chatting and laughing. You're ever so charming as you listen, making all the right noises to make me think you're genuinely interested. Cheeky grin and roguish charm get you far. I must admit, I understand what Amy thought she saw in you. You wear that mask very well, but so do I.

It isn't difficult to convince you to come back to my place. Luckily the level of flirtation needed to get you there isn't much, just a few hot words of promise. The taxi ride is a battle of wills: Your desire to molest me, and my desire to not throw up.

In the darkness of the car you push what you can get away with, testing my boundaries. I gesture towards the driver and pretending I'm shy seems to be enough to convince you to play the gentleman again. You take to whispering indecencies in my ear instead. I blush and snicker and call you wicked, taking my lines from the worst of popular romance novels.

My place is a little out of the way; I'm a sucker for tradition. Yes, I live in a little cottage on the edge of the woods. My ancestors lived there for centuries, though it's much better now with the wi-fi and running water. The woods are ours as well, but I don't think you'd like them. Not tonight. Not alone, not in the dark.

"Quaint," you say as you size up the place. What you mean is expensive. Though you're right, it does still have a nice, thatched roof.

Giggling I search in my bag for my keys, acting tipsier than I am. I want you to feel in control, though you most likely do already all things considered. I just manage to unlock the door in time to avoid your advances. Now comes the tricky part. I stride towards the kitchen, swift in the hopes you'll follow. I don't want you looking around too much; that might break the mood.

"Drink?" I offer, grabbing glasses.

Suddenly you're at my back, arms weaving around me like serpents, like constrictors.

"Hey," I protest, trying to wriggle free.

Your breath is hot on my ear, "Forget the drinks, I know what you really want."

Your voice drips with sin as your hands enact it.

"Stop, not yet," I protest. I really need you to have that drink.

"Don't be shy. This is why you invited me here, isn't it? You want this."

"No!" I shout as you force me down, bending me over the counter. If only you had taken the drink, then things wouldn't have to be this way. But no, it turns out that you're not just an abusive asshole, but a rapist too.

As you struggle with the one-piece that I'm very deliberately wearing under my dress I lick my fingers and draw upon the counter top. Amy had told me of your temper, which was why I told her to put that pouch under your side of the bed. I told her it would help make you calm. A little lie; it was simply insurance. My spittle sparks as the sigil completes, and the onslaught stops.

You try to gurgle words, but that isn't happening. Poor Grant, suddenly so confused, so rigid. Let me fill you in:

"You can't move, but you've guessed that already. I was going to make it easy. I was going to drug you with my special skullcap and valerian mix, and you would have been out like a light by this point. But no, you had to be terrible. So here you are, stuck. Admittedly you would have never woken up but considering all that is about to happen, you might have considered that a mercy," I move you back a bit, so that I can walk around you.

Lighting a few lamps reveals my kitchen. Modern take on the old cottage style, but I can see it is the jars that have your attention. Oh yes, those are what you think they are. How else would I preserve them? Plus, you never know what will be useful.

"There you are," I remark as my cat familiar Jenkins jumps up on the counter. "Ahh, you brought him then. Good. Put him down," Jenkins delicately releases the frog from his ginger maw into my hand. "Thank you for joining us."

I turn to you, presenting the frog in my palm. The frog with too many blue eyes and strange markings.

"Grant, this is Nazbula. Nazbula, Grant. Nazbula here is very loyal and very kind. He's funny, and charming too. The perfect familiar for Amy. Now, let's get this started."

I gently put Nazbula down and retrieve a poppet. Oh,

it may look like a little cloth doll to you, but I think you'll be impressed. Tears of anger and frustration run down your cheeks as I harvest some of your hair. Head, leg, and unfortunately pubic. A few drops of blood too, a long needle suited to that task. I wrap them around the pigeon heart and sew them into the doll as you watch. You're going to love the next bit.

Picking up the poppet I say a word, then I breath into it. Holding its tiny legs, I walk it across my counter. Noise erupts from you as your body disobeys your will. "I hope the irony of disliking being forced to do something against your will isn't lost on you Grant," I remark, wanting you to remember why you're here. I toddle your clumsy form over to my beautiful old oak table. It takes a bit of finessing to get you laid upon it, but we have time.

I gather up my tools, ready to work. It isn't really like what people think at all. They picture us naked, dancing under the moon or worshiping Satan, at some orgasmic sabbath. It's a Christian concept, and wrong. That's just an excuse to think of young women naked and sexually free. No, our way has a lot less orgies and a lot more practicality. Though I do like the occasional dance. However, there are observances to be made, so I light the candles and start with the unrewarding task of cleaning your body.

I throw your clothes in the washing machine; might as well launder them, and then I begin cleaning. At least the herbs I use to do it smell good as they scrub away the nicotine stains and pub smell. Looking at you as an object, as a doll of a person, you aren't bad. It's just your personality that is terrible.

"You know, I'm doing all this for Amy. Oh no, I'm

not killing you and stealing Amy away, that isn't the plan. You've probably guessed what I am by now. The poppet and use of magic gave it away, and I'm just doing what my kind has always done, helping the vulnerable. That tends to mean women, and it tends to mean dealing with people like you. I'm no man-hater, I've done this to my fair share of women too, but it's rare that a man will open up to me about his domestic abuse situation. All she wants is for you to be the lie you were when you first lured her in, and I can help with that."

You gurgle at me, probably trying to convince me you can change, be a better man, but no. That isn't how this works.

Once you're clean I begin to mix the ink. Squid ink, blood, herbs and spit. All of it goes in the blender till smooth. Modern technology is so useful, just like the suction machine I got for vacuum-packing clothing. I plug it in as I fetch the scalpel.

"Now Grant, I have to be honest with you, this is going to hurt. You might pass out, but to be honest I don't know if you can in this state. Probably not. Don't worry, you won't bleed to death. The wash should have done it's work by now by slowing down your bodily functions."

Using a hair-tie to secure the nozzle of the suction machine to my wrist I make the first incision. Blood wells up as I part you. I open you up autopsy-style, peeling back skin from your chest. What little gore there is gets instantly sucked up, the wash having done its job of making you corpse-like. Delicately I unravel your skin until it hangs from your torso like parchment. I clean as I go, using the nozzle and more wash to preserve you.

Standing, I look you over. Laying on my table, un-petalled as you are, you're open to an experience that will change you forever. As I wait for your skin to dry I get to work on your sternum. Lighting my pyrography pen I start to burn sigils into bone. The smell is unique as blue flames spark, marking you for your purpose. I bet you're starting to feel small in there, Grant, detached from your form. I suppose there might be some relief in that. As the final symbol completes they all alight, pulling your consciousness down. I collect all that you are into a cage for your soul.

It takes hours to ink all of the sacred tattoos into the inside of your torso. Every single one has to be painstakingly perfect. Some require me to stop and invoke, offer or fulfil some other required ritual element. Finally, as the sun rises, I'm done. With weary hands I sew you up, stitches vanishing as I go. My work leaves behind flawless skin.

I allow myself a cup of tea before sitting you up. You're quite compliant now. Not empty, just trapped inside the depths of yourself. I know you're able to see and hear but can do nothing.

"You see Grant, I've been friends with Amy for months. We have tea at my town apartment. She was so nice when I first moved here, very kind and helpful. I was surprised that she wasn't surrounded by friends, but you wouldn't allow that. You drove them all away with your jealousy and controlling behaviours. I made her feel safe, and I promised I could help. Then one day she came to me, broken-hearted with a black eye. She was so certain it was a one off, but when I scryed her future it wasn't."

I pause, glancing at my captive.

"But I agreed for her sake and offered her some friendly witchy help. Charms and the like, you know, to get you back on track. Like the one she put under your pillow, the one that allowed me to paralyze you. No, she doesn't know I'm doing this, or where you are, but when you return you'll be a new man."

I pick up Nazbula from the table, and he lets out a fluting chirp.

"Nazbula isn't a frog, he's something else entirely. Soon he'll be you. Slowly he'll eat away at your soul, allowing him a human life. All he wants is to be loved, and to love in return, which is something you've forsaken. He'll have all your memories and mannerisms, but without the icky brutality. Amy will be none the wiser, only happier. Now open wide!"

I pull down your jaw and Nazbula does the rest, changing shape as he slithers down your gullet. I can almost hear your last cries of protest before he becomes your eternal jailer. You brought this on yourself.

"Thank you," Nazbula croaks, trying to get your voice to work.

"My pleasure. You might want to give it an hour or so, take a shower and get used to all his functions."

Jenkins meows at me from the table, a quip about human forms. I pick up my familiar and curl up by the fire. The night's work has exhausted me.

Tomorrow I'll see Amy, and she'll introduce me to you. Whilst you're paying for a coffee she'll thank me for my work, and she'll note that you seem like a changed man. She'll smile and be safe, and in a few years I'll get a wedding invite. I've been getting quite a few of those. The best part? Your children will be interested in witchcraft, and so our coven grows.

DELIVERED

Chris Lilienthal

Donte Evers hid his board under a large bush by the sidewalk. He was usually the one everyone else was waiting on, but he was a good ten minutes early. He leaned his back against a tall oak near the agreed-upon rendez-vous point and unlocked his phone. He scrolled for a while before impatiently shoving it back into his pocket. A family of trick-or-treaters crossed in front of him, the youngest boy excitedly chattering about every piece of candy he had collected so far. After they passed Donte looked up and down the street, and he waited.

He looked at his watch again. It was past seven now, and the trick-or-treaters were fewer and farther between. The air settled and quieted, save for some late season cicadas singing nearby. Donte could hear his breathing, in and out, and it was starting to annoy him. Where were his friends? He was early, and now they were late.

A quick rustling of leaves overhead, followed by the pounding sound of feet landing on pavement, nearly sent

Donte clamoring up the oak tree. The figure that had just dropped from the branches, a zombie girl of about 5 feet, lunged at him with mock ferociousness. Brennon Anderson appeared from the other side of the bush, bent over and pounding his thighs laughing. His elongated Scream mask fell to the ground.

Alissa Stone, the pasty-faced zombie with hollowed-out eyes and a spattering of red around her lips, smiled and took a bow.

"Very funny," Donte said.

"You should have seen it," Brennon said. "You nearly shit yourself."

"No, I didn't," Donte said.

"Consider this your Halloween present," Alissa said, taking Donte's red cheeks in her hands.

"Where's your costume anyway?" Brennon asked.

Donte turned his back to them and slipped something into his mouth. He spun around, flourishing his black cape and smiling a toothy Dracula grin.

Leaning in toward Alissa, he whispered, "I vont to suck yer blood."

"You could just lick it off her face," Brennon said.

"That'll do," Donte deadpanned.

"Shut up, assholes," Alissa said, as she strolled down the sidewalk toward lit porches and Halloween candy.

They were well past the age for trick-or-treating. Every third house or so they'd get some disapproving variation of "Well, how old are you now?" or "A bit old to be out trick-or-treating, aren't we?"

It wasn't long before they reached the neighborhood playground. As soon as she caught sight of it Alissa took off running toward the swings. Donte followed while Brennon lagged behind, rooting through his candy bag as if there were a golden ticket in there somewhere.

"You're not going to find any Take 5s, Brennon," Alissa said.

"Shut up. I know I got a few," he said.

"Yeah, and I stole them when you stopped home to take a piss."

"What!" Brennon cried. "I trusted you to guard my candy bag from this idiot."

Dejected, Brennon plopped down on the bottom edge of the spiral slide and took a bite out of a Twix bar. Alissa and Brennon swung slowly, taking in the cool evening air.

After a while Donte took out his pocket flashlight and lit up his face just below the chin, like his dad used to do on camping trips.

"This feels like an excellent time for a spooky story," Alissa said hopefully.

"I don't know," Donte said. "I don't know if you've been good enough."

"Oh, I have one," Brennon said.

"No. Shut up, Brennon. I want to hear Donte try to scare us. I mean, it's only fair. We did scare the living shit out of him."

Brennon laughed. "I guess he can try."

"I'll do better than try," Donte said. "I'll hit you with a story so hard you'll still feel it in the morning."

"Nah," Brennon said. "I don't feel anything."

"This story takes place not far from here," Donte began. "Just a few blocks that way, but it was long ago. Decades. Back when the school buses didn't run through this neighborhood, so the kids had to walk home after school. And it was a long walk through all the connecting neighborhoods. There weren't many busy streets to worry about, except for one: old Sycamore Drive. There was a crosswalk, but no traffic light in those days, and you know how drivers were in the '70s. They'd blow right through a crosswalk like that while jamming to Janis Joplin, or some shit like that, on their eight-track players."

"Eight-track players! Ooooh, this story is sooooo scary," Brennon said.

"One morning," Donte went on, ignoring him, "little Penelope Flowers gets up and goes to school, just like any other day. But that day was special, and she wanted to get the school day over and done with. Halloween is one of the longest school days of the year, everyone knows that, and all day little Penelope just couldn't stop thinking about her Wonder Woman costume. She was going to put on that costume the second she got home, she was so damn proud of it. It was the first year her mother let her pick a costume of her very own, and that's who she chose."

"Good choice," Alissa said.

"Little Penelope Flowers was so excited that day, she kind of lost track of the school's rules and requirements. She kept talking during math class. She didn't hear it when the teacher called the class in from recess, and she day-dreamed her way through science class, failing to get her worksheet completed. So, Mrs. Hunsicker had no choice but to keep little Penelope after school to get her work squared away."

"Are you kidding me?" Alissa exclaimed. "It's Halloween!"

"Hey, rules are rules," Donte replied, "and Mrs. Hunsicker couldn't bend them just because it's the 31st of October. No, she had to keep Penelope on the straight and narrow. Problem is, by the time Penelope left school that day it was close to six. She's missed dinner; dusk was setting in; and the trick-or-treaters were already out knocking on doors. Penelope was absolutely frantic. She couldn't miss trick-or-treating. She was Wonder Woman, for God's sake, and she won't have that taken from her. So, she put on her green coat and ran out the school door. She ran and ran and ran — all the way. All the way until she got to Sycamore Drive. Usually she was part of a big pack of school kids making their way home, at least one or two older kids reminding the young ones to stop and look both ways before crossing. Not that day, though. So, little Penelope Flowers just kept running, straight across Sycamore Drive, right into the path of a moving postal Jeep."

"That's your scary story?" Brennon asked. "Little girl gets hit by a mailman?"

"The postman jumped out of the vehicle, completely beside himself — crying and weeping and shit. He scooped up the little girl and carried her to a nearby front lawn. Now, they didn't have iPhones back then, so he had to go up to the house on the hill there and bang on the front door. *Please, help. I hit a little girl with my postal Jeep. Go dial 911 on your rotary phone.*"

"Oh, man, my Great Grandma had one of those," Brennon interrupted. "We bought her a cordless, and she threw it in the trash."

"So, this woman, old and wrinkly, stringy white hair

down to the back of her knees, is at the door, and she sees the mailman all hysterical and falling apart. She snaps her finger in his face to get his attention, and tells him to bring the girl inside right away."

"Nope, nope, nope," Alissa said. "Don't go inside."

"So, he took the girl inside."

"I said NOPE!"

"Well, he did," Donte said, "and he's surprised to see the woman isn't alone. Two other old women, one with shoulder-length silvery hair and the other with short blue hair, were there in the parlor waiting for them. The mailman placed the girl down on a coffee table right there in the middle of the room. She wasn't breathing at that point, and she was covered in blood. It was a real gorefest."

"Would this be a good time to point out how effing irresponsible this mailman is?" Brennon asked. "I mean first he runs over a little girl with his mail truck. Then, instead of calling 911, he decides to consult the local witch coven!"

"So, the three women gathered around little Penelope Flowers and placed hands on her. They had candles lit, incense burning, the whole nine yards while they whispered some incantations in Latin or Greek or something. The mailman, meanwhile, was just standing off to the side, heart pounding, praying quietly in his head: *Please, God, let this work.*"

"IT WON'T!" Brennon announced through cupped hands, megaphone-style.

"Well, it didn't quite work the way the mailman had hoped," Donte said. "After several minutes of whisperings and rituals, the witch with the long white hair broke from the circle and hobbled over to a curio cabinet…"

"A curio what?" Brennon asked.

"A curio cabinet," Donte said. "It's where old people keep knick-knacks and ceramics and shit like that. Anyway, the witch went to the curio cabinet and took out this wooden music box, the kind that's handcrafted somewhere in Italy. Real expensive looking. On the top of the box was a picnic scene painted in elaborate detail, with tiny little bears dancing around flowers and baskets. They're having a swell time, and when you open it, it's supposed to play an old song called 'The Teddy Bears Picnic.' But when the witch opened it nothing happened. The mailman leaned forward, straining to hear the song. Instead, all he heard was the sound of the music box clapping shut."

"The white-haired witch, the one who opened the door, came over to the mailman and said their little 'Double, double, toil and trouble' was a success. Now the mailman was looking at the dead girl he just ran over, lying all bloodied and mangled in the middle of the living room, and thinking, 'Yeah, not so much.' But the witch said that, while her body is broken beyond repair, the girl is not. The witches safely intervened, and lassoed her soul into the magic music box. Now all the mailman had to do was take the girl in the music box with him. Give her a home, be the steward of her spirit. This was a lot more than the mailman bargained for when he left for work that morning, but he was in deep by that point, so he took the music box."

"BIG mistake," Alissa said.

"So, little Penelope Flowers never got to be Wonder Woman. She never got to go trick-or-treat. For that matter, she never got to walk to or from school again. Instead, she's trapped in a music box that doesn't even seem to work. This, you may imagine, really pissed off Penelope. Isolated and cut off from everyone and everything she loves, the girl became confused, scared, and angry. She tried to make sense of what happened, but she couldn't remember everything. She could see herself running home from school. She could see the trick-or-treaters coming out. She could see the postal Jeep in the periphery of her vision. Then, SLAM!"

Donte clapped his hands together suddenly and violently, making Brennon flinch. Alissa giggled at the theatrical flourish.

"Meanwhile, the postman had some cleanup to do. The witches were nice enough to dispose of the body for him, but his mail Jeep was all busted and shit from hitting a kid. So, he concocted some story about it being stolen; then he drove it to the edge of the ravine at the top of Samuels Gap Road and gave it a little push. And, BAM!"

Brennon flipped Donte off this time.

"As for the postman, life went on more or less as it always had. He continued to deliver mail and listen to Janis Joplin on his eight-track player. He managed to switch his route around so he never has to cross into that neighborhood again. He didn't want to pass by the witches' house, or behold the intersection where his Jeep struck a child. The police only found traces of the girl's blood in the street, but without modern DNA techniques, and no eyewitnesses other than the witches, there was no way to trace it back to our mailman. So, he got to live the life he's always lived, while poor little Penelope Flowers was stuck in a music box."

"By the way, as soon as the mailman gets home that fateful Halloween night, he went into his basement and threw that music box as far back as he could into a storage closet under the steps. He thought about pitching it in the dumpster out behind the Post Office, but didn't want anything about the whole affair to be connected back to him. He also never wanted to see that horrible reminder of what he did ever again."

"Solid plan," Brennon said.

"The weeks go on, and before you know it it's Christmas time. It was real snowy that year, and you know what they say about the post office. Neither rain nor sleet nor murdered children…Anyway, our mailman came home one night from his appointed rounds and noticed that the furniture in his living room had been moved around. The couch swapped walls, and the recliner's in the middle of the room. He naturally suspected an intruder, but he found no signs of a break-in. Maybe there was an earthquake, or road work jackhammering, that shook the house and shifted the furniture around. You know how easy it is to explain things away that you don't want to believe."

"Next night he came home, and discovered honey smeared all over every mirror in his house. The circular mirror that hung in the entryway, the full-length mirror in his bedroom, the medicine cabinet mirror — all covered with honey. Now he knows something's going on; an earthquake can't make your mirrors get all honied up. So he went into the basement and dug deep into the back of that closet until he finds it. He brushed the dust off and opened it up."

Donte cleared his throat and began singing in a slow,

shrill high pitch,

"'If you go down in the woods today; You're sure of a big surprise. If you go down in the woods today; You'd better go in disguise!' The mailman slammed the music box shut and tossed it back in the closet, onto the highest shelf, as far back as he could reach on tiptoes. Next morning he woke up and all the cabinets in his kitchen were open, and shit's thrown out all over the counters and the floor. A big bag of sugar is torn open, dishes are broken, spaghetti sauce is spilled on the floor. The sight of the red marinara mixed with broken glass made him sick to his stomach. This was getting out of control, and something had to be done. He called out sick from the Post Office, got the music box out of the basement closet and he drove over to the witches' house."

"Caveat emptor," Brennon said.

"He pounded on the front door, but there was no answer. He pounded some more. Nothing. He wandered around back to see if they're out on the patio smoking, drinking or skinning squirrels or something for some creepy ritual. Keep in mind there's a foot of snow, so it's a real mess. He's got no choice; the witches are the only ones who can straighten this out, so he opens the side gate and trespasses into the witches' snowy garden."

"This guy is totally giving the Post Office a bad name," Alissa said.

"First he walked up to the back of the house and peeks in through a sliding glass door, pervert-style. He got close, pressed his nose against the glass to get a good look, but it's a bust. No one's in there. The witches just aren't home, so he spins around to give the snow-covered yard one last going over, and he notices something way in the back. He should really just leave, try again tomorrow, but no. He just couldn't help himself. He trudged, step-by-step, through a foot of snow to the very back of the yard, where a two-by-four-foot rectangle of very cold earth has been cleared of any snow."

"A grave!" Alissa said.

"Before he could make any sense of it something came swinging out of nowhere, right by his head, Tarzan-like. He sidestepped it just barely and pivoted around, wondering what the Hell it was. He could see it, but he's not sure what he's seeing. It's round and dangling from a vine hanging down from an overhead tree branch. He leaned forward and squinted at it, and the severed head of the white-haired witch squinted back. Somebody, or something, had cut off her head and somehow strapped it to a vine, then looped it up over the tree branch. A decoration maybe? Who knows?"

"What got the mailman was how it came swinging at him, like it knew he was coming. The mailman was ready to retch, and he instinctively clutched the music box to his chest. He was breathing real fast and heavy now; he needed to get the Hell out of there. He looked up, just in time to see a silvery-haired head come flying his way. He dodged it, like the first. The third head, though, he wasn't so quick. The cold, blue head came dropping down from a branch directly overhead, colliding with his forehead and knocking him on his ass."

"What happened to the music box?" Alissa asked.

"He dropped the music box into a snow pile not far from the grave. It fell on its side, the soft landing saving it from any real damage. So the mailman is laying there, flat on his back in the snow, just seeing stars. And this is what he hears."

Again, in the same eerie, high-pitch voice, Donte sang, "'Watch them, catch them unawares; cut off their heads if you dares; 'Cause that's the way the Teddy Bears have their picnic.'"

"The mailman propped himself up with both arms, squinting to see who's singing. His head was spinning with pain. His vision was blurred and hazy, but he could see the outline of a girl about the height and build of little Penelope Flowers. She was wearing that green coat, blood in her hair, standing there on top of the muddy grave."

"Jesus," Alissa said.

"She walked over confidently and picked up the music box from the ground, pulling it in close to her chest. The mailman was freaking out. He was crab-walking backwards through the snow, as the girl descended on him. He was begging for mercy. *Please, please. I only wanted to help.* Penelope Flowers isn't having any of it."

"She leaned over the mailman and began singing: 'Beneath the trees where nobody sees; They'll cut your head off with de-lighted ease; 'Cause that's the way the Teddy Bears have their picnic.'"

"He saw the glint of a blade in her right hand; it was sharp, and curved like a tree trimmer tool. Still humming she lifted it high in the air, so it caught the sharp winter sun, the quick flash of reflected sunlight stabbing at the mailman's eyes. It only lasted a second, before everything in his world went dark."

Donte killed the flashlight for effect, the story finished. The three friends sat quietly for a few seconds in the now very dark neighborhood playground; Brennon was the first to say anything.

"Pretty good," he said.

"That was the shit!" Alissa said. "Your best one yet."

"It's mostly true," Donte said.

"No, it isn't," Brennon said.

"You think I just made that up on the spot?" Donte asked. "I'm flattered, but no, I saw it on the news a few days ago. Tonight's the fortieth anniversary of Penelope's disappearance. They never found her body, but they did end up finding all four heads hanging from that tree, swaying back and forth like wind chimes." He softly hummed the melody to 'Teddy Bears' Picnic.'

"You're shitting us," Alissa said. "That is not a true story."

"Google it," Donte said.

It was past nine now, and Brennon's mom had messaged him more than once. The latest read, "Get your ass home now!" He bid his friends goodnight and Happy Halloween, before skating down the road back to his house.

Back at the rendezvous point Donte fetched his board from under the bush, then offered to walk Alissa home. They strolled in silence for a few minutes, eventually arriving at the Sycamore Drive intersection. Alissa froze on the corner, trembling slightly.

"Hey," Donte said. "I *was* shitting you guys earlier. It's not true, not all of it."

Alissa didn't seem to be listening to him.

"Some girl named Penelope Flowers did disappear around here forty years ago," Donte said. "The rest of it, though, was just the dark recesses of my imagination."

Alissa slowly extended her right hand, her finger pointing across the street. Donte followed with his eyes, and standing there on the opposite corner was a little girl in a green coat. In the glow of the streetlight they could see her face was bruised and dirty, her hair disheveled. She was clutching something to her chest, but they couldn't tell what. She held their stare for several seconds until a Jeep came flying past. Was it a mail Jeep? Alissa couldn't tell. It sped by so quickly, easily going sixty miles an hour.

"Did you see that?" Alissa asked.

Donte nodded, even though Alissa wasn't looking at him.

The girl in the green coat was gone now, the street serene.

"You know how easy it is to explain things away that you don't want to believe," Donte said. "To shrug it off, to say your eyes were playing tricks on you. It's really very easy."

"It is, isn't it?" Alissa agreed.

After looking right and left, more than once, they quickly crossed Sycamore Drive. On the other side they searched for some evidence of what they had seen.

"Donte," Alissa said, bending down and reaching for something in the grass.

She held up the curved, serrated blade of a tree-trimming tool.

"Drop it," Donte said.

It fell back into the grass.

"You don't want to take that anywhere with you," he said. "You don't want that attached to you in any way."

She backed away cautiously.

It was probably nothing, Donte quickly added. Alissa nodded. Probably.

She looked at the house up on the hill. The exterior lights were off, and the windows were dark. She figured the homeowner must have been out doing some yard work earlier in the day, and had simply left the blade out by mistake. That's what happened, she decided. Careless, yes, but nothing more than that.

As Alissa and Donte continued on their way a motion light was triggered, illuminating a tree that had been hidden in the shadow of the house on the hill. Hanging from the lower branches were the severed heads of several teddy bears, the plush heads having been doused in red for added effect. An unconventional Halloween decoration, Alissa told herself, nothing more. Still, she couldn't help but imagine the little girl in the green coat out there on the corner. She saw her wielding the tree-trimming tool and hacking away at the unsuspecting teddy bears, chopping each head off and stacking them in a neat pile to go hang on the tree later on.

Alissa stroked the skin of her throat, and picked up her pace.

My Last Assignment

Johnny Hempseed

The alarm kicked on, and I slowly came around to awareness. I pushed the thin sheet away from my body, slick with sweat, the heater still throwing dry air into the motel room. I hurried into the bathroom to take a shower, toweling off in the ninety degree room afterward. I opened the curtains to allow the weak sunlight to filter through the thick, coastal clouds into the room.

I grabbed my camera and keys, along with the backpack that contained my laptop and digital audio recorder. The light rumble in my stomach directed me toward the small diner down the street, my nostrils flaring as I took in the cool, salty air. Even though I hated cheap motels, and crappy beds, there was nothing like a good breakfast to get me ready for a day of crazy interviews.

As I entered the diner the host greeted me. "Just one?" I nodded, following the man as he led the way to a small booth near the corner of the dining room.

"Can I get you something to drink while you decide what you would like to order?" I stared for a moment at the glossy booklet, quickly making a decision.

"Coffee with milk and sugar, please?" He smiled, jotting it down before he walked away. When the waiter returned with my beverage I ordered a stack of syrup-covered pancakes, along with a side of fried potatoes and gravy. I idly stirred the steamy coffee for a moment as I glanced around the small building, taking stock of the other patrons. A few truckers were sitting at the bar, and a small family sat huddled around a table waiting on their food. I looked away before my gawking got creepy, and I sipped my coffee as I organized the interviews of the day in my mind.

I had come to this small Oregon town to investigate a local legend about a specter who had been haunting the area for over thirty years, a dirty figure clad in reeking bandages. My food arrived, interrupting my thoughts, and soon enough I was ready to be on the road. It didn't take me long to clear the edge of town, and I eased off of my accelerator when I saw some familiar street names.

I found the right address and pulled onto the rough driveway, one of the potholes almost bouncing my head off the ceiling of my old car. I contemplated pulling over and walking the rest of the way, but the trees soon gave way to the small home. I pulled my vehicle next to a run-down pickup truck and turned off the engine, getting out of the car to grab my recorder, pen and pad. I also grabbed a small folder to hold any evidence my witness may have.

A moment later I knocked on the door, which was opened by a short, slightly hunched old man.

"You must be the writer?" he asked, his voice stronger and an octave deeper than his aged, withered body belied.

"Jason Smith. You must be Eddie." I said as he stepped back to allow me into the place.

He nodded. "Who did you say you were reporting for again?" he asked as he led me to the living room, which was minimally furnished.

"It's a paranormal eZine called *Angel's Eyes*. We're a small outfit, but we have quite a committed group of readers." He motioned to a dusty, but comfortable looking, couch. I sat, and he almost settled into a plush recliner before pausing. "Would you like something to drink? Tea or lemonade?"

"Lemonade would be great, thanks."

He shuffled away, and I contemplated offering to help him when I heard the amount of commotion coming from the other room, but he re-emerged just as I was rising from the cushion. I finished standing and clasped the glass that he extended toward me, taking a seat again before sipping the sweet citrus water. I pulled my recorder from my pocket, placing it where it would catch his voice.

"You're alright with me recording this conversation, as well as taking notes, right?" I asked after turning the device on.

"Yes, that's fine with me. What was it that you wanted to know?" he asked, sipping from his own glass.

"We would like you to tell our readers your experience with the cryptid called the Bandage Man." I replied, and readied myself to take notes.

"This was back in the late 70's, and this town was much smaller back then, if you can imagine that," he paused to take a sip of his drink, and I said nothing.

I'm not sure what it was, but something about Eddie

just didn't sit right with me. Maybe it was the way his wrinkled skin seemed to stretch across his face too widely, or the way the tips of his fingers were cocooned in ragged, bloody bandages.

"Anyway," he went on, "It was the end of the summer, probably the week before graduation, and I was out with my lady at the time, though her name escapes me right now. We had just finished eating, and the sun was getting ready to settle in for the night. Being young, and impulsive, we decided to go for a drive down the highway and up to a little quarry to get a little bit...frisky. I found a nice, hidden nook between piles of gravel to hide the car from prying eyes or curious cops, and things were just getting good when I had to step out of the car."

Eddie took another long drink from the glass of lemonade, and I followed suit. He seemed to be thinking about something that amused him, judging by the slight smile on his lips. He hiccuped quietly and wiped his mouth, and then took a long breath inward, clearing his throat before he started to speak again.

"So we were parked, doing what teens do, and I had to call a time-out to take a leak. I got out of the car, walking around the back of the gravel pile to my right, and I heard a soft, wheezing cough coming from the darkness." The old man's eyes seemed to glass over a little and widen with the memory, "He was just standing there. At least six and a half feet tall and twice as wide as I was, on the edge of the tree-line. At first I thought it was just a hobo so I called out to him, just the normal 'Hey there, you scared the Hell out of me!' kind of thing.

The hobo didn't respond, or even move, and as my

eyes adjusted more to the moonlight I could see that he was wrapped up in bandages. I started to back away, and that's when he finally moved. It disappeared into the woods, nothing too scary, though that was just my first encounter with him. I ended up taking the girl home right away, and went back to my own place soon after." Eddie finished speaking, quickly draining the rest of his glass.

"Would you mind telling me about your other encounter while I'm here?" I asked, finishing my own glass of lemonade.

"I don't mind, but could I have a few minutes? I have to take my pills." Eddie said, and I nodded.

"As a matter of fact, could I use your restroom?" I asked as I stood up, casting my eyes around the room, and he smiled.

"Of course. It's just down the hall, second door to the right." Then, almost as an afterthought, he spoke again. "Would you like some more lemonade?"

"That would be great," I said, never one to deny hospitality when it was offered, and hurried down the hall to relieve my aching bladder. When I returned the old man was seated, looking at the floor with a far-away gaze. He looked up when I stepped on a creaky floorboard, his eyes clearing the smile returning to his lips. The pleasant expression didn't seem quite right, or as genuine as it had before, and I felt something in my gut telling me that I needed to leave. I pretended that the phone in my pocket was vibrating, and pulled it out.

"I'm sorry, I have to take this." I said, fake-answering the phone. I walked outside, glancing over my shoulder as I approached my car. I slowed down, miming a conversation as I peeked back at the manufactured home. Eddie hadn't followed me, and as I wrapped up my faux conversation I hurried up to the door, knocking before stepping back inside.

"I'm sorry, Eddie, but I just had another person I'm supposed to interview call to say they had an emergency. If I don't make it over there within the next hour or so I'm going to miss my chance. Can I come back tomorrow, or can we meet at the diner by my hotel?" I asked.

"Sure, I can meet you at the diner tomorrow for lunch. We can finish up then," he said as we shook hands.

I packed up my stuff and walked back to my beat-up old car, sliding behind the wheel and exhaling a sigh of relief. As I drove away I was stricken with the urge to find the quarry that the old man had mentioned, and maybe I could find a trace of the Bandage Man. The GPS said it did still exist, but when I arrived there were large trucks entering and leaving the place, so I made a note to return later.

The time for my next interview approached, and this time I arrived in a small, idyllic residential area where the houses were clean and nicely painted, with each lawn neatly manicured behind chain-link fences. I pulled to the curb, once again grabbing my recorder, notebook and pen. I took a deep breath as I slid out into the breezy, coastal morning once more, the clouds overhead growing darker as they threatened rain.

I stared up at the sky for a few seconds before moving through the small gate to the house where my next subject lived. I raised my hand and knocked, expecting another weathered face to open the door, and was taken slightly aback when it was a young woman.

"Hello," she said, looking at me as if she was confused.

"Hi. I'm looking for Madeline Griffin." I said, and then continued, "I'm supposed to interview her for *Angel's Eyes* eZine." I said, recognition lighting her green eyes.

"Oh, you're here for me." She offered a gentle smile, stepping back and taking the lead into a large dining room. I placed my recorder and notebook down as we idly chatted for a few minutes. When she offered me a drink I told her that water was fine, and as she returned I switched on the recorder.

"You're okay with this being recorded, and with me taking notes, right?" I asked, as I always did.

"Yes. So, what was it that you wanted to talk to me about?"

"You told my editor that you had an encounter with the Bandage Man. I would like to hear your story." I said, and the relaxed expression dropped from her face.

"Oh, that. Okay," she said quietly, seeming to struggle to keep her composure. She took a drink of her water, then lit a long, slim cigarette. "You don't mind if I smoke, right?" Madeline asked, and I shook my head, eager to begin writing.

"Okay, so...I was driving back from my brother and sister-in-law's house, and it was late at night. The clouds were thick enough to block the moon and stars out, which made it even darker than usual, and I had my brights on, being worried about a deer or elk jumping out in front of me..."

She paused, taking a drink of her water, and flicked the long ash from her cigarette.

"I wasn't going to stop, but I did slow down a little. That's when the rain started. It was torrential within moments, and I felt my heart break for what I thought was a wounded person, so I pulled over when I passed the man. I watched him approach, his clothes tattered and kind of dated, and he reminded me of photos I had seen of the logging camps. He also seemed to have bandages on his hands, and when he opened the door to get in I noticed that the dirty gauze also covered his neck and face. The next thing I noticed was the smell."

She paused again, stubbing out her cigarette after another drag. Madeline seemed disturbed for a moment by her own memories, then started up again.

"I tried to ask him where he was going, but he didn't answer, so we sat there for a while. I kept my head facing forward, the smell forcing me to breathe through my nose. 'Where to?' I remember demanding, trying to sound tougher than I actually am. This time the big man, or whatever the Hell it was, grunted at me. When it vocalized I nearly choked, the odor increasing to the point that I could taste it." Madeline halted again, and I took the opportunity to get a sip of water. She took a drink as well, and lit another cigarette.

"I finally gathered the courage to turn my head and look at him, when he, or it...whatever...finally spoke. 'Drive', it said, that stench again filling my car. I did as I was told, trying to control my urge to floor the gas pedal. I had only traveled for about a mile when a huge animal bounded into the road in front of me, forcing me to slam on my brakes. In the heart-wrenching seconds of stopping short of the elk the big man opened the door, ducked out into the night, and was gone. That smell lingered, though."

She fell silent, and flicked her cigarette again. I was about to ask if that was the end of her encounter, but she cut me off by starting to speak again.

"I turned, trying to spot him running away from the car, but I couldn't see him. A man that big should have stuck out like a sore thumb, but it was just me and the elk staring at one another until I reached across to close my door. That's when I saw the dark stain on the upholstery of my passenger seat. I drove to a twenty-four hour car wash, trying to steam clean the stain away. It, and the smell, remained for almost a week until I gave up trying to get rid of it, and had the thing redone. You should have seen the looks the men at that garage gave me."

"You mean when you went in to have the seat reupholstered?" I asked, hoping to prompt her to continue the story, but she nodded and clammed up.

I made a note of her gesture and switched the recorder off, and I glanced at her as we walked to the door together. I noticed how pale she was, as well as the strange, glassy look in her eyes; the same haunted gaze that I had seen in Eddie's eyes earlier that morning. It was the look that had chilled me to my core, so I was happy that I was leaving and done for the day. I wasn't ready to hear another tale, or see that look in anyone else's eyes, at least not so soon.

My cellphone ringing gave me pause as I was slipping my key into the ignition. I lifted my rear from the seat and dug the device out, not checking the caller identification before I answered. I probably should have at least taken a glance at the screen, because the call changed everything.

"Hello?"

"Jason? It's Robin. How are you this afternoon?" I could practically envision the cheerful brunette's lips curling into a smile as she spoke.

"Hey. I'm alright, just finished my final interview for the day." I said, trying to match her enthusiasm and chipper demeanor.

"Actually, that's why Frank wanted me to call you. He finally got through to a man named Brady Jones, who says that the Bandage Man is attacking his livestock. He wants you to head out there this evening, to see if you can see the thing. He's also transferred some money into your account to hire a local photographer."

What followed was her reading a list of names and phone numbers as my heart sank into the bottom of my stomach; I had been looking forward to having the rest of the day to myself. As soon as we hung up, I drove back to the hotel room, starting to try and contact a few of the photographers. I left messages for two, then decided that it was lunch time.

Back at the diner the hostess that had seated me earlier smiled when I stepped forward in the line.

"Becoming a regular here, mister?" She grabbed a menu, leading me to the same small booth I had been seated in that morning.

"Coffee again?" I nodded, skimming the menu and placing my order. I checked my phone, excited to see that a voicemail came through. I checked the message, my spirits lifting as I dialed the callback number.

"Hello?"

"Hi, Jordan? My name is Jason Smith, and I was calling you about that gig tonight," I started. We spent almost ten minutes discussing payment, as well as arranging a place and time to meet.

It's safe to say that the photographer was a non-believer, but that wasn't going to stop him from making an easy hundred and fifty dollars. I couldn't blame him for it; that was how I had stumbled into my current writing gig, after all. I had seen some strange things since starting that had changed my mind though, and was glad to have company. This was especially true when I searched the address of the witness and found that it was halfway up one of the mountain passes.

There was no evidence of cryptid sightings on that road, and I started to doubt the man's claim as I researched the area he lived in. I started writing my article, setting an alarm on my phone for an hour before the time I was meant to meet Jordan, and I focused my attention on transcribing the old man's stories from the recordings, adding my notes for flavor. Time became a blur as my fingers moved from the keyboard to my recorder and back. Suddenly the alarm tone that I had chosen interrupted me, and as I moved my eyes away from the screen I felt a strange sense of apprehension.

It was the same electric feeling I had when I captured my first EVP, which I took as a good omen that something supernatural would happen. I packed my stuff up and readied myself to leave, then I drove to the nearest gas station to meet my photographer. It only took me about fifteen minutes to reach the place, and he arrived a few minutes after I had. We quickly shook hands, officially introducing ourselves.

"Do you want me to follow you, or do you want to

ride together?" Jordan asked.

"We can just ride up there together." I replied as he grabbed his camera and other equipment. I typed the address into the GPS and followed the directions, slowing when the road narrowed and the pavement ended. Mailboxes and street lamps became fewer and farther between, and I would have missed the turn if it hadn't been for the computer-generated voice that penetrated the silence in the car. When we arrived I was again surprised by the youth of the man that exited the house; he wasn't the gray-haired old man that I had envisioned based on Robin's description of him.

"Are you Brady?" I asked as I walked around the hood of my car, extending my hand. His grip was so firm it was almost painful.

"I am," he said. "You must be Jason, and who is this?" he asked, turning to my new acquaintance.

"My name's Jordan. I'm just here to shoot pictures if we see anything." He said, also exchanging a quick hand-shake with our host.

There wasn't much more small talk as he showed us to the large, open pasture at the rear of his home, where I could see cows roaming in the deepening gloom. There was a small table and a pair of deck chairs beneath one of the trees, which Brady gestured to.

"You guys can set up here for a few hours; hopefully you get what you came for. I'm going to go make you guys some coffee. If you need anything, I'll be in the house." With that our host was gone.

Jordan and I looked at each other for a moment and I simply shrugged, unsure of what to say, so we each settled into a seat. Brady soon returned with a thermos and a pair of ceramic mugs, leaving us alone once more. I was starting to doubt the story we had been told as the cold night wore on, and soon the cows began to settle in. At one point the clouds shifted, and I got the feeling that I was being watched as moonlight began to illuminate the field and trees beyond the fence.

That's when I saw a calf bolting away from the treeline. I watched as a tall, gangly figure appeared after it, clearing the fence with a loping jump. As it neared a foul stench preceded it, and I rapidly tapped on Jordan's shoulder. He startled, as though I had roused him from sleep.

"What?"

I simply pointed, unable to muster my voice. The figure must have seen us because it halted, its long, stilted steps retreating back over the fence and into the trees. Jordan didn't have time to raise the camera, or turn on the small light that would have enabled him to take pictures, before we were both up and running past the frightened calf. We had just broken the treeline when we heard a blood-curdling wail off to one side. Jordan finally managed to turn the light on as we spun around, and the man, or whatever it was, had tackled a half-ton cow from the other side of the pasture. It had its hands, which were wrapped in dirty, blood-stained gauze, thrust into the bovine's stomach.

The animal made a pathetic choking sound, but my attention was on the creature straddling it as it looked our way, the light reflecting off of the deep-set sockets where the eyes should have been. We both stood there, frozen in fear, as the beast grunted, its head cocking like that of a feral dog. It began stalking us, moving up the path toward the light, until the sound of a rifle firing split the night.

Brady had come to our rescue.

I heard the second shot whine over my head, and a solid, sickeningly-wet sound reverberated as the projectile made contact. I turned my head and could make out the monster charging towards Jordan. The third shot rang out, and this time I saw the large figure jerk when the bullet impacted it's chest. That finally deterred the creature enough to make it back down. It retreated with the same large, stilted steps that it had used to approach us, seeming to almost fade into the distance. The smell was more stubborn, the vaguely sweet, off-putting scent of rot hanging in the air.

I called Robin on the way back to town, quitting my job immediately. I didn't want any more assignments; this one had been too close for comfort.

Play It Again

Elizabeth Davis

Records are my life; Were my life. I fell in love with them during the afternoons I spent with my grandma while my mother worked. I was greeted by Philip Sousa when I came home, my grandma switching to the blues as evening fell, her doo wop saved for special, joyous occasions like the weekend.

There was something in the sound of vinyl that clearer definitions could never catch, something warm. The lucky thing was that I wasn't the only one who felt that way, and enough other people agreed that I could operate a small storefront and a thriving online business. The small storefront was for the customers that touched my heart—customers like my grandma, for whom vinyls held the keys to a golden past.

However, the customers that paid the bills were the collectors. That's why I found myself haunting antique shops, bidding on whole collections at estate sales, and sorting through the dumped boxes of those eager to offload an unwanted inheritance for a few bucks. All to find those few rare records that collectors would foam over.

It was one of those boxes that I found it right next to a stack of Genette Jazz records. It was a platter in a cheap, plain sleeve, with its title written in pen. My heart drummed as I made out that messy cursive—*My Heartbreak*. Without even looking closely at the records I could already guess its history—1920s when recording became cheap, and recording booths were booming and everyone wanted a piece of that shellac pie.

These were my favorite finds, these rare snapshots of those forgotten by history. Perhaps even a lost record of one of the greats such as Louis Armstrong or Robert Johnson.

I eagerly placed the record on the phonograph in the store, ready to entertain whoever walked in with a past that hadn't been heard in decades. The first thing that surprised me was the sound—it was clearer than I expected, with only a hint of the scratchiness that all vinyls had.

I was used to platters that were stored in terrible conditions, warped and wearing years upon them, but the languid violin was not marred at all. I listened to it, wondering who the musician was before the crying started.

The first voice sounded like a woman, gently sobbing as the violin carried on. A man joined in, his sobs nearly comedic in their intensity. A third voice, gender unidentifiable, their wails nearly hysterical laughter. More and more voices joined in, even as their wailing became muffled. The crying nearly faded into the music before more wails joined in, some of them nearly screaming out their pain, but even they faded back into the music as the record ended.

Silence dropped into my shop as I snatched the needle off the record. My hand shook as I re-sleeved it. I knew that I should check to see if there was a side B, but I couldn't bring myself to. As I filed it with the other misfit records I thought over why someone would record this. A desperate show of affection to get a lover back? Somebody misjudging the market after Okeh Laughing Record made the charts? Or was this just someone recording their grief for eternity, flinging it far ahead into the future?

I have heard many odd records in my line of work. Haunted house records, horror sound effects, and even odder, but this shocked me beyond any that I had heard before...For the first time since I opened my shop, I didn't linger beyond closing time.

In a couple days I had listed the album on my catalog and had refused to give it anymore thought. That's when she walked in. An older woman, grey streaking through her black hair. She hugged herself as she entered, trying to sink into her hoodie. She made a show of browsing through the floor stock before she approached the counter. In a quiet voice she asked me, "Do you have *My Heartbreak?*"

"Probably, what's the band or label?"

"It doesn't have any of that." She said it as if reprimanding me, "It's just *My Heartbreak.*"

I felt a tremor dance on my spine, like someone had set a needle on me. "Just one moment."

When I returned, I could feel a palatable sense of relief when I placed the plain sleeve on the counter in front of her. Still, my nerves were high and my mouth started running.

"So, why did you decide on this recording? Was it one of your family that recorded it?"

She shook her head.

"If you don't mind me asking, purely professionally, why this record? I have to admit that I've never heard of it until it came into my store, and I like to think I've seen a thing or two in this business."

"Have you actually never heard about *My Heartbreak?*" Her soft tone still bore a sting of accusation. "They say that if you play this record, it will take your tears away from you. That it will feed on your grief, and leave you lightened."

"Oh, neat," I said while running her credit card, "What's supposed to happen if you play it when you're happy?"

She gave me an intense stare as she took the bag off the counter. "It must always take something." Without saying anything more she left.

I shrugged my shoulders at her after-reflection in my windows. I didn't believe her, of course, but I was glad to have the record gone.

The next morning, when I opened my shop, the record was sitting on the counter. I thought at first it was the woman from yesterday, unsatisfied and making a return. Then I double checked the stock and cash register, but nothing was missing. I looked for any broken windows, jammed doors, or even new scratches on the lock. Nada.

As soon as I picked up the record I could feel the violin bow draw on the strings, and a few soft sobs play in my mind. I tried to shake the tune out with a jaunty whistle from the 1970s disco records. Yet as I brought the record to the back my whistling slowed down, becoming that of the melancholy violin. Maybe there was something to this record after all

I locked the album into my safe in the back, reserved for the few museum gems I wanted to someday find. I hoped the few inches of steel would help. Even still the album continued to play in the back of my mind, the mournful violin and all of the sobs on repeat, with a needle heavier than the world.

It followed me home, still playing on the phonograph in my mind, even though I put on my happiest 50's vapid pop and constantly refilled my glass with bad scotch. I fell asleep on my couch, finally dropping away from the music.

I anxiously pulled at my uncomfortable tie as everyone gathered in clouds of black, softly chattering among them. I looked at the faces around me, family I hadn't seen in a long time.

And that heavy coffin, lined with roses...

I nodded at my mother, who I would stop speaking to in a few years, too tired from the constant arguments over my new stepfather and my own future. Uncle Tyrone, whose funeral I would be attending next year thanks to a drunk driver on the road. Cousins who I might see again with the next funeral, but even that wasn't certain.

And my grandma lying in the coffin.

The cancer had shriveled her up, mummifying her before the coroner had even started. As she was dying I had learned how to properly set the phonograph needle, to sort through her collection, to soundtrack the mood—all tasks she no longer had energy for, but that still gave her a smile. I leaned over, trying to think of words to say.

And that's when my memory went off the rails. Her hand reached forward, clinching mine in a vice grip. Her eyes opened, her milky eyes staring at mine. A violin wailed in the corner, overpowering the quiet conversation. My eyes darted to the women from yesterday, her graying head resting on the violin. Her face was at peace, even as the violin wailed louder.

"This was the last time you cried," my grandma said, her scratchy voice not sounding like the warm tones that accompanied her records. "Would you cry if anyone else here died?"

I looked around at the crowd. I didn't cry at my Uncle's funeral, who was always frustrated that I showed no interest in the football that my cousins seemingly built their lives around. Not at my mother's, her words always sharp and tired. In the black and grey crowd, brighter colors emerged. College roommates, high school lunch buddies, coworkers from previous jobs. They had never gotten close to me, always viewed my interest with less than benign curiosity, the kind that lost me priceless pieces of my collection. Regular customers, the girl running the 7-11 at the end of my block, the man with the sandwich truck that parked outside my shop every Tuesday. I had to dredge my memories for their names—if I had ever bothered to learn them at all.

"None, not one at all?"

I looked down at my grandma. She was dressed in her last Easter dress, the one I helped pick out. Her folded hands that had snapped along with trumpets and trombones. Her face wore a faint smile, a smile she never used—only having big smiles or deep frowns.

"No, nobody else but you."

"Then give me your tears, Honeybun."

But I couldn't. Every time I thought about crying, I remembered the vinyls I played after her death. The smoky voices over muted saxophones that cried for me. Even after my mother told me to keep it down, that she couldn't take listening to those songs on repeat, I still played them. My mother never understood that those records cried my tears for me.

With a sudden spasm, my grandma's hand crushed mine.

I cussed in pain, trying to pull away.

"Honeybun, I see, I see. But I still need my tears."

I woke up with my pain wrecking my spasming hand, and a wailing violin with sobs playing in the background. I stumbled out of the couch, massaging my pained knuckles and joints while the record continued to play. With a few heavy steps I stood in front of the record player and snatched "My Heartbreak" off, not bothering to carefully lift the needle, letting it scratch along the platter. I held the platter in my hands, feeling all seven inches still warm from playing. And then I did what I have never done, never thought I would do even for the most damaged record.

With a single twist, I snapped it in half.

Not satisfied, still hearing the record playing in my head, I opened my window. I watched as it sailed through the air, satisfied to hear the cracking as the shellac met the pavement. Finally the record stopped playing in my head. Triumphant, I returned to sleep.

I was woken early in the morning by a call from the next door yoga studio, which specialized in sunrise classes. The owner's voice was choked, her cough muffled.

"I'm sorry—the fire was already going when I got here."

In the distance I heard shouting, and sirens. Without bothering to put on my shoes, or coat, I ran to my shop. There wasn't much left to see. The buildings next to mine were untouched, not even the hint of grey soot on their walls. My shop was nothing but ruins, the few beams left slumping against each other.

After the last firetruck pulled away I dove into the ruins. My hands and arms were cut by melted plastic and broken brick, but I still searched for the safe, thinking it might have survived the inferno. Past a wall of blackened paper that broke with a single touch I saw the melted vault door. I reached forward, touching it, my panicked brain focusing on it, on what I would need to open it.

As my fingers brushed against the surface the door fell down, smashing onto the rubble. I blinked at the remains inside—a single record resting on a pile of ash. A single record in a plain sleeve. I pulled it out, holding it close as tears slid down my cheek, and I knew I wouldn't be able to stop them as I slid to my knees in the wreckages.

My tears splashed on the sleeve as "My Heartbreak" drank in my sobs.

The Calling

Blaise Langlois

Her knees were damp, and her cheeks burned. Kneeling in the grass Lyvie Dean placed a small card on top of a sturdy, cardboard shoe box, her shoulders shaking uncontrollably as she wiped her nose with the back of her hand. Charlie, named after Charlie Chaplin due to the small, black mark on his lip, had been the family cat, but he really belonged to the little girl at his graveside.

They hadn't been looking for a pet when her best friend had walked into her life; Charlie had found them, appearing from nowhere one summer day. Although Lyvie's parents had made it clear that a kitten was out of the question her father faltered in his resolve, especially when the tiny tuxedo cat had leapt up onto the picnic table and then jumped onto Lyvie's shoulder, purring madly. He hated seeing disappointment on his daughter's face, and conceded to at least look for an owner first. Needless to say, Charlie became a permanent fixture in their lives.

Clouds darkened the sky just after she sat the card down, followed by a deep rumbling. Lyvie eyed it nervously. Smoothing her dress as she stood, she leaned over the tiny marker and repositioned the small flower arrangement.

Her mother placed a hand on Lyvie's shoulder, turning so the girl could see her lips. "Come on now, honey. It's time to go home," she signed.

Rain began falling as the mourning child grasped her mother's outstretched hand, allowing herself to be led to the waiting car. Once again the threatening sky rumbled, this time followed by a large *crack*. Blue light flooded the sky, illuminating the large house standing sentry over the graveyard. Able to be viewed from most areas in town, the large, dark victorian stood with shuttered windows and peeling paint. It loomed from the hill, an ever-present observer gazing upon the growing town, and today it witnessed a small girl lay her best friend to rest.

The residents of Little Lake had only ever known one family to own the house, and the last of them, Agnes Howard, had died a number of years back. Since then the house has been unoccupied, save for the weeds which had invaded the front porch, or the family of racoons nesting in the garage. A "For Sale" sign, rotting and half falling off the post, had been there for well over three years. Before that the house had stood empty, pale windows and sagging doors seeming to tell a tale of grief. A sadness emanated from the entire property, and one merely had to drive by in order to be overwhelmed by feelings of melancholy and despair.

In the early 90's the paramedics, and subsequently the coroner's office, had arrived and removed Agnes from the premises after she suffered a fatal heart attack. The heart attack may not have been deadly, had Ms. Howard not been a hoarder. For years, she routinely wandered the streets with an old stroller, hunting through the trash of her neighbours for what she called 'goodies'. She had collected anything and everything, her eyes lighting up like a child at Christmas when she spied something that she considered to be worth saving. Her favourite treasures were of the four-legged feline variety, and at her death she had accumulated (by her neighbour's count) approximately thirty-seven.

Another flash of lightning caused Lyvie to hug herself tight, her gaze pulling away from the creepy house as she unsuccessfully tried to get the image of Charlie out of her mind. She had been the one to find his lifeless body underneath the large oak in the front yard. The veterinarian, gesturing to the electrical burns, had told them it was a lightning strike. With a sigh Lyvie settled into the backseat, allowing the rhythm of the windshield wipers to lull her to sleep.

In her dream a small kitten sat sunbathing on the porch of the Howard place. Lyvie imagined herself lying with the kitten, stroking its silky fur. It vibrated under her hand and butted up against it, giving her a love bite. Startled, she pulled her hand away. *That hurt*, she thought. She woke with a start and rubbed the fleshy part between her thumb and forefinger. Again she closed her eyes, feeling the hum of the car as they continued down the road. A sadness had taken over her, a darkness really, and she felt an unexplainable need to see the tiny creature.

The next morning the sun peeked through her bedroom curtains. Lyvie sat up, looking down at her hand; she noticed two tiny puncture marks, instantly recalling her dream from the car ride. Leaning over the edge of the bed she grabbed her hearing aids and popped them in, making a slight adjustment. With a still-heavy heart she fought off the covers and stumbled out of bed.

Mrs. Dean was already down in the kitchen, coffee in hand.

"Your dad packed your lunch, it's in the fridge."

She nodded.

"Lyvie, please, remember you have piano lessons after school today — and you need to be on time!"

"Okay, Mom."

"Honey, you look a little pale. Are you alright? You can stay home if you're not up to going to school today. I can call in."

"No, it's okay. I'm fine," she signed back intently.

Lyvie retrieved her lunch, dropping it into her backpack and kissing her mother on the cheek before heading to school.

After a long day, the bell, finally signaling freedom, prompted students to collect their belongings and head home. Although she was thinking about nothing in particular, Lyvie's face carried a look of deep concentration as she walked. Glancing at her watch she noted that it was already four o'clock, and she remembered it was Tuesday — piano lessons. She picked up her pace, then suddenly stopped. Something had brought her to the edge of the woods. She stood there for a moment contemplating the small trail, which was partially hidden by an overgrowth of Moonseed vines. A high-pitched mewling caught her attention, its call drawing her down the pathway.

"Here, kitty," she called. The culprit failed to appear. Curiosity got the better of her and Lyvie pursued the animal, ignoring the fact that time was passing.

"Psst. Psst. Psst," she called, her fingers moving in a snapping motion. Pursing her lips, she made small kissing sounds. "I know you're here, little kitty." This time the kitten answered her call and appeared from the brush, halting at the crest of a small hill. The sun shone behind it, creating a halo around its tiny, sleek frame. It was white, just like in her dream.

"Come here," she coaxed, as she squatted down to its level. The setting sun reminded Lyvie of the time and she leapt to her feet, her sudden movement startling the feline. Disappointed, she watched as it scampered off into the woods.

Upon arriving home Lyvie mounted the stairs to her small, but extremely tidy, bedroom. Her parents often joked that she should be the one cleaning the whole house, rather than paying their biweekly housekeeper. Slumping down next to Charlie's old bed she clutched his blanket to her chest, breathing in as if to bring some part of him into herself. The blanket was one her mother had made after Lyvie insisted he have one to match her own. She buried her face in it as tears welled in her eyes, but they remained trapped. She got into bed, but was now thinking about the kitten from earlier. Her heart felt a longing, but it wasn't for her beloved Charlie — it was for the strange cat from earlier that day.

The next morning Lyvie made a point of leaving early for school, forgetting that her father would already be up.

"Quite the early riser," he signed. "Would you like a

ride to school today, kiddo?"

"No thanks, Dad. I think I will get some air and walk."

"Okay. Are you sure?" he asked, bringing her in for a hug. He kissed the top of her head and stepped back, looking her in the face. "I really don't mind."

She stood on tiptoe and gave him a kiss on the cheek, catching his eye and mouthing, "See ya!"

The morning air was cool, but Lyvie had no difficulty ignoring it. She wanted to, had to, see if she could find the kitten again. She hastily headed toward the trail from the day before. *Maybe it won't be there*, she thought. Reaching the path, Lyvie found herself walking further into the forest than intended. As she crested the hill it appeared in all its decrepit glory — the Howard place. A trembling of leaves caught her attention, and the kitten suddenly appeared from the woods.

It headed toward the house, pausing on the top step. Looking jauntily over its left shoulder it almost grinned, giving it an impish quality. The porch sagged under Lyvie's weight, despite her petite size. The kitten ran its purr in full gear, rubbing up against her legs. Reaching down she attempted to pet it, but it dodged her touch and climbed through a small hole in a broken window. Creeping up to the window, Lyvie peered inside.

The light was practically non-existent, and darkness seemed to breed within the walls of the house. She rubbed the smudged pane with her sweater sleeve, soiling it with soot and grime. *Click.* The front door suddenly swung open, imploring her to enter.

She walked through the doorway, her eyes scanning her surroundings as they adjusted to the shadows. A pungent odor made her eyes water, leaving a sour taste in her mouth. She coughed as thick dust invaded her lungs. Each step forward sunk her feet further into filth, a composting heap of expired food and cat excrement. Blinking she spied a flash of white behind a stack of newspapers taller than she was. Lyvie made her way through the maze of boxes, slipping on garbage bags and tripping on piles of clothing.

Anxiety crept up on her as walls comprised of large boxes shifted under their own weight, threatening to crash down upon her. However, Lyvie continued, obsessed with finding the elusive kitten. She squeezed through into what appeared to be the kitchen, its functionality and purpose long forgotten. Dishes, old take-out containers, bottles and cans were overflowing on every surface. The refrigerator door was hanging open, a musty smell mixing with that of ammonia. Black mold clung to the interior of the fridge, along with its long-rotted contents.

Lyvie's feet no longer felt as though they were stuck in mud, instead she felt a crunching beneath them. It was like walking on a pile of sticks, and she struggled to maintain her balance. Her eyes, having adjusted to the gloom, could now see that they weren't sticks at all, they were bones — animal bones. Unbeknownst to Lyvie, a scurrying, scrabbling sound, was coming from within the house walls. It was as if a rat, or something even larger, were trying to climb, but his paws, thick and clumsy, couldn't accommodate.

To be precise, it sounded like something trying *not* to be heard.

The scurrying-scrabbling sound halted, and there was a movement amongst the bones that caused Lyvie's weight to shift. Falling backwards she sucked in a painful breath, coughing violently as she clambered backwards in terror. The bones began to vibrate, piece by piece reassembling themselves into the form of a cat — several cats. Lyvie screamed and the bones turned their heads, clicking in one unified motion. Desperately she attempted to push herself backwards, but the cardboard beneath her continued to slip, preventing her from gaining purchase and righting herself.

A yowling drew the gaze of the creatures, and the skeletal, feline army seemed to come to attention. Acting as commander the white kitten sat at the top of the sagging staircase, yowling once more. The ossified cats shifted in some sort of twisted formation and began to make their way toward their miniature, fully-fleshed leader. With their bones clacking in tandem, like a card attached by a clothes pin to a bike wheel, they moved in a calcified wave.

Cutting in front of the pack Lyvie made for the staircase, with the compelling need to follow the kitten propelling her forward. The staircase was overrun with clothing, furniture, boxes, bags, old paintings and even a 10-speed bicycle. Lyvie fought her way through, disgusted yet too scared to stop. As she neared the top a small hatch opened, leading her to the attic.

Despite the disastrous state of the rest of the house the attic was relatively clean, with only a few boxes piled in one corner. The tiny, white kitten sat in the center of the room grooming itself, purring contentedly. As its right paw rubbed behind an ear and across its nose, a tiny chaplin-style moustache was revealed.

"Charlie?" she whispered, gingerly approaching him

as tears fell freely.

The kitten answered with a gentle mew.

The sound of clacking drew nearer, causing the floor to tremble. Lyive scooped Charlie into her arms protectively but he squirmed out, leaping onto the boxes in the corner. The clowder of cats filed into the room, their hollow sockets fixed on her. She moved toward the new Charlie and he leapt off the boxes, landing on her shoulder. They methodically formed a semi-circle around her and sat at attention, appearing to be waiting for instructions.

Lyvie had been chosen once more.

The Curse of the Grootslang
Chris Hewitt

My ears pop as the detonation reverberates down the tunnel, an explosion of rocks ricocheting off the walls as a billowing cloud of orange dust swallows my world. I hold my breath; the muted whining of the extractor fans is the only sound. The dust fades to reveal the man-monster Willem lumbering around in the rust tinted gloom, oily shemagh pulled up over his sweaty, red face, a dusty mop of greasy black hair visible under his battered mining helmet. He barks orders at his crew, and a handful of ghosts flitter in the dying sandstorm as he trudges over, pulling down his mask. I exhale and suck in the hot blasted air, chest convulsing.

"Smoke 'em if you got em," grunts Willem, pulling out a crumpled pack of Camels. He lights up, using a tarnished Zippo, and takes a long drag. His hacking cough dislodges a dusting of cinnamon as he steadies himself and fixes me with blood-shot eyes. "Fok, man, these are tough rocks. Be lucky to make forty foot today."

I take my pencil and scribble in my tatty journal for show; I don't need to carry the zeroes to know we're three days behind schedule. Removing my glasses, I try to clean them, but only succeed in scratching the lenses; luckily, they're just for show too. "Looks like you're gonna lose your bonus then."

The burly foreman stiffens, his jaw grinding as he spits a slug of black tobacco. "We shook hands on a deal, larney!"

I let the slur slide and start crossing through items in my journal. "No, we had a contract, the terms of which require you and your team to get the shaft and tunnel dug in thirty days."

Willem reaches into his jacket and pulls out a well-hit bottle of Bain's whiskey. He drains the dregs and launches it across the tunnel where it shatters against the granite wall. He flicks his cigarette after it.

"Yah think me a fool? I know why you came to me, and I know where your calculations have put us," he says, running a dirty, fat finger across my journal.

I snap the book closed, slide on my gritty glasses and meet his gaze. "Really? Do tell."

I'd found Willem passed out in a smoky dive in the back streets of Cape Town and hired him on the spot. Beggars can't be choosers when looking for a mining crew, especially one that doesn't ask questions. We'd sailed for Port Nolloth the next day, and despite the sea air, the old miner remained intoxicated. The bruising off-road drive out to Kuboes, however, did the trick. As we reached the craggy, volcanic foothills of Richtersveld, Willem growled like a bear awoken from hibernation. His temperament hadn't improved in the twenty-eight days we'd spent underground.

"Go on," I goad.

Willem grins, yellow pegs a testament to a lifetime of abuse. "You couldn't get no Nama workers down here, not here, not under the reservation. Ain't that right? But do you know why?"

"Well, it is a protected UNESCO's World Heritage site."

"Yeah, right! That what the locals told you?" Willem cackles, lurching over to a large trunk. He returns with another bottle of Bain's, this one only half empty, and taking a big swig, he offers me a sip. I shake my head. He shrugs and gulps down another mouthful, wiping the excess away with the back of his hand. "They won't mine here on account of the Grootslang."

Now that's a problem, although I have to admit the old miner just went up a notch in my estimations. "Is that so?"

"Yeah. Legend has it the Grootslang sits on a cache of diamonds down here. A cave. Ah, what did they call it… the… err…"

"Wonder Hole?"

The words hit him like a slap, and he lowers the bottle from his lips. "Yea!? Yea, that's it."

A commotion down the tunnel, and Willem turns at the sound of excited voices. He glances back at me, torn between targets for his venom. I think he's going to say something, but instead he stomps off into the murk, cursing under his breath.

❮——◦——❯

I catch up with Willem, who's at the mine entrance shaking his head. His crew surrounds him, four dirty reprobates all scratching their heads. I'd like to say I knew their names, but I've kept myself to myself these past weeks. They say familiarity breeds contempt. Contempt had been my starting position; hence getting acquainted would only have made matters worse. I shoulder my way past two of the crew. "Another problem, Willem?"

The foreman looks perplexed. "I dunno. Seems like we hit something."

"Diamonds, I hope."

The big bear snatches up a pickaxe, and without hesitation buries it into the rock face with a thunderous clang. The crew gasp at the sight of the buried iron pick and Willem raises a hand for silence as a filigree of cracks radiates across the rock surface. "Get outta here," he yells, turning and running as the tunnel comes crashing down. I jump aside as the crew rush past me. A gust of wind howls in the opposite direction, towards the fallen face, as if some mighty beast had taken an immense breath.

I stare into a beckoning dark void.

"What the fok you got us into?" bellows Willem.

My hands tremble as I remove my glasses, letting them slip to the floor. "Riches beyond imagination."

The big foreman pins me against the wall. "You crazy domkop, you think those tales of diamonds are true?"

"I know they're true," I reply, fumbling in my pocket to retrieve a handkerchief wrapped object. Unwrapping the fabric, I hold up the family heirloom. "See!"

The ten-carat diamond reflects in Willem's wide eyes, and he snatches the gem from my hand. The perfect stone gleams in the light of his headlamp as he scrutinises it, turning it over and licking his lips. A glance after his retreating crew and he buries my inheritance in his pocket. "That's for my trouble."

"Plenty more where that came from," I say, nodding down the tunnel.

"Yeah, and what else?"

"You scared of Nama fairy tales? I thought you were the baas man, not a frightened kid."

I can see him thinking; can almost hear the cogs whirring.

"Fifty-fifty."

I can't help but laugh. "Are we negotiating?"

"Equal share. Take it or leave it."

I try to look surprised, but it's hard in the face of such comical threats. We both know he isn't going anywhere. I spit in my palm and thrust it towards him. He hesitates a moment, before his enormous paw crushes my hand and as he hollers after his crew, he leans in close. "Don't think of fokken me on this, larney."

"Moi!?" I grin back.

⊷——⊶

Five minutes later the crew reappears brandishing axes, sledgehammers and spear-like drill rods. It seems Willem is taking no chances. I make a note in my journal; that's twice the old dog's surprised me today. I hope I can return the favor.

Willem arrives a minute later, empty-handed, a heavy rucksack slung over his shoulder.

"It's a bit of overkill, isn't it?" I say, nodding to the crew.

"Best be prepared," he says, twisting to reveal the sawn-off shotgun hanging from his belt. "Ain't that what you Scouts say?"

I laugh; he's got a point. "Anything for me?"

"I thought you said it was a fairy tale?"

"As you say, best prepared," I say, giving a three-finger scout salute.

He rummages in his rucksack, and I gasp at the sight of several sticks of dynamite jostling amongst the bric-à-brac. With a grin, he tosses me a small package and I gawk at the small medical kit.

"Case, you get a splinter, larney," he roars, heading off down the tunnel.

I unzip the kit and fumble through the bandages, plasters and antiseptic until I spy something shiny. I hold up the plastic-sealed scalpel. It will have to do. As I join the group, my limply brandished blade is the source of much amusement.

We set off down the tunnel; a passageway not made by human hands. Rather, it seems to be an ancient lava tube or maybe a dried-up underground river. I run my hand along the smooth walls as the wind continues to flow into the depths. Our echoing footsteps are the only noise as we descend, the raucous miners now silent.

We stop. Willem bars the path, and I understand why. No flashlight can illuminate the impenetrable darkness ahead. The foreman pulls out a handful of red flares and lights them, scattering the fizzing, sparking sticks into the void. I watch them fall, and my jaw drops as I realize we're standing on the precipice of an immense cavern. The flares come to rest in a landscape of jagged stalagmites; columns of stone that stretch like fingers to the ceiling.

Willem leans out and hocks up a glob of cancerous tar so dense that I hear it hit the ground below. "Eish, that's fifty-foot and no mistake."

"Ropes?"

"Do I look like a fokken mountain climber?"

"Baas!" yells one of the crew, pointing at the side of a ledge. Willem grabs the man's flashlight and shines it along the cavern wall. He lights another flare, the red sparkler tumbling down a steep ramp to the cave floor.

"Oh, fok this," cries Willem, nodding at the ramp. "Fairy tales be damned, that ain't natural. What aren't you telling me!?"

"That diamond…"

Willem looks sheepish and pulls me aside.

"What of it?" he hisses.

"It was part of my grandfather's estate. When he died, it became my father's, along with the journal, and when he passed it became mine."

"And?"

"It took me years to decode the cryptic notes, but this is where my grandfather found that stone, and it wasn't the only one. He and his partner made it out of here with a bag of gems. A lifetime…no, a legacy, of wealth."

Willem glances over his shoulder at his crew, rubbing his chin. "This is between us, right?"

I nod.

Willem commands his crew, and they return a few minutes later with a jury-rigged framework of spotlights hooked up to a generator. They haul the contraption into place and crank up the generator. The engine bursts into life, illuminating a galaxy of twinkling stars embedded in the cavern walls. Down below, more diamonds glitter in shallow shimmering streams that wind their way around the stalagmites. Long toothy stalactites drip from the ceiling, and I can't shake the feeling I'm staring into the salivating maul of some monstrous beast.

I see the ramp now, carved out of the granite wall, it's as smooth and well-worn as the tunnel. Halfway down, the crew, with Willem in pursuit, are falling over themselves to be the first to fill their pockets. The secret's out.

I take my time joining them, careful not to slip off the narrow ledge. The dull drone of the generator reverberates about the cavern as I descend. By the time I catchup with the miners they are hollering and laughing as they shower each other with fistfuls of diamonds. I find Willem appraising several large gems.

"Didn't I tell you," I say, deciding against patting him on the back.

He can't take his eyes from his bounty. "It's incredible."

"That it is, and they're all ours, fifty-fifty. That's the deal, right?"

He waves a dismissive hand. "Ja, Ja, of course."

Right on time, the diesel generator splutters, and the lights flicker before plunging the cavern back into darkness. The sparkling stars are gone, and a deafening silence descends over the cavern. In the gloom, no one can see my smile as I duck behind a large boulder.

"What the…" growls Willem, switching on his helmet's light. His crew follows suit, their lights crisscrossing the cavern floor like anti-aircraft searchlights. They'll not find me.

"Where's that fokken larney? Split up and find him. Now!"

An icy chill slithers down my back and I freeze, closing my eyes and holding my breath as death slides past my foot, a hissing of scale on stone. There's a scream, and I open my eyes as one of the crew levitates into the air, his headlamp flailing. With a crunch, his screams are cut short, the yellow light turning red as his lifeblood rains down. The droplets spatter my face, warm and wet. I must not move, not yet.

The crew turn as one, their lights illuminating the demon; a gigantic serpent that towers above all. Its head is as large as an elephant, the tusks or fangs, I cannot tell but to say they're longer than my arms, are dripping blood. It's all I can do to hold my ground; only the certain knowledge that fleeing would be suicide keeps me rooted.

Two of the crew lack my instincts and they don't get far. I watch as the second man move simultaneously left and right, his torso striking the cavern wall, while his intestines and legs are tossed into the rabid jaws of another skulking beast. The third miner makes it to the ramp, only to run into a rising wall of scale. His headlamp tracks upward, iridescent scales shifting from green to blue to black as the light, and the fool are extinguished.

The last miner hasn't moved, not an inch. It doesn't

stop his flashlight from shaking, or his quiet sobbing. He's soiled himself. I can smell it, and so can they. A shadow slinks out of the gloom and coils itself around him. The poor man is pleading, as am I, for his quick death. It's not to be. The serpent takes its time squeezing the life from its prey, gargling screams and cracking bones culminate in the miner's head popping off and rolling across the ground. It comes to rest at my feet, the intact headlamp illuminating me.

I panic.

"Get behind me," cries Willem, dragging me from my hidey-hole as he unloads his shotgun into the coiled beast. The monster roars as we withdraw towards the ramp. There's movement on the right, more slivering shadows, and Willem unloads the shotgun again and again. I stumble onto the ramp. It's now or never. My hand shakes as I reach into my pocket and pull out the scalpel. The knife meets little resistance as I plunge it into Willem's throat, before slipping the razor-sharp blade around his neck. A fountain of blood turns my world crimson once more, and I tear the rucksack from his back as he falls. He hits the floor hard, and scowls back at me, hands clutching at his neck, unable to stop the life flowing through his fingers. I reach down into his jacket and grab his lighter before fishing once more. "I believe this is mine," I say, retrieving my heirloom.

Heart pounding, I hold the diamond high. "Grootslang, hear me! I return to you that which was taken and ask for my freedom, that my bloodline's curse be lifted."

Willem's eyes roll back into his head, and he gurgles as I throw the diamond into the darkness. There's a cacophony of hissing, and I push myself back against the wall. I can't see them, but I can feel them, an icy chill in the darkness that threatens to swallow me as I slide up the ramp; fingertips scrabbling as I feel my way.

Willem's body shivers and moves, and for a heartbeat I think he's coming for me, intent on revenge. I watch as they drag away his body, and with it the last of the illumination. It's just me now, my panting breath loud in the darkness as I climb up and up, hoping, praying, that the Grootslang have accepted my offering.

✦──○──✦

At the top of the ramp, I stagger into the tunnel, the faint glimmer of the safety lightning gives me hope as I trip over the generator. I reconnect the fuel line, and strength failing tug at the starting chord. On the third attempt, the engine coughs into life, illuminating the cavern.

Every fiber of my body is telling me to leave, but I need to see and staring over the edge, I despair. A splattering of rubies populates the constellation now, and down below the rivulets of diamonds run thick with blood. I watch the Grootslang slip back into the shadows, and I pray I've seen the last of the terrible serpents. Now I understand what drove my father and grandfather mad; why they both ended their days banging their heads against the walls of an asylum, terrified of the shadows, convinced the Grootslang would reclaim their stone. It's cost my family's fortune to return the cursed gem, but if it means I can stare into the darkness without fear, then I'll consider it a bargain.

All that's left to do is to end this; to ensure no one else

is tempted into that cursed hole of wonders. I retrieve the notebook, my forefather's tatty journal, and with a flick of Willem's Zippo set it alight. The journal burns as only old paper can, and I let it fall onto the burlap rucksack as I turn and run, run like my life depends on it.

The Sea Remembers

David Green

Jacob stood on the slick rocks as he gazed up at the light-house. The stone tower tore into the purple-black sky, a white beacon of hope against an encroaching doom — if only Jacob could recall that ill feeling. The night filled him with dread. He came out to watch the spotlight swing around, forcing the darkness away, though it soon returned.

Ocean spray spat at him, but he paid it no mind. Water surrounded the lighthouse, the approaching storm raising its level and flooding the wooden dock. A boatman came with supplies once every so often, but Jacob couldn't re-member the last time he'd visited. For Jacob, it seemed the rest of the world ceased to exist; the lighthouse, the rocks of the island, its surrounding water and the terrible sky were his world.

Water caught in his white, overgrown beard, dripping onto his boots. It fell from his scruffy eyebrows too; it seemed to soak into him. He kept his eyes on the sky, the hypnotic turn of the lighthouse's beacon lulling him into a calm state. Jacob listened to the waves crashing about him, the patter of the droplets colliding with his trench coat.

"The sea remembers. Have you learned?"

Jacob staggered as the voice echoed from the ocean's depths. The sky exploded into orange and red, and the lighthouse cracked across its foundation; the sound driving Jacob to his knees. Blood poured out of the fissure, crashing over him like a wave. The sea reached up to meet the crimson torrent, their collision like the sound of a gong.

The lighthouse swayed, then toppled sideways, devoured by the sea as lights danced in the malevolent sky. Jacob curled into a ball and covered his head, his screams lost in the cacophony.

"You belong to the sea."

Silence fell, and Jacob lowered his arms. A man he recognized stood above him, framed against the starless sky.

"I'm sorry," Jacob whispered, scrambling to his knees.

The man raised a scythe and swung it, splitting Jacob's head in two.

⊷—o—⊶

Jacob woke. He lay on his side, on his wooden cot. He had been alone in the lighthouse for weeks.

"Nothing but dreams," he muttered, swinging his legs to the floorboards. "Though they're getting worse."

Jacob reached out with a shaking hand and grabbed an ever-present bottle of rum. He lifted it to his lips and drank, the alcohol spilling into his beard. It helped him cope. Samuel, his former workmate at the lighthouse, had complained of dreams until the day he walked off the rocks and into a watery grave.

Jacob struggled to recall the man's face. The silent ferryman had brought supplies since then, shrugging when Jacob told him of Samuel's death.

"Can I leave with you?" Jacob had asked, eyeing the boat.

The ferryman shook his head and pushed away from the dock, rowing away as he ignored Jacob's curses. The details of their meeting often slipped away, and trying to remember them felt like catching smoke.

How long has it been? Jacob thought, examining the chalk marks on the wall by his cot. He'd mark fourteen, then the supply man would arrive, and he'd rub them away and count again. Jacob shook his head at the marks facing him; over that many by far, and crude drawings of the lighthouses and half-familiar faces he didn't remember etching.

Jacob grabbed a piece of chalk and wrote on the wall, urging his hand under control.

"The sea remembers."

⊷—◦—⊶

The waves washed the dirt and sweat from Jacob's naked body. He stood on the rocks, arms stretched wide as if he addressed a crowd, challenging the water as if to prove it held no sway over him.

"Come to me!" he screamed, his voice breaking from lack of use. He raged at the ocean. It tormented him and he feared it, the water dominating his thoughts and dreams.

Desperation drove Jacob's fury; he desired nothing more to escape the island, though he knew police searched for him on the mainland.

"A prison here, a jail there," he screamed, throwing an empty bottle into the ocean and slipping as he did. He crashed down, striking his forehead on the rocks. In a daze he smiled as he watched his blood drip to the ground and mix with the water, each wave swallowing it and carrying his life source into the sea.

Jacob lay on his back and laughed, the waves continuing to crash into him until his skin pruned and the cold stung.

***

The gash split his forehead across the middle. It wasn't deep, but Jacob knew it needed stitching to heal. He peered in the mirror as he dabbed at it with the sleeve of an old shirt, which he had soaked in rum. Each touch made him wince. Something inside the wound caught his attention; a yellow glint reflecting in the stained glass. Placing two fingers either side of the gash, Jacob leaned closer and pulled the cut apart.

A cluster of yellow eyeballs stared back at him. Jacob gasped, his stomach heaving. He closed his eyes, sure the blow to the head was playing tricks on him, and his heart hammered in his chest. He inched open an eyelid: the wound had returned to normal.

Jacob sighed with relief. He grabbed a bottle of rum, the urge to drink strong despite the twisting of his guts. As he turned back to his reflection he saw the flesh around the cut move, as if something inside was pushing out.

A tentacle spurted from his forehead, smashing the mirror.

Jacob fell backward with a cry. The bottle of rum shattered on the floor, its contents dripping between the floorboards. He felt his injury, expecting to touch the cold, alien skin of the thing protruding from his forehead. His trembling fingers came away with a little blood on them, but no tentacles. Jacob peered around, surprise blossoming as the bottle of rum sat whole on the table, the floor dry.

Jacob looked into the mirror, its glass shattered as if struck. In the reflection his face peered back, skin pruned and green-hued. He looked away with a jolt, shaking his head; shock bubbled in his confused state of mind, unsure if he lived in a nightmare or just teetered on the verge of madness. The words on the wall caught his eye.

"Will you return to the sea?"

Jacob stood, bringing the bottle with him as he left the room. Those weren't the words he remembered writing.

Jacob watched the sea writhe. The water reflected the sky's maelstrom, a kaleidoscope of reds, purples and greens dancing across its surface. He thought he should be able to smell the salt of the ocean, but the air remained scentless as it howled around him. Jacob didn't remember walking down to the rocks, yet there he stood, his trench-coat and hat protecting him from the waves that pounded the island with a ferocious insistence.

Jacob glanced upwards and the lighthouse's beam

passed overhead, its familiar beacon comforting him. After a moment he frowned; the spotlight swung by again, faster than it should. Its circular journey picked up speed, and as it did the waves redoubled their effort. Jacob hunched over as the spray beat into him. He wanted to go inside, but his legs wouldn't respond.

"Leave me alone!" he screamed. "I acted in self-defense, I swear."

Despite the crashing of the waves, and the creaking of the lighthouse's searchlight, Jacob heard a soft whisper in his ears.

"The sea remembers. Why haven't you learned?"

He laughed, a sound of madness and regret as he dropped to his knees, no longer able to withstand the sea's punishment. A foghorn blared through the night, like the one from the lighthouse, though no one else lived on the island to sound it. Jacob covered his ears as the turning of the spotlight and the waves reached a crescendo, peaking into a frenzy in answer to the horn.

Then…silence.

The water stilled, and the searchlight blinked out, plunging the island into darkness. Shadows swirled around Jacob as he wept with fear, shame and regret.

"I'm sorry," he cried into the gloom. "What do you want from me?"

The sea didn't answer.

The lighthouse's light clanked back to life, and the sky returned to the normal black. On the wooden dock lay the body of a man, his clothes soaked through. Jacob crept towards him on all fours, observing the new arrival with care. The man's chest rose, though he shivered in his sleep.

Jacob wiped his face, running fingers through his damp beard. The man dressed in clothes like his — the coveralls and rubber boots typical of a lighthouse keeper. Jacob scanned the horizon for debris, or any signs of a wreck, but the waters were calm and unblemished.

Climbing to his feet, and looking around at the now peaceful night, Jacob grabbed the stranger under the armpits and dragged him towards the lighthouse.

◆——◦——◆

Jacob lay the man on Samuel's old cot and lit a fire. He watched from a chair as he drank his rum, a wrench secreted up his coat sleeve for safety. The flickering illumination played across the strangers' face, casting odd shadows; he looked youthful, then ancient, his features morphing into remnants of other faces from Jacob's past. He chalked it up to his imagination, alcohol and a guilty conscience making him see things.

The fire's warmth, and the peaceful slumber of the stranger, made Jacob's eyelids heavy as he wandered somewhere between sleep and wakefulness. The image of the man from his past standing over him, scythe in hand, fluttered through his sleep-addled mind.

"Am I dead?"

Jacob opened his eyes with a start. The stranger watched him, his legs drawn up against his chest and arms wrapped around his knees.

"No," Jacob answered, taking a swig from his bottle. "Not unless I am, too. You're in my lighthouse, on an island ten miles from the mainland. May as well call it a hundred. What's your name? Are you Samuel's replacement at last?"

The man peered around, his eyes lingering on the chalk marks above Jacob's cot.

"Daniel is my name," he replied, the depth of his brown eyes made Jacob look away. "Who's Samuel?"

Jacob drank before answering. "He's dead."

"Did you kill him?"

The image of Samuel walking into the ocean played in his mind, interrupted by a memory of his hands around Samuel's throat as he held him underwater. He pushed the vision away.

"I can't…no. I couldn't. Never." Jacob muttered.

"How long have you been here?" Daniel asked, his stare unblinking.

"You ask a lot of questions, boy." Jacob snarled, lowering the wrench into the palm of his hand. Daniel's eyes narrowed for a split second, his face breaking into a smile that reminded Jacob too much of Samuel.

"I'm sorry. I should thank you for pulling me out of the storm."

"Aye," Jacob replied, holding out the bottle of rum. Daniel leaned forward and took it. "You were heading here? You're dressed like a lighthouse keeper."

Daniel drank his fill from the bottle.

"I don't remember," he replied, wiping his sleeve across his lips. "Isn't that strange?"

"Aye." Jacob replied, taking the bottle from him.

"Do you have any food?"

Jacob frowned, then looked at the chalk marks. Fresh supplies hadn't arrived for weeks. He stared at the bottle in his hands. *Who brings the rum?*

"No," he replied, shaking his head. It made no sense to him. "There's rum."

"Aren't you hungry?" Daniel asked, leaning back into his pillows.

"No."

The men stared at each other until Daniel drifted to sleep.

⊷—o—⊶

Jacob fell from the top of the lighthouse.

Plummeting towards the rocks, he couldn't recall if he jumped or someone's hands did the job. The slick rocks approached and he closed his eyes, ready to meet his end. Instead he slowed, hovering six feet above the ground. Opening his eyes he saw a skeleton wearing a trench coat laying on the jagged surface, its bones pointing in impossible angles.

Jacob twisted and looked towards the lighthouse's summit. He saw himself leaning from the window, laughing and screaming into the bruised heavens.

Jacob's vision pulled back, and he viewed the entire island; waves assaulted the rocks while the white lighthouse stood out against the black waters and purple-yellow sky, thrusting upwards into the night.

Jacob watched as the waves built, renewing their barrage as if they aimed to wash the island from the face of the earth. Water crashed into the lighthouse, the sound of a foghorn splitting the night. The rocks rumbled as a crack tore through the lighthouse. Jacob watched himself fall from the top, feeling the thud as he smashed into the rocks.

Jacob opened his eyes. He lay on the floorboards, his bed covers twisted around his legs. Scrambling to his feet he grabbed a bottle, gulping rum down as if his life depended on it. He turned towards the other cot, expecting Daniel's eyes on him, but the newcomer's bed lay empty.

Jacob took a piece of chalk and etched another line on the wall, his hands shaking.

"He knows. Kill him."

He didn't remember writing it, but it resembled his unsteady handwriting.

"Why?" Jacob whispered, scratching at his skin. He felt filth building beneath his fingernails. He looked into the stained, broken mirror and saw himself stare back; but it was a Jacob from another life. His beard was short and well-groomed, his forehead unbroken. The mirror Jacob looked back, his mouth twisted into a predator's smile as a cruel light shone in his eyes.

"The newcomer knows what you did," the reflection said in a seductive tone. "Kill him."

"I can't." Jacob sobbed, afraid of the man in the mirror. The image laughed.

"You've done it before, remember? You're good at it; it's something you enjoy."

Memories slammed into his mind.

Jacob crept toward the farmhouse, an inviting light shining through the windows. He couldn't remember the last time he'd stayed somewhere warm, his belly full. He hid below the ledge and listened for anyone inside.

"I'll need a good night's sleep before tomorrow, wife," a man's voice called. "I'll miss your touch."

A woman's musical laugh answered.

"Best come to bed, Samuel," she replied, "I'll give you something to remember me by while you're away at that awful lighthouse."

The light blinked out as Jacob heard the woman laugh again, their voices fading. Thinking the farmhouse owners occupied, he reached up and climbed through the open window.

"Fools," he muttered, crouching inside the kitchen and looking around for things he could pilfer.

Jacob stuffed bread, cheese and ham into his tattered jacket pockets. He searched for coin, but came up empty-handed. Still, the food would be welcome. He spied a bottle of something and took that too — sniffing at it made him smile.

"Rum," he whispered, and headed back toward the window. He listened before climbing out — Samuel and his wife sounded busy, his intrusion undetected as Jacob crossed the yard towards the barn. He'd sleep there, nestled in straw, and steal a horse in the morning. Before Samuel and his wife could discover him he'd hit the road.

A few hours later Jacob's eyes shot open as he heard the clink of an empty bottle. A man stood above him, staring down with fury.

"On your feet, thief!" He snarled, pointing at Jacob with a pitchfork.

Jacob's head spun; he'd drank all the rum, then passed out. Staggering to all fours he gazed around, desperate *for a way out — a lifetime in jail already awaited him if the police arrested him. A farm tool by his side caught his attention; pushing himself to his feet Jacob pretended to fall, his strength leaving him. Samuel stepped back, Jacob taking the opportunity to grab the scythe.*

He surged to his feet, swinging as he stood. His arms vibrated as the blade stuck into Samuel's face, cutting a curved path through his cheek, nose, forehead and scalp. The man twitched as he sank to his knees, then toppled to his side.

Dead.

Jacob acted fast, pilfering through the man's trench-coat. His search turned up coin, tobacco and a key — to the aforementioned lighthouse, Jacob reckoned. He peeled the man's clothes off too; they were clean and well-kept, much better than the rags he wore.

"What have you done?"

Jacob looked up as he pulled on his boots. A woman stood in the barn's doorway, her eyes fixed on the dead body on the blood pooled around Samuel's head.

"I'm sorry," Jacob muttered. "I acted in self-defense."

"Murderer!" she screamed, running at him.

Jacob barged past, knocking her to the floor as he fled the barn.

"No!" Jacob screamed, knocking the mirror from the wall. It fell to the ground and shattered. "Samuel drowned. Here! On this island. I held him below the water and watched as the life drained from him."

He heard footsteps behind him. Daniel stood there, framed by the doorway, though he wore the face of Samuel for half a moment. He nodded and walked away. Jacob grabbed a shard of glass, its edge cutting his palm. He saw himself reflected; skin caked in filth, the gash across his forehead angry and tinged with green at the edges.

Daniel waited by the water's edge. Clear skies and blue waters greeted him, the first time Jacob could recall the island looking that way. Blood dripped from his hand, the shard of glass cutting into him.

"Are you going to kill me, too?" Daniel asked without looking around.

"I don't know. My thoughts confuse me. It's like I've lived too many lives."

Daniel turned and smiled. His face resembled a younger version of Jacob's, before a cloud passed in front of the sun. As it moved Daniel looked like Samuel again.

"Your memories always return before the end."

"I've killed you before, haven't I?"

Daniel's face flickered back to the one he'd worn when he washed up on the island.

"I'm all the people you've murdered, yes."

"Can't I just leave when the supply man arrives?"

Daniel laughed and shook his head. Ominous clouds raced in above him, thunder rumbling in the distance.

"Jacob, leaving here has always been your choice. You always resist. I know you're planning on it now. You tread the same well-worn path. Do you remember arriving here? How long you've lived here?"

Jacob frowned as he started at the face Daniel wore. A

memory itched at him. He knew it from somewhere, not as well as his own or Samuel's, but he'd seen it.

"No," he answered, staring out to sea. Waves built on the horizon. "Months?"

Daniel pointed over his shoulder. "Look."

Jacob followed his finger.

The lighthouse stood behind them, cracked and ruined, no beacon pouring from its summit. It looked like it hadn't been in use for decades. Jacob scanned the island. The wooden dock had rotted and fell away in places. A small boat lay anchored to it, half submerged in water.

Jacob flinched as thunder rumbled above him. He peered at the sky from under his eyebrows; lightning danced within the clouds. Water crashed into him as waves leaped over the rocks.

"It can't be," Jacob muttered, "you've put some spell on me. Demon!"

He thrust the shard of glass at him, but slipped on the wet rocks. Jacob's attack sailed wide as Daniel stepped out of the way, as if he knew the assault would come. Water flooded the rocks, the storm causing the sea level to rise. Daniel sat on Jacob's chest and held his face beneath the waves.

"Make your choice," Daniel said, his deep eyes boring into Jacob's. He strained and writhed, spluttering as he tried to lift his nose and mouth above the water, but the man holding him proved too strong. Lightning flashed above him and Jacob's vision spun, the sky shifting behind him.

Jacob spent the day in the forests that surrounded the farmhouse, edging his way closer to the sea. Samuel's wife had mentioned a lighthouse, and if Jacob could reach it then it'd prove an excellent hiding place. Night had fallen, bringing along an encroaching fog, and he spied torchlight on the road as people searched for him. He smiled and turned away. Jacob could smell salt on the air; the sea lay near, his escape close. He'd find the water's edge, locate a boat and row to his hiding place until he judged it safe to leave.

Jacob emerged from the treeline and spotted the lighthouse on a nearby island. Satisfied, he approached the rocky shoreline.

"Who are you?"

Jacob spun. A man, a boy almost, in a police coat stood nearby, his dark jacket hiding him in the gloom. Jacob tackled him, forcing him to the ground and wrapping his hands around his throat. The stranger thrust a knee into Jacob's stomach, knocking the wind out of him. The officer held him down, throttling him as water splashed from the sea onto Jacob's face, the man's serious, brown eyes staring down into his.

"Over here!" he yelled into the night. "I have him!"

Jacob thrust a hand out, searching for something to use. His fingers found a jagged rock, grabbing it and swinging it into the man's temple with a crunch. He blinked, then toppled over. Jacob turned and hit him for a second time, then a third, splitting the man's skull and coloring the rocks crimson. Jacob staggered to his feet, dizzy from the lack of oxygen. He heard shouts from behind and ran on the wet rocks, searching for a boat.

He found one fifty yards away. Jacob turned to see torches following him, but he'd make it if he doubled his *pace. He placed a foot down just as the lighthouse's fog-horn blared, startling him into losing his balance. Jacob fell, smashing his forehead into the rocks. Pain exploded, his vision going white, and he felt weightless as he slipped into the sea and beneath the waves.*

Jacob stared up at Daniel, his face the same as the officer he'd killed by the shoreline before he'd fallen to his own death.

"It's not possible!" Jacob cried. "I'm not dead."

Daniel smiled down at him. "You always say that."

Jacob screamed and thrust the glass shard at Daniel's head. It jammed into his temple, and Jacob pushed it further into his skull. Daniel's lifeless body flopped to the ground. Jacob followed him, wrapping his hands around his throat, his fury driving him on.

"You've made your choice yet again."

Jacob spun around as the thunder split the sky. Daniel's body disappeared in his hands, as if it'd never lain on the rocks at all. Panic built in Jacob's chest as the oppressive sky weighed down on him, the waves battering his body.

"The light!" Jacob cried. "It'll chase the storm away."

He raced towards the decrepit lighthouse and tore up the stairs to its summit. The wooden steps creaked and cracked as he bounded up them, though some were rotted away. Jacob reached the lens room and fell to his knees at what he saw.

The lighthouse apparatus hung abandoned and rusted. The beacon hadn't shone in decades, and never would again. Jacob cried, his ravings somewhere between laughter and tears. He staggered to the windows and looked out at the red-hued sky. Wind howled about him, and the waves threatened to swallow the island whole — they devoured the shore and almost reached the base of the lighthouse.

Below him, on the jagged rocks, lay a skeleton, washed in by the tide. Clothed in a lighthouse keeper's coat the body appeared too far below him to see, but Jacob knew the details as if the bones were his own.

Jacob jumped, the rocks rushing up to meet him.

He opened his eyes with a start. Jacob lay in a coat, in a small dormitory with wooden floorboards. A second bed by his side lay empty. He patted his body, and discovered he wore a lighthouse keeper's coat, even though he lay in bed. From outside he heard the gentle slosh of water. Jacob's head throbbed. On the bedside table sat a bottle. He took it and sniffed.

"Rum," he muttered with a smile, lifting it to his lips and drinking.

A piece of white chalk lay next to the bottle. As he took it, a foghorn broke the silence. As the cry faded, a whisper drifted into his ear.

"The sea remembers."

THE TRIAL OF ALSE LIND

MICHAEL D. NADEAU

CHAPTER ONE: THE SICKNESS

She watched them wheel another young boy in, his blotched skin beaded with sweat. This was the ninth child stricken with sickness in as many days, and it was growing. They were calling it an epidemic, and it was all that Alse could do to keep up with her patients. Their fevers claimed them in their sleep, if they were lucky. Alse Lind was a young woman who was trained in some herbal remedies, and she was currently helping the local doctor out with this sickness. She daren't mention any of her own cures or remedies for fear of being called out as a witch; one needn't that kind of attention these days. She had long, black hair and dark brown eyes, eyes which had seen too much death.

It was the fall of 1654 in the Province of Maryland, and the chilly wind was blowing colder than usual for the beginning of the season. Also changed the cold cloth on the forehead of a young girl, but her patient's only response was a slight moan, her fever blisters maring her little face.

"Miss Lind, how does the day go?" Doctor Young asked, coming in from the back. He let the white curtain drop, obscuring the latest fatality from view, though Alse still caught a glimpse of a tiny arm hanging from under a sheet.

"It goes, doctor. How do you fare this day?" she asked, inclining her head as he stopped in front of her.

"Not well, if I dare say. This epidemic grows quickly, and the cause is beyond me." He bent down to the young girl on the cot to check her eyes, sighing in frustration. "This one is getting worse. Is there no end?"

Just then the front doors slammed open, and an old woman barged in. Her stride was purposeful and strong. "I've told ye before, and I'll tell ye again," she started, looking around at the young ones on cots. "Tis the work of a witch!"

"Please, Goody Hawser, this is not witchcraft. If you start that you will have the governor here right quick," Doctor Young said, walking towards her. He took her firmly by the shoulder and escorted her back out. "Now, if you have anything useful to contribute then that would be most welcome, but since you never do..." He didn't even finish the sentence before she was out, the door shutting behind her.

"I hate to say it Doctor," Alse said, but he cut her off with a raised hand before she could continue.

"Don't say you agree with that old bat?"

Alse turned away, changing the cloth on yet another

child. "All I know is that we cannot find out what is making all these children sick, and the fact that they worsen, despite treatment, is absurd."

"I know, yet it cannot always be the Devil, or witches." He took his coat off and hung it on the hook by the door. "I'm going home to get some sleep. Do not stay up too late yourself Alse, Mary will be here within the hour."

"I will not doctor, good rest." She continued to work tirelessly, taking care of the children and wincing as another was brought in just before Mary arrived. She didn't leave till the dawn rose over the mountains.

Chapter Two: Accusations

Alse walked home in the early morning mist, the light rain falling on the packed, earthen road. She was exhausted from the night's tasks, and now she was glad to be headed home to get some much needed rest. She passed several early risers, mostly farmers making their deliveries of milk and eggs to the stores. In town she stopped, for a black cat stood in the road staring straight at her. "Move along cat, I have no quarrel with you this morn," she said, waving her hand tiredly at the small creature. It nodded its head at her and walked off the road, disappearing into the bushes.

"Is that your cat Alse?" one man asked as he watched the exchange from his carriage. She saw that he had stopped as well, probably more out of superstition that respect.

"No, Goodman Danvers, it is not mine," she answered, looking down at her feet and moving on. She only walked another ten feet before she saw a small girl walk into the road, her face pale and her gait staggered.

Alse rushed to her side, catching her as she collapsed in a shivering heap. "Help! Anyone! I have a sick child here," she called out, drawing the attention of two more farmers driving by. Sadly, that wasn't the only attention she gathered to herself.

"Another sick," Goody Hawser said accusingly, walking over as they took the child from Alse's arms. "And look who it is that finds her."

"Hush now Goody, this woman did nothing wrong. She caught the girl for the Lord's sake." The farmer loaded the girl up on his wagon and covered her with a blanket, the other man helping Alse up to her feet.

"Aaahh, but that is not all she has done. Followed her, I did. She spoke to that black cat, and it understood her command!" Goody Hawser threw her hands up in the air at the end, being dramatic as always, yet the first farmer looked back with interest.

"I did see that. I thought it was odd that it followed her command, which is why I asked her if she owned the cat." More and more people came over now as the sun tried to break through the low clouds. The mist was letting up, but everything was still soaking wet.

"What are you saying madam? Are you saying Miss Alse is to blame for the sick children?" one woman asked, her long hair tied up in a bun. She carried a basket of bread, and looked frightened by the conversation.

"That *is* what I am sayin'," Goody Hawser said, putting her foot down and staring at Alse in the eyes. "She is a witch!"

This caused a commotion the likes of which Alse hadn't seen in quite some time. People started to form their own opinions regarding the young woman standing there, and her protests went unheard. "I am not a witch!"

"She speaks to animals!" one said.

"She commands the beasts." Another yelled from the back.

A stone shot out and grazed Alse's head, spinning her to the ground. "Stop this!" she screamed as she threw her hands up to protect her face. As she did a wind picked up that sent two of the men flying back, and the women all cowered to the ground.

"Witch!" they all cried out, scrambling back from Alse in terror.

CHAPTER THREE: THE TRIAL

"What is the meaning of this nonsense?!" a man called from horseback as he reigned in his steed amid the confusion.

"She be a witch Deputy, we all seen it!" one of the farmers called, jumping in his wagon to bring the sick girl to Doctor Young.

"Aye, she called up a witches wind to keep us away," another woman said, making the sign of the cross upon her bosom.

"Please sir, all I did was help a sick child..." Alse was shaking now, huddled on the ground.

"Who is the accuser?" he asked, dismounting and putting his hand out for Alse. He helped her up to her feet, running his finger over the slight graze near her hairline. "And who struck this woman?"

"It was the crowd, your honor," Goody Hawser said.

"They were fearful of her power, they was." She inclined her head a bit as the crowd slowly dispersed. "I am the accuser and I stand by my words."

"Very well. To me then," he said as he mounted up again, looping a length of cord around Alse's hands. "These are serious charges, and have to be stated in front of the governor for trial."

Alse walked quickly behind, lest she be dragged by the horse. Goody Hawser was right alongside the deputy; her gums flapping as usual. In quick time they were at the courthouse. The deputy escorted her through the gathered crowd outside, who were booing and throwing small stones at her. Where at first the deputy had been shocked at the wound on her head, he now ignored the rock-throwing in favor of getting her inside in a timely manner.

Within the hour the trial was started; quick frontier justice being the way of the world in these parts. As long as a case was documented, and filed properly, it was pushed through before rumors could spread across the province. It started with Goody Hawser telling everyone there about the sick children and the cat, and it ended with the tale of the witch wind. Alse was put up on the stand and questioned then as well, a damning line of accusations that she wouldn't be able to deny. Instead she tried another tack.

"If I were a witch," she began slowly, making sure that she had their attention, "Wouldn't I need some sort of magic hex bag near the sick children? Did you find any of those at the hospital?"

"We did indeed send someone to gather Doctor Young and search for foul play," the Governor said, sitting up on his high seat behind his desk. "Ah, here they are now."

Two men came in pushing the doctor in front of them. "We found some strange bags your honor!" one called, throwing them on the table in front of Alse.

"Witch!" the room cried out, standing up and wailing in despair.

"Order!" the governor called, banging his gavel several times. Once order was restored he looked to Alse on the stand. "What do you say for yourself now, young miss?"

"It seems like they are made from Goody Hawser's dress material, Your Honor." Alse said in a quiet voice, looking at the old woman as she said this. "And as I recall she was always bothering the doctor and I in the hospital, yelling about a witch...."

CHAPTER FOUR: THE TRUTH COMES OUT

"Tis true your honor!" Doctor Young said from the middle of the room.

"And," Alse went on before anyone could change the direction of the questioning. "I remember her saying that she had been following me when I saw that cat. Could she have been in command of that creature?" Alse had the room now, the superstitious folk already turning on the old woman. They did not disappoint her at all.

"She was there when that Devil wind took us as well!" a man said, standing up and pointing at the old woman.

"She never even fell over. Besides, was it not Goody Hawser that named Alse?" another woman asked, her voice trembling.

"Wait! I am not the witch!" Goody Hawser pleaded,

backing away from the condemning stares.

"Order! Order I said!" the governor stated again, banging his gavel until it broke. The room hushed as it did, taking it as a sign. They all turned towards Goody Hawser to see her looking right at the man behind the desk.

"*Witch!*" they cried.

It wasn't long after that Alse was released, with the real witch being dragged towards the gallows kicking and screaming. As if to add fuel to the fire the little black cat came running out of the bushes and clawed two of the guards holding the old woman, their cries of fear ringing across the entire square. They strung Goody Hawser up late that afternoon, the noose her last embrace. When she fell the noose failed to break her neck, and her eyes bulged in horror. The crowd only cheered on the death that would take a long time to come, chanting that the Devil would receive his servant back soon.

Goody Hawser kicked and thrashed, her face turning blue and her bloodshot eyes almost popping out of her head. After a while she was dead, swinging in the slight breeze as the crowd broke apart, their bloodlust sated.

Alse walked back to the hospital, a spring in her step. She had been spared the noose this day, but she must be careful. These days witchcraft was on everyone's lips it seemed. She walked in and saw Mary, sitting in a chair, almost nodding off as she held a young boy's hands. "Nocturn almorta," Alse said, putting the young woman in a deep sleep. She went from bed to bed, draining the last of the life from the children and collecting the real hex marks; tiny bones placed under their fingernails. Their flesh turned to black ash, flaking off and spiraling into the breeze.

"Mistress, all is well?" the cat asked, meowing in his singsong tone as it came into the room, his tail swishing back and forth.

"Why yes, dearest Cat, it is." Alse finished, then she grabbed a couple of her books and walked towards the door.

"And now we are off again?" Cat asked, purring next to her leg.

"I'm afraid so Cat, for these people will know something is wrong soon enough. The epidemic will be over though, so they will know they killed the 'witch'," Alse said, letting her hair down for the first time since moving here. She had done this in over four colonies now, extending her life with each child consumed. At the tender age of one hundred and six she still had a very long life ahead of her, and the cat was her closest friend.

"Nice touch, having me claw those guards," her familiar said as she picked him up into her arms. "Where are we off to this time?"

"I was thinking of going a bit north, possibly Massachusetts," she said as she walked out into the street. No one even noticed that she was carrying the cat, for they didn't see it if she didn't want them to. Benefits of being a witch, and all that.

The Cover of Storms

Ashley Burns

The weather had been progressively worsening. A dreary rain turned the sky a mournful shade of grey, which became the steady ping of sleet hitting roof shingles like fingers drumming on a hollow, wooden desk. This was followed by the sounds of cars honking in harsh rebuttals as they drove on polluted, oil slicked mush that gave way to hidden stretches of treacherous ice. It had hit so suddenly the salt trucks were hopelessly overrun. Sitting in my old Lazy Boy recliner I settled in as I watched the weatherman make his frenzied broadcast, telling citizens to bunker down, latch the windows and doors and so on; all the usual preparations most people had already made when December began in earnest. Only it wasn't December.

We were only in the infantile first week of November, where the last vestiges of autumn should have still held strong. Trees were supposed to be enviable shades of russet, and sunshine not violently stripped bare by cutting winds and freezing temperatures. I imagined plenty of people were not prepared, no pantries stocked or wood chopped in reserves. Shaking my head I tried not to envision the poor, homeless men and women who would undoubtedly freeze to death. I had read somewhere that it was a peaceful way to pass, all things considered, but I could only hope. There are much, much worse ways to go.

Just thinking of the cold seemed to summon a draft. I shivered, pulling my fleece blanket tighter around shoulders that had become sloped and weakened with age, despite my protestations. The chill had a way of seeping through your pores and gnawing on your bones like a dog worrying his favorite chew toy. The hearth crackled and spit as the logs burnt brightly in deep shades of hectic reds and oranges. It seemed the warmth could not thaw my negative thoughts, so I tried to think of other, happier memories. The news bulletin remained as a thin strip under the regularly scheduled programming, a benign game show with a warning pulsing underneath. It demanded I begin the arduous task of preparing for the hunt. Turning it off eased some of my worry; I had survived worse than freezing temperatures and a nor'easter storm's wrath. Besides, the news was just a distraction, their superficial weather reports meant little to me other than knowing the type of storm and roughly when it would peak.

Subconsciously I rubbed my forearms, tracing the edges of scars that had healed poorly. I had been waiting for my young protégé; the clock ticking on the mantle taunting me as it moved steadily ahead. I was an only child, but my father's brother had married and was blessed with several children, one of which had married and given birth to a lad named Gentry. I was his tutor for many years, watching and observing. Adding here and there to his curriculum - folklore, mythology, and trickles of his heritage. I saw real potential when he saved a feral dog being abused by some local teenagers; even outnumbered he did not back down. I watched him being beaten, taking it in stride with nary a sound, and the pain he endured so the dog could be spared gave me hope. Despite our history together I still worried that maybe he had reconsidered.

I knew it was his choice to make, but the knock on the door filled me with hope. Easing out of my chair I made my way to the front door. Unlatching the deadbolt I opened it a body's worth, battling against the forceful winds. Gentry stepped inside, brushing errant snow and ice off his jacket and boots. He hung his coat and scarf on the iron hook behind the door, rubbing his numb hands together as he followed me to the living room. He sat down next to the fireplace, and I eased back into my chair. The words came easy...

Most people will blissfully live their whole lives un-encumbered, ignorant to what hides and hunts under the cover of storms. Those very same people never acknowl-edging or thanking you for saving them from monsters they did not even know existed. It is thankless work, dangerous too. My patchwork quilt of scars is a testament to the veracity of their rending claws and razor-sharp teeth. My journal, a worn, leather affair, serves as both living will and record of my tireless work. Inside it you will find detailed descriptions of beasts and the storm types they favor to take refuge in, the best methods to track and kill them.

With no children of my own to pass my legacy to I

have worried ceaselessly about my life's work, hoping to succeed it to a younger, more able-bodied man or woman. Then divine providence smiled upon me! You came along and fit all the necessary requirements. Intelligent, athletic, an open and curious mind, and a spirit of altruism. An empathy towards your fellow peers. Most importantly, though, you possess a desire to use your strengths to protect those who are unable to. The ultimate decision is, of course, up to you. I will not try and impress upon you the merits or detractors of such secretive work as there are many on both sides, I am afraid. I promised myself if you came tonight I would share with you my history, and perhaps after hearing my story you will be able to make a more informed decision. I know from experience it is not something to be taken lightly. It is an unbreakable pact with darkness, to secrets, to living a double life where one part of you is forever unable to confide and unburden yourself with a loved one. Secrets take on depth, and weight, over time.

Are your shoulders strong enough to carry it? Your heart steady enough against its ravages?

Throw some fresh wood on the fire Gentry, and I will pour you a glass of spirits. It will provide the heat to fend off the chill of my story. I am partial to scotch, J. Walker Red or Glenmorangie. The latter? Neat? Two cubes it is then. Let me see, I was just 10-years old the first time I saw one. . .

Growing up my family lived on a farm. Our livelihood was in parts produce - corn and soybeans - and meat from the hogs, eggs from the chickens, and fresh milk and cheese from our prized bovines. It was year-round labor, but in my opinion a great way to raise children. The daily chores kept idle hands busy and growing bodies strong, not to mention the other valuable lessons such as the ebb and flow of life, or the way the Earth recycles natural resources. Mother Earth was ever gracious, giving us plants to feed ourselves and others, asking only to care for her in turn.

Our livestock was kept in two different enclosures - the cows in a fenced-in swath of acres, grazing aplenty, and the pigs in a corral of sorts, laid with straw, massive copper troughs where their feed would be poured in. My Pops, he was a gentle giant. Firm, but reasonable. He respected those pigs with the same reverence he would a person, even talked to them in kind. Meat, he used to tell me, is more than the slabs of bacon we consume. They are giving their lives to feed and nourish us, so we care for them, making life a comfort until their time has come. He stayed true to that principle until his dying breath. I always respected that about him, his unwavering values and ethics.

I digress. . .

It was encroaching upon winter, a time to tighten belts and work with grim determination. Once the harvest had been bundled, distributed into our pantry and the markets, we laid fresh compost in the fields, tilling the dirt to replace the nutrients the crops had stripped. Taking long rolls of insulation we laid down row after row, a barrier to protect the ground from freezing temperatures. The animals were rounded up to the barn, since it had more protection against the elements. The animals went gladly and without complaint, though some looked agitated - lolling wide eyes and stamping their hooves on the ground. I tried my best to comfort them, petting their flanks and cooing words of comfort, with little success. I assumed they could sense the bad weather coming, which was the source of their anxiety.

Moving with practiced ease I guided the animals to their respective enclosures, checking that they had food and fresh water before I left. After securing the barn doors I dropped the cross hatch to keep them closed. I headed back to the house, rolling my stiff shoulders as I went, more than ready to take a bath and eat a hearty supper. I felt like I had hay in every crevice, and despite working around it for all my young life it still itched horribly. Ma used to joke I should set up a scratching post to get to all my hard-to-reach places, but I insisted the best scratcher this side of the Mississippi was her wonderful nails. She would laugh, then put some chamomile in my bath to help ease the discomfort.

My parents were old fashioned, not big proponents of technology and mindless television. Instead we had a radio, one of those broadband types that could piggyback on telephone wires and get surprisingly clear reception given our distance from town. As I dusted off my coat and boots I could hear what sounded like an emergency broadcast. Ma and Pops were sitting at the dining room table, concerned expressions furrowing their brows. The storm, named Thomas, was coming with gale force winds and below-freezing temperatures. Sleet and snow would be up to 13 feet, if not more. Pops gave Ma a knowing look, and with a subtle nod she left the kitchen.

"Son, I know you're a bit young, but I need for you

to be prepared," he said, kneading his callused hands in knots. Reaching out I covered his large hands with my own, putting a brave face on for what terrible truth I could only guess. I had never seen my father in such a state, so unsure of himself. After a momentary struggle he continued solemnly.

"I don't rightly know the why of it, so I'll save you the trouble of asking. I just know it is. Has always been, if my grandpappy was to be believed. After seeing what I seen I'm inclined to believe it wholeheartedly. I guess you could say it's a tradition in our family. Cursed might be apt, too. Depends on how you see it, I suppose. I was never much for religion, Heaven and Hell always seemed too black and white in my book. Life, in my humble opinion, exists somewhere in the middle. I ain't too proud to say I prayed sunup to sundown the first time I seen one. There had to be a God, if those Devils existed."

He paused, dragging a weary hand down the salt-and-pepper stubble of his square jaw.

"Your Ma is probably the only exception to what I'm about to say. I doubt she really believes, just trusts me enough to know I ain't crazy, I reckon." Sighing, he looked me square in the eye, holding it there so I could see he spoke the truth. I did not really need the confirmation, I trusted him unconditionally in the way only children can with abject devotion. His deep voice, like a blanket of warmth, continued. "The storms are just camoflauge for what hides beneath them. They come from the stars and ride the storm's coattails, dodging in and out as they hunt. They prey on the weak, son, on animal and person alike. Sometimes I wonder if there are millions of them all over the world, and if so if there're other families like our own, who valiantly take up the cause to protect innocents. I like to think there are, it helps me sleep better at night. You seen the missing persons bulletin in town, I take it?"

The jarring turn in his tale made me start. "Yeah... uh...Pops, can't miss it in front of Mitcham's Convenience Store." I replied, confused where this was going.

"Have you ever noticed the majority of those folks only seem to go 'missing' right after a major storm?" Quirking a bushy eyebrow I realized, with dawning horror, that he was right. In the wintertime the bulletin, which normally hosted business cards and ads for services, became heavy and weighed down with dozens of faces - men, women, and children, pets too, beseeching people to find them.

"Ah, I see you made the connection. Good, good. Now listen closely, lad, for this is a matter of life and death. The alien creatures that hide in those storms are vicious, they'll take your life without batting an eye if you're not careful." He pulled up the sleeves of his plaid button-down shirt, and I gasped at the ragged scars littering his forearms. "Never go out there without two things - fire and a weapon. They abhor iron, it's the most dangerous thing for their kind. Salt is a way to trap them, but that's tricky with gale force winds. Keep it on you and in a pinch make a circle around yourself, they can't pass it. I'm getting on in my years; not as quick or agile as I once was. I want you to know it's a choice though, and I won't make it for ya. Nor will I judge it. Every man has to make his own path, but if you do decide to fight them I'll teach you everything I know. What say ya?" Pop's face held no judgement, no condemnation.

I thought on it, deeply. If my father, a tirelessly good man, had taken up the cause then I could do no better than accept the mantle and wear it proudly. I nodded, and he visibly sagged in relief. To this day I feel certain my Pops would have loved and respected my decision either way. Truly I do. He was just that type of person; a man of his word, back in the days where your word was sometimes all you had.

That night I tossed and turned, trying to picture what the creatures looked like. My only point of reference were the fictitious comics I had, and much of what my father had imparted rang true for many of the tales. The line of reality had never seemed weaker in my young, impressionable mind. A sudden desire to check my closet, and even under my bed, made me weak in the knees. I remember pulling the covers up to my chin, quivering in bed, straining to hear any sign of a boogeyman lurking in the shadows.

The storm was battering against my bedroom windows, threatening to break right through with each successive gust. Summoning my courage I eventually swung my legs out of bed and padded over to the window, searching through snow drifts for what might lurk underneath them. Suddenly a hideous growl accompanied the shrill screaming of pigs, as though it was right in my ears. I backpedaled away from the window, hesitant to avert my eyes before I raced down the hallway towards my parent's bedroom. My father was already loading buckshot into his shotgun, and when he saw me in the doorway he told me to get dressed. Running back to my room my heart was thudding so painfully in my chest that I thought it might burst. Adrenaline coursed through my veins as I hastily applied layer after layer. My father walked right past my room, never glancing at me, knowing that I would follow him. His steps were sure and confident, purposeful, as I followed in his wake while still adjusting my clothes and pulling down my wool cap. I must have gotten in front of him though, because when he opened the back door a swirl of snowflakes flew right in my face, momentarily blinding me.

"DUCK!" My father bellowed. I dropped to the ground as the gunshot rang loudly, rending the air with a solemn boom. Trembling I looked up at my father, his expression grim. He stormed past me, heading straight for the barn while reloading the shotgun in one fluid move-ment. Boom. Click. The snow came up to my thighs as I resolutely followed in my father's steps. A full moon gave ample light to see by, but it was the kerosene lamp he held that my eyes were riveted to. Like Moses parting the Red Sea he stormed through snow drifts as if nothing could keep him from his quarry. His anger was palpable, radiat-ing from him in waves. I could sense his fury and singular purpose with startling clarity. Hurrying my stride I kept to his heels, feeling certain of his protection.

When we reached the barn the door's latch had been broken clean in two. This was no easy feat, as the bar was solid steel and several inches thick at that. Seeing how ca-sually it had been torn asunder shook me to my core. The strength needed to do such a thing made me blanch, almost losing the battle for my bladder. As we got closer I could hear the animal's panicked screams. The storm had muted them substantially, but at this range it could not diminish their sheer terror. Pops used the tip of the gun to nudge the barn doors open, looking down the barrel for the creature he sought. As I eased in behind him I gasped. Blood and gore were splattered on the walls and roof, bits of sinewy flesh and bones hanging from the rafters like macabre confetti. The stench of copper stung my nostrils, making me gag violently. There was a sourness, a foul odor that interweaved with the carnage that made my eyes water. All of the animals were straining to get as far away from the carnage as the enclosures would permit, and I could hear the wood straining against their combined weight.

None of that compared to the audible crack of bones snapping in half, accompanied by a nauseating slurping noise which dragged my eyes from the carnage towards the far end of the barn. The creature, nestled partially in an alcove of shadow, back to us, was oblivious for the moment of our arrival. I doubted it would stay that way long as my father pulled the trigger. Shot after shot echoed off the walls. It was deafening being this close; my ears were ringing, throwing my equilibrium off balance. As I fought to steady myself I was not prepared for when it turned around. I had thought it was small at first, but I was wrong. As it unfolded, joints popping hideously, it stood almost seven feet tall. The arms dragged the ground, tipped with nasty-looking claws that could disembowel anything.

It was covered in a mangy, coal-black fur that seemed to ripple with its movements, like it was a separate living entity. My father began chanting, the words unintelligible, but the creature seemed to comprehend their meaning and narrowed its eyes. It hissed, rasping grating, guttural sounds that mimicked the language my father spoke, but it felt wrong somehow. Jaundiced eyes with slit pupils dilated with rage. Just when it looked ready to pounce my father reached behind him, and in one fluid movement threw an iron axe, embedding it in the creature's forehead with an audible crunch. It spit the skull almost clean in half; the creature staggered drunkenly, then collapsed. It was dead on impact. My father swooned before dropping to his knees, looking years older than when we left the house. He was still mumbling, almost a whisper, before his wide eyes met my own. I couldn't quite place the emotions cascading in quick succession across his face. Relief, maybe?

In the midst of all this my mind went back to something Pops had said in the kitchen about Ma trusting he was not crazy. Surely if she saw that creature she would have no room for doubt? Breaking eye contact I turned to where the creature had been. The axe was still there in all its glory, tinged with something blood-like, but the monster was gone. Running to the spot I spun in circles, trying to locate its body, but all that remained was the carnage left behind. I had so many questions that it caused a physical ache; you don't see something like and walk away unscathed. Walking on unsteady legs I managed to stumble over to Pops before I collapsed flat on my bottom.

He laughed, a strained version of his normal joviality. "I know you have questions, son, just give me a minute, alright?" He said with strained patience. Cheeks flushed from exertion, brow dripping in sweat.

I nodded. My throat felt so tight I did not trust my voice.

We sat there for maybe an hour, maybe five minutes, before Pops started talking. I think the momentary reprieve was as much for my sake as his own. I listened raptly, my decision solidifying with inner conviction. The Language of the Storms was a way to bind and hold the creatures until iron meted out their final judgement. It wasn't the why of it that bubbled up inside me, it was the where that truly disturbed me. When Pops was done with what I guessed was my first lesson I spoke the question burning on my tongue.

"Where do they come from, Pops?" The words tumbled out in a rush. Our parents at that tender age are like Gods, with infinite wisdom and experience. We turn to them for guidance to navigate the tricky twists and turns of life. This was no different, at least not to me. He looked contemplative, weighing the wisdom of telling my impressionable self more than he had already divulged. I think in the end he knew I would never let it go; he acquiesced, though with visible reluctance.

"Lad, that's the million-dollar question ain't it?" He chuckled dryly. "Our ancestors believed they came from above." He gestured towards the roof and the sky beyond. "That the stars we so admire in the night sky are actually those monsters in celestial form. The journals passed down say that shooting stars are really just those monsters falling to Earth. It makes sense if you think about it - the cold of space and the freezing temperatures of winter storms means likely they can't exist in warmer climates. But who knows, maybe someday they will learn to adapt. I hope not." He said sadly, clenching his hands into fists. "Let's put this barn to rights." He stood, tall and solid like an oak tree, and I tried to do the same.

We worked side-by-side, gathering up the remains of our butchered livestock and throwing the mutilated bits into a wheel barrel. The axe was hung back up on the backside of the barn doors. The blood had turned to ash and now the blade gleamed, sharp and deadly. I climbed up the hayloft ladder and used rags to wipe away great arcs of splatter, my belly full of nausea. The smell was worse than the bite, heady and pungent with flecks of rotting meat. Once we finished, sweaty and tired, we took the wheel barrel and dumped it in a barren pit. Pops wandered over to the shed and came back carrying kerosene fuel, which he poured over the bits. Before I could ask why Pops spoke.

"The creatures excrete poison when they feed. Any critter who ate some of that," he pointed at the hunks of flesh, sinew and bone, "would die just from ingesting it. Painfully at that. That's why you gotta burn it. It's hard enough when it's just animals, but when it's people...Men and women, God forbid a child, you have to burn them. No matter how much it pains you to do so." Even at that age the gravity of what Pops had endured staggered me. Raw anguish has its own mark, if you will. It resides in the eyes, dulls them a bit, robs you of your innocence and puts duty over your own conflicted emotions.

I can see your curiosity; it is a Hell of a tale to conjure from imagination alone. I assure you it is real, and tonight I will prove it. Will you follow? Will you take up the axe and harden your heart? Will you put the lives of others over the very breath you breathe?

I stood, leaning heavily on my cane, and eyed the young man that providence had sent me. His deep-set green eyes, a trademark of our lineage, flashed like Holy retribution. I sighed in relief. Wandering over to the bay windows I saw the dark clouds congealing in a thick, ominous blanket. I signaled for Gentry to come take a look, and he hurried to my side.

"Are you ready?" I asked, looking out the window. Eddies of snowflakes, whipping and whirling, in dizzying circles, blanketing the ground in a pristine white. It was a shame it never stayed that way.

"Yes." He replied, straightening his broad shoulders.

"Let us begin," I slipped on a heavy overcoat, patting the pockets for the buckshot I always kept loaded within. Gentry moved to grab the shotgun, but I stopped him with a hand of his forearm. Pointing to the closet he nodded in understanding, passing me the gun while he retrieved the iron axe. He hefted it from hand to hand, acclimating to the weight. We shared one final look, conveying the last opportunity to back down, to walk away and never think of such dark things again, but Gentry only clenched his jaw with firm resolution.

Without another word we stepped out into the blizzard of snow and ice to hunt the abominations that hid in them.

Death Whisper
Tor-Anders Ulven

The Apocalypse was supposed to happen with a big bang. A huge, extravagant, over the top, mass extinction event. That's what we were led to believe. Some asshole pushes a button that sends a million nuclear warheads flying to some other asshole, and in response that asshole does the same. Or a meteor the size of a continent sets the atmosphere ablaze as it hurls towards us at a million miles per hour. That's what Armageddon should look like. Big, flashy, excessive. Impressive.

Instead it happened with a whisper.

It was like a vague rumour, something you'd never really expect to have consequences. Just an inconvenient nuisance, multiplied silently a billion times in a billion places until finally we were all gone. Extinct, a fragment at a time. We never saw it coming, never saw it happening.

There is no extinction date, no single occurrence. It happened over weeks, months even, and all attempts made at finding a patient zero were doomed to fail. There is no patient zero, simply because we are all patient zero. There isn't an overarching narrative that would explain it, and there isn't a master tale that unravels a complex chain of events that eventually led to our demise. No. There are a billion stories, each one unique, each one just as important as the next. Not a single one will explain anything. They are Epitaphs, words to remember a life, to remember how we died. Nothing more.

Now I'll tell mine.

My wife woke up with a headache a few months ago, just an inconvenient nuisance. She swallowed some pills and rushed to work. She went in late, half an hour maybe. Her right index finger was hurting. Probably strained it at the gym, no big deal. A couple of people had called in sick. Headaches, body aches, nothing to write home about. Her boss was usually a decent bloke, but that particular day he was grumpy. Stomach ache, she told me. So he warned her not to come in late again. She had a shitty day at work.

I felt fine. Had the day off, did some laundry, took a shower, mowed the lawn. Thought about painting the fence. It was looking a bit worn, faded. There's always tomorrow though. There's always a tomorrow.

My wife came home in a mood. Her headache hadn't faded, and her right index finger was feeling weird. I made us some dinner, pasta carbonara, and she told me about her shitty day. I did the dishes, she took a nap, and suddenly the day was over.

You know, it's weird. I don't remember the good times anymore. I don't mean the *good* good times, but the everyday good times. Like watching TV in the evening, holding each other tightly, discussing what that character should or shouldn't be doing. Laughing over dinner at some stupid joke, or a simple kiss before work. Those moments are gone, faded from memory.

My wife only got worse. Everyone did. In just a few weeks the vague, inconsequential nuisance had spread from her index finger to cover the entirety of her right hand. She couldn't hold it still, she said. Kept shaking and spasming. See the doctor, I told her. Probably just a minor thing, an inconvenience. So she did, but the doc couldn't do anything. Simple muscle spasms, due to stress most likely. Call in sick for a day, relax. It would pass in a day or so, surely.

Weeks go by, but she doesn't get better. At the same time it isn't really a huge deal either. The weird spasms persist, and they now cover the arm too. I've been feeling sick for a few days now. Weird itching in my left leg, like it's on the inside of the skin. Can't shake the feeling that something is up, like a creeping whisper, but I brush it off. The news tell me that there's some unusual flu strain going around. They can't quite figure out where it all started, but they urge children, pregnant women, and the elderly to get vaccinated. You know, just in case.

There are riots in Asia. What else is new? There's always a riot. Civil war in the Middle East, same old thing. Some country in South America that I can't pronounce the name of had their economy go belly up. People are going crazy in Eastern Europe, looting stores, overthrowing governments. Status quo, I think to myself. That's the world for you, but we're safe though. Civilized, democratic, shit like that doesn't happen here.

One day my wife calls me from work. She has to go to the hospital, she tells me. Cut herself badly. Gonna be a scar, she warns me. I'm just worried about her, but she tells me it's fine. A few stitches, some painkillers, back to normal in no time. My leg is killing me, I can't stop it from convulsing. Where did you cut yourself, I ask. The neck, she replies. Accident with scissors. Strange, inconvenient, nuisance.

A week passes, maybe two. The vague whisper is slowly becoming a static buzz. Explosions, riots, presidents and state officials desperately trying to calm us down. People are acting strange. Cult-behaviour, the news anchor calls it. Mass-hysteria is another term they use. People, young and old, walking into oncoming traffic. Jumping from tall buildings, stabbing themselves with scissors. Some kind of drug, perhaps. Toxic fumes, maybe.

A few days later and the static buzz is now a thundering roar. I wake up covered in blood. Turning to my wife I realise I can't feel my leg anymore, it's like it isn't there. It's all I can think about as I stare at my wife's dead body, her throat slit almost from ear to ear, the knife resting in her right hand. Her blank gaze is lifeless and cold, but I can't stop worrying about my leg. I can see it moving, convulsing violently under the sheets, but I have no control over it. Hopping clumsily on my one good leg I make it to the living room. Time to check the news again.

People have lost control, the woman on the TV shouts. She is stabbing herself again and again and again with what appears to be a simple wooden stick. Blood gushes from her neck, and I watch with disinterest as she collapses, her body suddenly off-camera. In the background I see people running. Many are bleeding, all are screaming, some are frantically chewing on their own arms, hands and fingers.

My wife returns moments later, foaming at the mouth. There isn't much left of her arm. The flesh is torn away, bitemarks reaching down to the bone, fingers missing. Her eyes are the same. Blank, cold, dead. I realise I can't talk to her, can't calm her down. Her voice is a continuous death rattle, blood gushing from her neck and mouth simultaneously, perfectly synchronized. When she charges me I'm ready. I tackle her to the ground, bash in her skull with my bare fists. No real emotions behind it, haven't had those for a while.

The world has gone mad. From a whisper to a deafening roar. We never saw it coming, we were never prepared. A billion voices screaming in unison, but we were too busy to notice. Too busy to care. It came disguised as mundane atrocities happening elsewhere. Horrible fates hidden in TV-filters and sensationalist headlines. A tidal wave of suffering and death that we were indoctrinated to ignore.

My legs want me to go find a vantage point, somewhere high we can plummet from. It's like a murmur, a soft, comforting reassurance. I can't see any reason to stick around. Nothing here for me anymore, nothing here for anyone anymore.

And just like that we disappear, with nothing but a whisper.

A death whisper.

ALL HALLOWS' HANGOVER
S.O. Green

What was the worst part of a hangover? The shit-mouth, the fizzing battery acid in your guts, that warm bubbling in your pelvis like you'd gotten lucky? Or maybe the trembling panic of the realisation that you didn't remember any of it?

June stared at the ceiling, probing the black hole that had been Halloween like a missing tooth.

"Holy shit. How much did I drink last night?"

"Maybe the same as me."

Sam sat up next to her, gouging her palm into her eye socket. If she was anything like June then it felt like someone had jammed a screwdriver in to pop the lid off her head like a paint can. June lay and gaped at her roommate as she stretched and adjusted her vest.

"Did we...?"

Sam flashed her a smile, then leaned over to fondly pull a strand of blonde hair out of her mouth.

"Would it be so bad if we did?"

June didn't know how to answer that. She wasn't gay, but she *was* on the rebound. Neither of those were encouraging thoughts to confront with the woman who'd shared her bed last night.

Sam didn't press her. She slipped out and limped to the lounge, their shared living space before...whatever had happened. She heard the coffee pot bubbling and oil hissing in a skillet.

June dragged a pillow close and buried her burning face in it. Trust alcohol to complicate an already complicated situation.

Only she couldn't remember drinking. She remembered shouting. Screaming. Crying. She remembered Mark telling her it wasn't going to work, failing to mention that Natalie and her blossoming relationship with his lower half was the reason it wasn't going to work. She'd figured that out for herself later, skimming social media to figure out where the shattered pieces of her life had fallen.

Then Sam had shoved a rubber mask into her hands and told her they were going out for Halloween.

Because, "She who makes a beast of herself forgets the pain of being with men."

Yeah, apparently that was literal.

The mask was impaled like a severed head on the bedpost. It wasn't a monster she recognised. Just some grey, toothy creature. It fit real snug, she remembered that, and it had been oddly breathable. When she'd pulled it on it hadn't felt like she was wearing a mask at all.

God, it hadn't been watching them *all night*, had it?

She threw the pillow at the mask, knocking it to the floor. She didn't think Sam had taken advantage of her;

she'd never been anything but the best of friends. A shoulder to cry on, a partner in crime. Sure, she had odd friends and strange interests and that witchy look June had never been into. Black hair and piercings. Denim and fishnets. Smiles with too many teeth...but that didn't make her a bad person.

She hadn't gone as a witch last night. They'd both been beasts, and she wondered where Sam's mask was.

She decided it must have been a mercy sleepover. June hadn't wanted to wake up to a cold bed and remember that Mark was never going to be hers again, *could* never be hers because he'd traded five years of love and good times for a girl he'd met last month on Facebook. So she'd asked Sam to hold her, and that was exactly what her friend had done. That was how they'd fallen asleep, and that was how they'd woken up.

She almost believed it.

Didn't explain why she was naked. She reached for her shirt from last night,but she'd overdone it with the fake blood. *Really*overdone it, and she'd ripped one of the sleeves. Her jeans were in pretty bad shape too.

She grabbed the Hello Kitty dressing gown from the back of the door. It hadn't fit her in a couple of years, but Mark had always hated it so it felt right. She wondered if she was going to spend the rest of her life defining herself by what a man had ripped out of her.

She hovered at the window, tweaked the curtains. The day had dawned cold and clear. Blue-grey sky, and maybe the promise of a new beginning. She'd throw her old life out like a spoiling pumpkin. She'd be sad for a while, but it was better than carving on a grin and going through life like a June-o'-lantern. Sam would understand if she couldn't be happy for a while.

Sam always understood.

The neighbours across the street looked like they'd partied last night. Nothing new there, since June could hear the bass thump-thump-thumping in her teeth most weekends while she tried to rest up from work. The remains of demolished gourds were spread out on the grass,and someone had set fire to their decorations. The word 'WHORE' was spray-painted across the front of the house.

Party guests probably hadn't done that.

The white trash girl who lived there, different dad for her kids every month, shuffled out. No sign of her usual blonde curls and leopard print. She stared plaintively around her ruined garden, and June tried to figure out what was wrong with her face.

Their eyes locked for half a second. June let the curtains fall, flattening herself against the wall. It wasn't the reproach in the other woman's eyes, it was the row of four parallel grooves in her face. They were stitched shut, but still raw, like someone had tried to tear her face off.

June gulped down bile and staggered into the lounge, the smell of breakfast almost making her puke.

Sam seemed to be taking the hangover in stride. She was blasting Combichrist from her phone and brutally scrambling eggs in a pan. June clutched her head as the words pounded into her brain. *Hey! You! What the fuck is wrong with you?*

"Did we...go over to the neighbours' house last night?"

"Your guess is as good as mine, babe."

She ignored the term of endearment and slumped onto the couch. She flicked the television on, trying to focus on something other than the nausea and guilt frothing in her belly.

The news was playing. There was a house covered in yellow police tape, a ring of onlookers and press people with cameras flashing. Lots of cops.

She knew that house; it was Mark's house.

She cranked the volume. Sam let out a whine of complaint, but June ignored her so she shut off the music just in time to hear the anchor's voice cut through.

"*...two bodies recovered from the scene as Mark Neusbaum and Natalie Johanssen. An anonymous source within the department has stated that wounds on both victims are consistent with those of an animal attack, but that there is overwhelming evidence of human involvement. Police are searching for witnesses to identify two females seen fleeing the scene late last night. The bodies were discovered this morning by...*"

"Good fucking riddance," Sam said. She swiped the dust off her hands and turned back to breakfast.

Except that June didn't think it was dust on their hands.

"Sam, did we...kill them?"

"Get real."

"I *am* getting real. We put on those masks last night, and I can't remember anything that happened. There's blood all over my clothes, my whole body *aches*, the woman across the street had her house wrecked and her face slashed up...and now Mark is *dead*."

"Sounds to me like everyone's getting what they deserve." Her lips quirked into an enigmatic smile, and her voice dropped low and husky. "You and me, too."

"That wasn't what he deserved. He was an asshole, but...I didn't want him to die."

"Why the Hell not?"

Sam slammed the frying pan off the heat and stormed into the lounge. God help her, June cringed in her seat like a lion was prowling into her living room.

She'd never been afraid of Sam before.

"He didn't give a fuck if you lived or died. Five years of your life you wasted on that piece of shit and then he *cheats* on you. He never knew how good he had it. He threw you away like you were nothing. If I hadn't been there for you, you'd have..."

"Okay," June said. She held up a hand, and the wild look in Sam's eyes softened just a little. "You're right. I was in a bad way last night, and you were there for me. You're a good friend."

"You'd have been better off with me."

"I...didn't know you felt that way."

Sam made an ugly noise in her throat and stalked back to the kitchenette. Suddenly, June wondered if she'd been blind for the last five years. Sam had never brought a girlfriend home, not once in all that time. Every time June had needed a night in Sam was there. Every time she'd cried, same. Sometimes she'd catch Sam staring at her and ask her, "What?"

And she'd tell the biggest lie of them all.

"Nothing."

No, she hadn't been blind. She'd been in love with a guy who wasn't in love with her. Apparently they both had terrible taste.

Her stomach churned. It was too much. She leapt off the couch and bolted for the bathroom. Sam called after her, but she didn't have time to explain. She reached the toilet just in time to hurl. She'd only been sick a couple of times in her life, but this was Biblical. Muscles snapped rigid. Tendons bulged. Blood vessels broke. Her back heaved. Her knuckles whitened around the porcelain and her body ejected *everything*. Complete factory reset.

She stared down into the bloody mess she'd just made, head spinning. Bobbing on the surface was a human finger, pallid from acid erosion, one painted nail and a ring Mark had once given her that had belonged to his grandmother.

A ring he'd asked her to give back.

She screamed and kicked herself into the corner, crushing a towel over her face and weeping. It wasn't what she'd drank last night that was making her sick.

It was what she'd eaten.

"Holy fuck! Holy fucking fuck! This can't be happening!"

"It's polite to flush after," Sam pointed out.

June leapt to her feet. She hit the wall, knocking towels to the floor. Sam was leaning against the doorframe, a smirk flickering across her lips.

"Where did you get those masks?"

"Does it matter?"

"Yeah. I think it does." She spat in the sink and adjusted her gown. "Sam, I think they did something to us. I think that's why we can't remember anything."

"Is that what you think? Or is that what you want to think?"

"Jesus, Sam, two people are dead!"

"Yeah, and none of it was my idea. I don't give a shit about that lady across the road,and I wouldn't have gone within a restraining order's distance of your asshole ex if you hadn't had such a boner for crashing his party with Miss October. But I did it for you, because *you* wanted to."

She'd lied. She'd said she didn't remember, but she did. How could June trust her when there was still nothing in her head but empty space?

Sam was staring at her, waiting. Her eyes were dark, vicious slits. There was something wrong with her face. June could see it now, in this light. Her skin looked rubbery and off-colour.

"Where's your mask?"

She scratched her cheek. Her smile didn't falter. "Where do you *think* it is?"

"This isn't you. You're not this person."

"Fuck off. Five years of living in a fucking music video, watching you piss our lives away with *him*, and now I'm finally getting what I want. This is who I want to be." Her eyes glittered. "And it was who you wanted to be too, until you took it off."

It *was* the mask. She needed to take it and burn it, then she needed to find some way to get Sam's off. She had spell books in her room, right? Practical Magic and hokey shit like that. Maybe something in those would work. Or maybe...

Someone knocked at the door. Hammered on it would be more accurate. It was the kind of knock that had handcuffs and flashing blue lights behind it.

"June Summers! Police!"

"I'm going," June hissed, holding Sam's gaze. "Don't

try to stop me."

She pushed past her into the hall, willing herself to be more defiant than she felt. She'd almost made it back to the lounge when Sam pulled a bag over her head. She let out a muffled scream as the plastic pulled taut around her face.

Except it wasn't a bag, it was a mask.

She didn't scream for long. Actually, it was only about twenty seconds before she started laughing.

She who makes a beast of herself...

The Mirror That Tells Truths and Lies

McKenzie Richardson

Kelsey had always been exceedingly aware of her appearance. Even as a child she'd been drawn to any reflective surface, mesmerized by the reasonably-symmetrical face mirrored back at her.

As she grew she learned to maintain that face, to create an illusion of effortless beauty. It required a lot of work to appear so natural.

By the time she got to college she had perfected the art of perfection. Head held high, like she owned the world, never a hair out of place. Morning classes after late-night parties, Friday nights at the campus bar, internships, trips to the grocery store and executive board meetings were all faced with the same easy attractiveness.

But deep down she held a secret, a chink in her armor she refused to reveal.

Kelsey's eyes lit up when the bright, foil paper fell away from the mirror. It was a full-length one with a metal frame worked into a pattern like intertwining ropes, flickering with a beautiful gleam in the light of the scented candle. The frame was painted ivory-white, and the surface was highly polished.

She squealed with excitement and swept Hannah up in her arms, thanking her for the present.

"I found it in an antique shop," her friend explained. "I just knew you'd love it. It's weird, as soon as I saw it, I thought of you. It was like it called to me, telling me to give it to you. Crazy, huh?" She laughed at her strange thoughts. "Anyway, happy birthday, beautiful!"

Kelsey only half listened to her friend, already lost in her own reflection and thinking how great the mirror would look on her bedroom wall.

"So, are you going to come out with us to celebrate? It'll be fun," Hannah coaxed, cocking an eyebrow as she observed her friend.

Kelsey disengaged from her reflection and gave Hannah an exasperated glance.

"Are you kidding me? I can't go out with my hair like this."

Hannah eyed Kelsey's hair, which was done up in a complicated array of braids that met in a tight bun at the top of her head. "What's wrong with your hair?"

Kelsey rolled her eyes. "These split ends are out of control." She waved her hand up in a sweeping gesture across her head, then went back to picking at the cuticle of her thumb. "Just look at how dull it is."

"Oh, come on! No one is even going to notice."

Kelsey scoffed. "I tried making an appointment at the salon, but the stylist says she can't see me until next week. Nope, I'm staying in this weekend, then it's a trim first thing Monday morning before class." She gave a definitive nod, as if to punctuate her sentence and end the conversation.

Hannah opened her mouth to point out that the ends weren't even visible, they were carefully tucked out of sight, but they'd been friends since freshman year and she knew only too well that Kelsey was notoriously stubborn. Once she'd made up her mind there was no use arguing.

As Kelsey walked her to the door Hannah swatted her friend's hands, which had pulled a tiny chunk of flesh from the bed of a nail, blood oozing from the small opening. Self-consciously Kelsey staunched the wound with the hem of her shirt, leaving a red stain.

"You need to stop picking at your fingers, girl," Hannah remarked.

Kelsey shrugged. "The less skin I have, the less I weigh," she countered, only half-joking. Then she closed the door as her friend's form retreated down the hall of the apartment building that led to the elevator.

That night Kelsey uncorked a bottle of red and set it on the counter to breathe.

"Happy birthday to me," she muttered.

While a bowl of leftovers heated up in the microwave she stood in the bathroom and unwound her hair. The ends were dry and brittle, and she glared at them in annoyance. She wondered why she'd let them go so long without a trim, though she had been a bit overwhelmed with midterms the previous week on top of her excessive skincare routine. She was glad she'd stayed home, knowing she wouldn't have been able to have a good time anyway with being perpetually aware of her less-than-perfect hair.

Around her were a cosmetic counter's worth of creams and elixirs to clear skin, defy age, make hair shine, reduce pore size, and countless other magical effects to bring her closer to perfection. It was a lifetime's worth of collected knowledge on how to appear young, bright, and attractive.

Over the years she'd learned the right clothes to wear to hide her imperfections, to cover up the flaws she saw in herself.

She preferred simple earrings as to not draw attention to her ear's attached lobes, jealous of the elegant slopes of Hannah's unattached ones. She never wore open-toed shoes, no matter the weather, as a way to conceal the feet she was so self-conscious of. She had countless ways to mask, to hide, to disguise, and methods to play up the features she did like such as widening her eyes or elongating her already thin legs. They were all tricks to convince others she was without flaw.

When the microwave dinged Kelsey went down the hall and poured herself a glass of wine, and as she ate her sensible portion of dinner she flicked on the TV. Despite her efforts to distract herself with a movie once she'd finished eating she kept fiddling with the ends of her hair, scrutinizing their harsh tips. She was unable to focus on anything else.

Switching tactics she got up and retrieved the mirror from the corner. It really was beautiful, its frame so detailed and lifelike. She grabbed a hammer and a nail from the drawer in the kitchen and brought the mirror to the bedroom, where she set to work mounting it on the wall next to the door.

Once it hung securely she sat on the bed across from it and gazed into the shining surface.

She sipped the healthy pour of wine, examining her reflection. Her cheeks were already a little flushed from the alcohol, reddening her features and giving her a pleasant glow.

She still couldn't ignore the state of her hair, and remained fixated on it. She couldn't wait for Monday; she needed to do something.

With wine-infused confidence she took matters into her own hands.

With a pair of kitchen scissors in her grasp she set to work snipping off the dull ends. Each cut was euphoric, as though the flaws dropped away as unruly hair fluttered to the floor under the mirror's gleaming gaze. She felt lighter, shedding her worries along with each flawed tip.

When she was certain she'd severed every fragmented hair from her mane she admired her handiwork in the new, floor-length mirror. She was certain her hair looked better, less frizzy.

Yet something still wasn't quite right. The start of a pimple was forming on her forehead, magnified in the mirror to the point that she couldn't focus on anything else. She tried a warm compress and creams, but was impatient with the results. Finally she took a safety pin to it, digging around beneath the skin. Despite the chance of scarring she couldn't stand looking at the bump, so accentuated in the mirror's reflection.

After her work on the blemish other flawed features became glaringly noticeable in the space inside that lovely white frame. The mirror's impeccably clear surface was unforgiving, showing all of her flaws, each little piece of her lacking in perfection. She brought one hand to its surface, nibbling the cuticle on the other.

She snuck a glance down, and a snarl marred her wine-stained lips as she curled the toes of her bare feet out of sight. The second toe of each foot was slightly longer than the big one. To most the transgression was imperceptible, but in the reflection of the mirror it was painfully obvious. Her long, thin toes were witch-like and grotesque. In a vain attempt to even things out she clipped the ends of her pedicured nails, but it wasn't good enough. Still her reflection haunted her.

An insane desire to fix them once and for all crept into her mind. As soon as it did she shook her head, surprised. It felt foreign, an intruder, a thought not her own. Once again the feeling overcame her, no longer content to be hidden away. Still slightly high on the effects of her victory over her split ends, she threw back the rest of her wine and considered her options.

Toe shortening surgery was out of the question, since between her unpaid internship and tuition there was no way she could afford it. In high school she'd briefly dated a guy who'd convinced her to marathon a lot of gory action movies with him. She recalled the numerous, gross scenes of finger shortening and digit removal used as punishment or torture. Cigar cutters and pruning shears were often used, cleaving clear through the bone. The corner of her upper lip twitched in disgust and annoyance. She didn't have either of those just laying around her apartment.

Still, looking at her reflection revealed so repulsively, she was convinced that she needed to do something. Right now, tonight. There was no time to waste.

Edgy and irritated Kelsey went back to the kitchen for a refill, then stood in the middle of the room as she sipped her wine and thought. She'd always been a creative problem solver.

After a moment she opened the drawer next to the sink. Inside, among the clutter, was a scissor-like gadget she'd bought when she'd been on the raw vegetable diet that had only made her uncomfortably bloated.

She grasped the spring-loaded handle in one hand, squeezing it firmly. She watched as the other ends came together, the stainless-steel cleaver snapping sharply against the flat surface that rested perpendicular to the blade, acting as a miniature cutting board for easy chopping.

Her brow was set with determination, and she brought her glass and the scissor-like contraction back to her bedroom. The device could easily hack through cucumbers, cabbages, and carrots; she estimated her toe was about the same thickness as a carrot, and theorized it would work well enough.

For a fleeting moment she realized how crazy this was, and prepared to abandon the insane attempt. Yet, when she looked back to the mirror, the desire for perfection intensified, hardening her resolve. The mirror gleamed as though egging her on, promising its supportive presence throughout what was to come.

Taking the clever resolutely in her hand she slipped the tip of the offending toe of her left foot between the blade and the cutting board close to the pivot point, maneuvering the other toes downward and out of the way. Before she could think too much she closed her eyes, clamping the handles together as hard as she could.

It hurt, of course it did.

White-hot pain coursed up her foot, her leg, her whole body as the bone cracked audibly. The tip of her toe tumbled to the floor with a clean cut and a spurt of rosy blood.

She wrapped the bleeding stump in a wad of toilet paper, and after a moment she examined the result in the mirror. Despite the blood she decided the foot looked better, the stunted toe now extending properly just below the tip of her big toe.

Over the years Kelsey had learned that perfection took hard work and determination, and she was no quitter. Beauty was pain, and she would do anything to unleash her true self, the perfect specimen she knew lay buried within.

She repeated the process on the other foot, collecting the bloody ends from the carpet where they'd fallen and depositing them in the wastepaper basket with the hair clippings. It was messy business, but instantly the mirror revealed two perfectly-matched feet, with toes of descending size. It shone in the light as though congratulating her on a job well done. She was ecstatic with the results, and her mind filled with all of the footwear options now available to her.

After painfully hobbling to the kitchen she gulped down a celebratory glass of wine, emptying the last of the bottle. A glance at the clock on the stove told her the night was still young, so she opened a second bottle of pinot noir and poured another glass.

When she went back to the mirror to admire her new perfection her feet looked lovely, but the desire to fix her earlobes set in. They were a fine size, but she longed for unattached lobes, so elegant and admirable. She pictured Hannah's eccentric earring collection, envious of her ability to draw attention to those glorious lobes.

Snatching a paring knife from the wooden knife block on the kitchen counter she once again faced her reflection. It looked simple enough, just a quick slice. After cutting through the nail and bone of her toes, the fleshy lobes would be easy.

Holding her ear firmly she pulled it outward, lining the blade up with the connective tissue. Then, with a graceful slide of the knife, she cut through the skin as simply as slicing raw chicken.

Within moments she was the proud owner of two un-attached lobes that hung down slightly from her head. As she wiped away the dribbles of blood she could just picture how regal they would look with a pair of diamonds dangling from them, no longer forced to wear plain earrings.

There was a fair amount of blood seeping from her ears now. The tissues wrapped around her toes were completely drenched in crimson, and they left dark, wet splotches with her every step. It didn't matter to her though; it was worth it for the beauty she had attained.

By this point she was feeling a little lightheaded, from the wine she assumed. Still the mirror's reflection pulled her in. It promised her a window into perfection, the thing she had wanted for so long. In the mirror she could see her true self locked inside, waiting to break through her flawed frame. She just needed to help it come out.

As she raised her glass to her lips she nearly dropped the wine, shocked at the flabby skin under her arms. It hung loosely and swung a bit when she shook her arm.

She'd toned them mercilessly, but it seemed she'd been slacking lately.

She glared at the skin, grabbing it in her hand and pulling at it in a humiliating display. Blood still trickled down her neck, but she was hypnotized by the sway of her arms. Unable to take her eyes from the mirror a voice inside urged her to fix them. There was only one way.

But she shook her head; that was too much. She couldn't go that far. She was already losing a lot of blood. The voice persisted, but Kelsey could be stubborn. She wouldn't do anymore. Such things were a slippery slope.

As she watched the image in the mirror blurred and swayed, then zoomed in on her every flaw. The point at the end of her nose, the wideness of her hips, her thin lips, her far-set eyes, her fleshy knees.

Her stomach churned with the realization that she was still so far from her dream body.

She lifted up her shirt, examining her stomach in annoyance, her frustration building. No matter how little she ate, or how many crunches she did, there was still a bit of flab there.

Letting her shirt hem fall back into place she closed her eyes. She felt a bit dizzy, and knew for certain it was time to stop this madness.

Then, something grabbed her wrist.

When she opened her eyes she found a long, white rope twisting around her arm. Following it with her eyes she saw that it led to the mirror.

She gasped; eyes wide with fear as the mirror's metal frame extended out to her like tentacles. The ivory ropes snaked their way around both wrists, biting into the skin and pulling her toward the bed.

She tried to fight it, tried to tell herself it was all an illusion, but the tendrils wrapped around each of her fingers. With hard jerks and yanks they forced her hands to pick up the knife from the bed.

Then, under the mirror's supervision, her hands cut away the excess skin on her arms, the ropes helping to guide it against the edge of the blade. She cried out at the pain that flamed through her body, tears bursting from her eyes.

After a few moments, and a great deal of agony, she was left with a satisfying sleekness in her limbs.

The ropes continued to wrench her arms with ease. They orchestrated the removal of every bit of fat from her body; from the back of her legs, from under her chin. Controlling her like a puppet they stripped away the skin of her stomach, revealing sculpted abdominal muscles. They peeled off excess flesh in thin ribbons, layer after layer dropping to the floor with sloppy splats. Each removed wad of skin made her thinner, smaller, better as shown through the eyes of the mirror.

Unable to force herself from the mirror Kelsey watched as her body dwindled. She couldn't stop it. She was torn between her horror of the mirror's hacking, and the image it reflected back to her; her mind conflicted. She was so near perfection that she could almost taste it behind the pooling blood from the surgical cuts to narrow her tongue.

The mirror showed her what she could become, what she was supposed to be. It just needed to cut away the things that got in the way, to shape her into that ideal form.

It sculpted her, subtracted the failings to unveil the perfection that lay within. It was helping her, it assured her, and the results would be to die for.

The blood and the pain intensified her dizziness, but she was so close, so close, so close. She wanted to stop, to pull away, to free herself, but even in her horror she saw her perfected shape becoming reality. The ropes squeezed harder against her attempts to escape until the room filled with the popping and snapping of finger bones breaking.

The metal tendrils flung her limp arms in a violent dance of cutting and hacking, nearly there now. With each slice the mirror shaped its clay, never satisfied with anything less than perfection.

As her hands pulled a messy lump of an organ from her abdomen she felt the overwhelming sense of arrival, having reached her perfect form. Head up she looked into the mirror, her entire body reddened with blood, her inner workings exposed. For one glowing moment the reflection in the mirror erased all the carnage, revealing herself as she truly was. Kelsey stared into the face of a goddess, a woman so lovely her whole body ached with the achievement.

Then the ropes, now stained with blood, released her, retreating back to wrap around the mirror that housed the most perfect human specimen it had ever created. She stood there for a second, then crumpled to the floor, no longer able to hold herself up.

After days of missed classes and unreturned texts, worried friends talked the building manager into sawing through the deadbolt on the door. They found Kelsey on the bedroom floor in a pool of dried blood that had turned black as it hardened into the carpet.

At odds with the grotesque scene Kelsey's face shone with a smile, widened by two slits at each corner of her mouth. They'd dried and hardened into an everlasting grin of satisfaction.

When the police arrived they were at a loss. All the windows were securely shut, no signs of forced entry. Knives, scissors, and kitchen gadgets were scattered around her on the floor and bed, a paring knife in her hand. Yet surely such abuse could not have been self-inflected.

Two of the officers vomited at the sight of her. It was a mess to clean up, bits of skin and severed body parts laying all around her, spilling out of the small garbage can. The body had to essentially be pried from the carpet, the blood having dried and pasted it in place.

It was sad to see such a beautiful woman reduced to a gory pile of flesh and organs.

When the coroner came to remove what could be scrapped from the floor he admitted to himself it was the worst he'd ever seen. He was glad he was working alone that day, so no one could see his uncharacteristic squeamishness.

As he loaded the remains onto the wheeled gurney he caught sight of his reflection in the handsome mirror on the wall. It was a lovely mirror, its deep-red frame gleaming in the light that poured through the bedroom window. He smoothed his hair, then squinted, having never noticed how large his cheeks looked. If only they were smaller, firmer, tighter; he could look at least five years younger.

Without really knowing what he was doing he unhooked the mirror from the wall and stowed it at the bottom of the gurney. He'd never taken anything from a job before, but something urged him to give that mirror a new home. It was as though a voice called to him, convincing him.

When the mirror was secured in place he wheeled the gurney down the hall and into the elevator, thinking how lovely the mirror would look on his wall. He knew just the place for it.

Absentmindedly he brought his fingers to his cheek as the elevator descended. His face really would look better if his cheeks were thinner. Perhaps he'd look into surgery.

About the Authors

Ashley Burns

Artist, writer, and Muay Thai fighter. Choreographed violence that spills into my love for horror in all its many forms. Read more of my work in the upcoming Kandisha Press Women of Horror Anthology coming out early 2021. Follow me on social media for sneak peeks and more of my ramblings.

Wattpad- @AshleyBurns524
Reddit- u/BufferCat
Instagram- @ashmuaythai
Facebook- https://www.facebook.com/ashley.burns.9678

ELIZABETH DAVIS

Elizabeth Davis is a second generation writer living in Dayton, Ohio. She lives there with her spouse and two cats - neither of which have been lost to ravenous corn mazes or sleeping serpent gods. She can be found at deadfishbooks.com when she isn't busy creating beautiful nightmares and bizarre adventures. Her work can be found in, Eerie River Publishing Patreon July 2020, Eternal Haunted Summer Summer 2020, and No Safe Distance: Stories from Isolation.

BRANDON EBINGER

Brandon Ebinger is a horror/dark fantasy author who lives in upstate New York with his fiance and two cats. He holds a BA in creative writing. He enjoys horror films,Gothic rock and punk music and video games. He is a huge fan of haunted attractions,and spends October as a haunt actor.

Brandon has written five horror/dark fantasy novels, Ash, Hollow Hills ,The Afflicted, Rose and the upcoming Broken Night. He has also published a handful of short stories within the genre. He is currently at work on his new novel.

Facebook: https://www.facebook.com/brandon.ebinger .
Twitter: https://twitter.com/BEbinger2
Instragram: https://www.instagram.com/brandonofmill-haven/

DAVID GREEN

David Green is a writer of dark fiction. Born in Manchester, UK and living in Galway, Ireland, David grew up with gloomy clouds above his head, and rain water at his feet, which has no doubt influenced his dark scribblings. David is the author of the Pushcart Prize nominated novelette Dead Man Walking, and is excited for his fantasy series, Empire of Ruin, debuting in June 2021 from Eerie River Publishing.

Newsletter: https://tinyurl.com/y6ah8brp
Twitter: @davidgreenwrite
Website: www.davidgreenwriter.com
Facebook: https://www.facebook.com/davidgreenwriter

S.O. Green

Simone Oldman Green is a genre-fluid writer and editor living in the Kingdom of Fife with husband, John. Author of over 40 published works with 10 different imprints including Dragon Soul Press, Black Hare Press and Eerie River Publishing. They also won 3rd Place in the British Fantasy Society's Short Story Contest 2018. Writer, vegan, martial artist, gamer, occasionally a terrible person (but only to fictional people). They thrive on the unusual, which might explain why there are so many cats.

Website: https://thebasementoflove.blogspot.com/
Facebook: https://www.facebook.com/thebasementoflove
Twitter: https://twitter.com/SOGreenWriter

Johnny Hempseed

Johnny Hempseed is a writer who lives in rural Oregon. He writes twisted horror and speculative fiction.

CHRIS HEWITT

Chris lives in the beautiful garden of England and in the odd moment that he's not walking the dog, he pursues his passion for writing fiction. With horror, fantasy, and science-fiction stories published in several anthologies from Eerie River Publishing and Black Hare Press, Chris has many stories coming out throughout 2021.

Twitter: @i_mused_blog
Blog: http://mused.blog/
Amazon: http://mused.blog/author

JOEL R. HUNT

Joel is a writer, proofreader, ex-teacher and part-time human currently residing in the UK. Among his other hobbies of eating, breathing and crouching in dark corners, Joel constantly plans stories and screenplays - a very small number of which actually get written. Most simply languish in his ever-growing 'Unfinished' folder, which is now approaching a mass capable of generating gravitational pull.

Joel's genres of choice are horror and sci-fi, although the odd bit of sentiment does manage to sneak in between the freakishness and disturbing twists. He hopes in time that he might earn a living from putting words on a dead tree in a particular order, or at least earn enough for the occasional cup of tea and vegetarian full English breakfast.

If you are so inclined, you can follow Joel's latest exploits on Twitter, where he also posts daily micro stories. But it might be simpler to cut out the middle-man and seek psychiatric help.

Twitter: https://twitter.com/JoelRHunt1
Website: https://joelrhuntauthor.wordpress.com/
Reddit: https://www.reddit.com/r/JRHEvilInc/
Amazon:https://www.amazon.com/Joel-R.-Hunt/e/B07SBX6G3W

Blaise Langlois

Emerging author, Blaise Langlois, will never turn down the chance to tell a creepy story around the campfire. After a long struggle with her inner critic, she made the plunge and now shares her stories, which she writes in between teaching and raising four beautiful children. You are sure to find her feverishly scratching out ideas, which are shared with her supportive husband, usually just after midnight. Her favourite genres include horror, sci-fi and dystopian and she particularly enjoys writing short fiction and poetry.

You can learn more about her writing journey by visiting her blog at: www.ravenfictionca.wordpress.com

Chris Lilienthal

Chris Lilienthal is a writer and communications professional in Harrisburg, Pennsylvania. He spent more than two decades telling himself stories in his head. In 2020, he started writing them down. "Three Balloons" is his first published story. When he's not writing, Chris enjoys sketching, kayaking, hiking, and reading in the hammock out back. He lives with his wife, two sons, and two dogs.

Follow him on Twitter @ChrisLilienthal and on Instagram @ChristopherLilienthal.

Tim Mendees

Tim Mendees is a horror writer from Macclesfield in the North-West of England that specialises in cosmic horror and weird fiction. He has had over fifty stories accepted for publication in anthologies and magazines with publishers all over the world. His debut Lovecraftian novella, Burning Reflection is out now from Mannison Press.

When he is not arguing with the spellchecker, Tim is a goth DJ, crustacean and cephalopod enthusiast, and the presenter of a popular web series of live video readings of his material. He currently lives in Brighton & Hove with his pet crab, Gerald, and an army of stuffed octopods.

https://timmendeeswriter.wordpress.com/
https://tinyurl.com/timmendeesyoutube
https://www.facebook.com/goatinthemachine

Michael D. Nadeau

Born in the usual way, author Michael D. Nadeau found fantasy at the age of eight with Dungeons & Dragons. He loved being different people as well as casting magic. By High school he discovered his love for reading thanks to a teacher. She fed his thirst for books by bringing her own books from home and lending them to him, even buying one towards the end of her class. He has now read hundreds of fantasy books, living in each of their worlds along with the characters. After awhile he started creating his own worlds for his games with friends. Cities, gods, ancient and terrible beings and histories...then he would burn them all down.

He is the author of the Lythinall series: The Darkness Returns book 1, The Darkness Within book 2, The Darkness Falls (coming soon), Dragon Caller; Rise of the archmage book 1, and Tales from Lythinall — an anthology (coming soon). He also has several stories in Kyanite Press's Journal of speculative fiction and Eerie River Publishing anthologies, as well as writing for Gestalt Media's monthly contest regularly.

https://www.amazon.com/Michael-D. Nadeau/e/
B07L3ZJXCL/ref=ntt_dp_epwbk_0
https://karsisthebard.wordpress.com/

Elizabeth Nettleton

Elizabeth Nettleton grew up on the Sunshine Coast, Australia, and is now based in Oxfordshire, England. She has been an avid reader and writer since she was a child, and particularly enjoys writing dark and speculative fiction. Her short stories and drabbles have been included in The Sirens Call eZine, Trembling with Fear, Short Fiction Break, and several anthologies by Eerie River Publishing. Elizabeth's novella, The Price of Gold, and middle-grade fantasy novel, Solum's Landing, are both available on Amazon.

Twitter - @ElizabethNett18

KIMBERLY REI

Kimberly Rei does her best work in the places that can't exist... the in-between places where imagination defies reality. With a penchant for dark corners and hooks that leave readers looking over their shoulder, she is always on the lookout for new ideas, new projects, and new ways to make words dance.

Kim is happiest tapping away on a keyboard or doing anything at all with her beautiful wife.

https://theancientmillennial.square.site/kimberly-rei-author
http://tales.studiorei.org/
https://www.facebook.com/ReiTales/
https://twitter.com/SeersDaughter
https://www.instagram.com/theseersdaughter/

McKenzie Richardson

McKenzie Richardson lives in Milwaukee, WI. A lifelong explorer of imagined worlds on the written page, over the last few years she has been finding homes for her own creations. Most recently, her work will be published in Eerie River Publishing's With Blood and Ash, coming 2021. Her stories and poetry are also featured in anthologies from Black Hare Press, Iron Faerie Publishing, and Dragon Soul Press. In addition, she has published a poetry collaboration with Casey Renee Kiser, 433 Lighted Way, and her middle-grade fantasy novel, Heartstrings, is available on Amazon.

McKenzie loves all things books and is currently working towards a master's degree in Library and Information Sciences. When not writing, she can usually be found in her book hoard, reading or just looking at her shelves longingly.

For more on her writing, follow her on:
http://www.facebook.com/mckenzielrichardson/
http://www.instagram.com/mckenzielrichardson/
http://www.craft-cycle.com

Austin Shirey

Austin Shirey has been telling stories ever since he first read THE HOBBIT as a kid. If he's not writing, he's probably reading or enjoying time with his wife, their two daughters, and their two cats in Northern Virginia. His fiction has appeared in Orca, All Worlds Wayfarer, Stonecoast Review, and Blind Corner, with stories forthcoming in the WEIRD FICTION anthology from Black Hare Press and the WITH BONE AND IRON dark fantasy anthology from Eerie River Publishing. You can find him and his work online at www.austinshirey.com.

Follow him on:
https://www.austinshirey.com
https://twitter.com/tashirey87
https://www.instagram.com/shirey_writes

K.T. TATE

K.T. Tate is an English author inspired to write speculative fiction. She draws on her love of horror to explore the themes of cosmic and occult horror, the supernatural, folktales and witchcraft. Writing mainly drabbles and short stories, her works have been featured in a plethora of anthologies. All of which can be found on her website below. When not at the beck and call of her monstrous muses she is a geek, enjoying comic books, video games and table-top rpgs.

Website – www.eldritch-hollow.com
Facebook – https://facebook.com/eldritch-hollow
Tumblr – https://eldritch-hollow.tumblr.com

V. A. Vazquez

V. A. Vazquez comes from New York City where she previously worked as a theatre producer and a ghostwriter for famous fashion editors (which you wouldn't be able to tell from looking in her closet). An author of urban fantasy and comedic horror, she specializes in stories that involve women (or men or non-binary folks) romancing monsters, preferably the slimy Lovecraftian kind. She currently lives in Scotland with her husband and their wee doggo.

You can find her on Twitter @vavazquezwrites.
www.vavazquez.com
www.facebook.com/vavazquezauthor

WILLIAM A. WELLMAN

William A. Wellman is a queer horror author, and a passionate lover of dark and anthological stories. Their writing explores questions of LGBTQ+ love and identity through the lens of the horror genre, resulting in unsettling but bittersweet fiction. William also works as a writing coach, helping writers to meet their authorial goals and overcome common (and uncommon) challenges. Peculiarly, William still finds time to write and produce the literary horror podcast 'Hello From The Hallowoods'.

William's journey has led from the frozen wastes of Alaska across the world, passing through ancient temples and decrepit bus stops with uniform curiosity. At this time they can most often be found with a typewriter beneath the trees in Parc La Fontaine in Montreal, or in a coffee shop of suitable proximity. If you happen to spot them, say hello. If this seems unlikely, connect with them using the links below instead.

To say hello, try Twitter or on Instagram at @williamawellman.

For Facebook, as long as it lasts, @williamwellmanwrites will do.

You can find more of their books and learn about coaching opportunities at www.williamwellmanwrites.com.

More from Eerie River:

It Calls From the Forest: Volume One

It Calls From the Forest: Volume Two

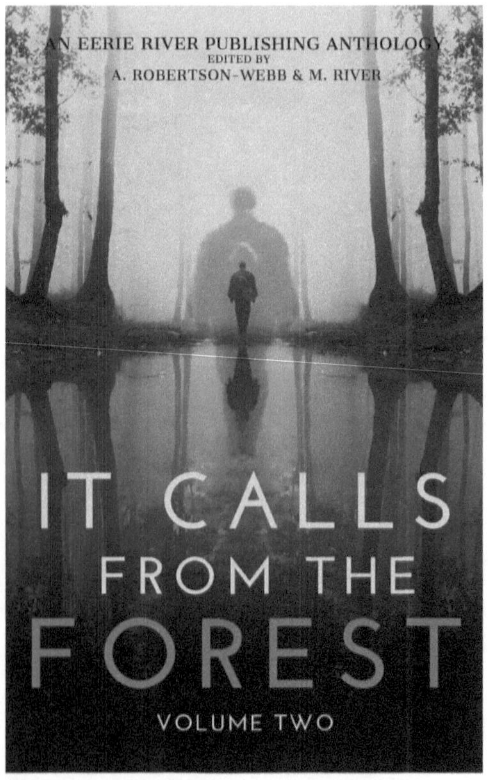

It Calls From the Sky

Don't Miss Out!

Looking for a FREE BOOK?

Sign up for Eerie River Publishing's monthly newsletter
and get **Darkness Reclaimed** as our thank you gift!

Sign up for our newsletter
https://mailchi.mp/71e45b6d5880/welcomebook

Here at Eerie River Publishing, we are focused on
providing paid writing opportunities for all indie authors.
Outside of our limited drabble collections we put out each
year, every single written piece that we publish -including
short stories featured in this collection have been paid for.

Becoming an exclusive Patreon member gives you
a chance to be a part of the action as well as giving you
creative content every single month, no matter the tier.
Free eBooks, monthly short stories and even paperbacks
before they are released.

https://www.patreon.com/EerieRiverPub